Lance Free

Border rhymes

Lance Free

Border rhymes

ISBN/EAN: 9783337259679

Printed in Europe, USA, Canada, Australia, Japan

Cover: Foto ©Andreas Hilbeck / pixelio.de

More available books at **www.hansebooks.com**

BORDER RHYMES

BY

FREE LANCE

LILLIESLEAF.

———

I am content to be so bare
Before the archers ! everywhere
My wounds being stroked by Heavenly air.

E. B. BROWNING.

———

HAWICK:

JAMES EDGAR, 5 HIGH STREET

1899

PREFACE.

I herewith send out into the world the children of my brain, trusting they will find their way into the hearts of souls that are akin.

F. L.

Liiliesleaf,
    May, 1899.

CONTENTS.

CONTENTS. ix.

CONTENTS.

CONTENTS. xiii.

CONTENTS.

CONTENTS.

ERRATA.

In the 21st line, page 109, for "be" read "is."

In the 11th line, page 170, for "taken" read "token."

In the 8th line, page 177, for "hidden" read "hid in."

In the 29th line, page 294, for "sweat" read "sweet."

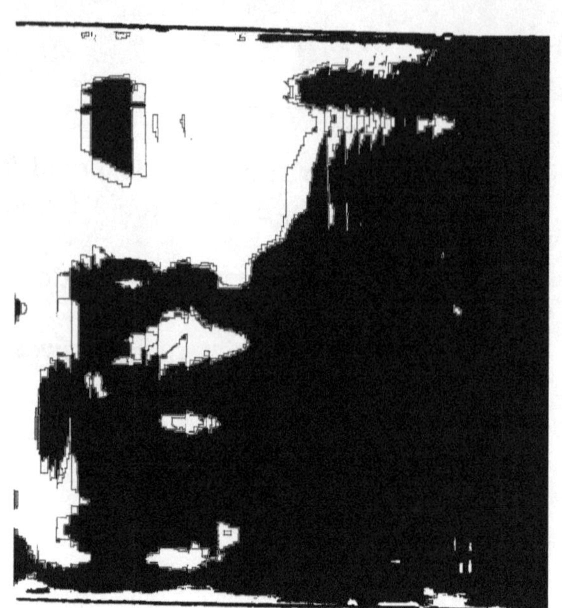

Border Rhymes.

LOO.

DEAR little Loo, queer little Loo,
   O, she loves the wild flowers well;
But the sweetest flower o' a' to me
   Is dear little Loo hersel'.

Through lang, lang years, wi' wistfu' een,
   I dream o' flowers aboot her,
An' rowth o' a' things guid an' fair
   That canna' be withoot her.

But wise wee Loo, the blasts are rough
   That blaw ower the gentlest life ;
An' a brave, strong heart is needed
   To warstle through the strife.

But there's a Faither's love abune
   To bield the tenderest buds,
An' the flowers are slockened wi' rain
   That fa's frae heaven's ain cluds.

A

I'll bring, if prayers can bring, frae heaven
    An angel sae leal an' true,
To keep frae every stain o' sin
    Oor ain auld-farrant Loo.

OOR AIN WEE LOO.

O, SOMEBODY'S een are blithe an' bricht,
    They laugh into mine an' mine laugh too—
Auld-farrant een wi' a sense o' richt
    Are the kindly een o' oor ain wee Loo.

Pure as the stars on a simmer nicht,
    An' sweet as the flowers in mornin' dew
That ope their hearts to the kindly licht,
    Is the winsome smile o' oor ain wee Loo.

Other folk's bairns nae doot may be
    Bonny an' guid an' clever an' true,
But nane o' them a' has a smile for me
    Like the leal smile o' oor ain wee Loo.

I like to look in her bonny face,
    Wi' her innocent soul shinin' through—
A rosebud openin' wi' quiet grace—
    Nae wonder we like oor ain wee Loo.

Angels abune may covet mair bliss,
    An' entice her away frae oor view ;
But wherever she is, I'm shure o' this,
    She will aye be oor ain dear Loo.

CATHIE AND FRANK.

O, THE vale o' the Tweed is bonny
    In the bield o' the heather hills,
Where the river, reflectin' tree an' flower,
    Is fed by a hunder rills.

O, the vale o' the Tweed is bonny,
    A' robed in its simmer prime,
Wi' the wild rose an' the hawthorn
    An tufts o' the sweet wild thyme.

An' fornent a bonny laburnum
    I ken o' a cosy fauld
Where twae wee twin lambs trot oot an' in,
    Weel bielded frae heat an' cauld.

O, the vale o' the Tweed is bonny
    Frae Yair to auld Elibank ;
Still, siller could buy the hale vale,
    But it canna' buy Cathie an' Frank.

May angels aye guide their little feet
    Frae everything that's wrang,
And lead them aye in the paths of peace,
    Where true love wad have them gang.

And when at the last the angel comes
    To open the gate of heaven,
May leal hearts meet their ain leal hearts
    Wi' welcome by true hearts given.

A LANG ROAD.

"MOTHER, mother, come away,"
  I heard a little maiden say ;
"We've a lang road afore us."

And all along the dusty way
The flowers looked up and seemed to say—
  " Little maiden, take me."

Her little hands were filled with flowers ;
Her gentle heart forgot the hours,
  Filling itself with sweetness.

I thought upon life's dusty road,
And raised my thoughts in prayer to God
  To line her way with flowers.

And when the weary end draws near,
May shining ones from Him appear
  To take our own sweet flower.

KATE.

O, KATE, Kate, you want to look nice—
    A sweet embodiment o' grace ;
That's why you love your silver brooch
  With " Truth " engraved upon its face,

Solomon was wonderfu' grand,
    As we read in the Bible story ;
But a greater than he has said
    The lilies outvied his glory.

Now, if you are adorned with truth,
    And love it in every degree,
Then even the lovely lilies
    Will be far surpassed by thee.

The fruitful palm in sunny lands
    Grows outward—upward from the heart,
And spreads out its crown of beauty
    To heaven from its highest part.

So may thy life from inner truth
    To outward beauty ever grow,
Crowning with opulence and grace
    A soul as white as falling snow.

YEARNING FOR THE SNOWDROP.

O, WE weary for the snowdrops
    In the hollow of the year ;
But life is creeping through the clod,
    And the flowers will soon be here.

The crocus will open its heart of gold,
    And laugh in the sun's bright face ;
Daffodils too will come, and hyacinths,
    With comely racemes of grace.

The lambkins will dance on the lea,
  And the daisies will kiss their feet ;
And the blackbird's heart will overflow
  With melody rich and sweet.

Roses will lurk in the blooming hedge
  And blush in the morning dew,
Showing their clusters half concealed
  And half held forth to view.

Autumn shall follow the summer
  Over the hill and the plain,
And the mellow fruit will fall in her lap
  Along with the golden grain.

Then winter will come and bind
  The earth with an icy chain,
And the snowdrops will know their time
  And foretell all the flowers again.

SPRING.

THE earth asleep
    In slumber deep
Lay underneath the snow ;
    The angel spring,
    With genial wing,
Swept over all below.

Then bud and bloom
Rose through the gloom
To greet the eye of day;
The earth grew green,
The streamlets sheen
Sang sweetly on their way.

Now 'neath our feet
Are daisies sweet,
Birds warble on the spray;
In the blue sky
The lark sings high,
And love is all his lay.

My soul is thrilled,
My heart is filled
And troubled with emotion;
For earth and air
And all things fair
Are full of love's devotion.

In my best dreams
All nature seems
A harp of many strings,
That angel throngs
Stir into songs
By rustling of their wings.

MAY.

THE green-robed earth is beautiful
    In dell and hill and grove ;
Life fresh and young is everywhere,
    And over all is love.

The tender grass, the sweet primrose,
    The daisy by the way—
A golden heart in silver set
    To greet the eye of day.

Life thrills through every branch and twig
    Of every forest tree,
Unfolds the leaves like bannerettes
    That tell of victory.

The birds pour forth the joy of life
    In raptures of delight,
The streamlets murmur sweetly on
    In music day and night.

And I could sing a song of heaven
    Revealed in all things fair,
Did not my heart with fulness fall
    Dumb on the altar stair.

THE DAISY.

THE sun withdrew his genial ray,
 I plucked a daisy by the way ;
Its white and crimson rays were rolled
Around its lovely heart of gold—
O, daisy by the trodden road,
I read in thee the love of God.

My soul is stirred whene'er I see
The emblem of myself in thee ;
For in the cold and dreary night,
When earth obscures the blessed light,
I fold my heart from curious eyes
Until God sends the bright sunrise.

Then heedless of the pain that's past,
I open all my folds, and cast
Myself into the kindly light,
When all is fair again and bright
As morning freshness after rain,
Or morning rest from night of pain.

And when the darkest hour draws nigh,
I'll fold my withered leaves and lie
In peace, while angels bear me through the night
Into the sweet and glorious light ;
And, daisy by the trodden road,
I'll take thee in my heart to God.

EYES.

LOVING, laughing, beautiful eyes;
    Wondering, thoughtful, and wise;
Eloquent eyes that to mine unfold
Treasures far nobler than beaten gold—
    Eager eyes ever so bright
    As they hail and drink the light,
Like the young plant pushing abroad
    The roots and leaves
    That foretell the sheaves
Flung down at the feet of God.
O, dear eyes! in the coming years
Only the noblest be thy peers,
And only love shine in thy tears.

    And when the hosts of right and wrong
    Are mustered face to face and strong,
Then, wise eyes! the perfect law read ye,
    And lift the sword of right
    With willing hands to fight
For laws that make men free.
And when the angel comes,
    After long years,
Lay down the sword and go
    With him to higher spheres;
Round thee a life well proven,
In thee, heaven inwoven.

SABBATH IN SUMMER.

WE must not let our spirits rust,
   Come ! let us shake the week-day dust
  From weary hand and heart and brain ;
And walk in peace with quiet feet
Where all around is pure and sweet,
  Forgetful of the world's dull strain.
O, come where flowers and song
The whole day long
  Fill every yearning sense with God,
Like holy angels in the air
That draw us up the altar stair,
  By stream and dale and beaten road.

Beauty fills receptive eyes,
  And music grateful ears ;
The soul of beauty never dies,
  Song sweetens all our tears
  And thrills through all the years.
O, come and walk by green-merged streams,
  And grow as the still flowers grow ;
Yield up our hearts to summer dreams,
  Let song and beauty overflow
    Our souls with peace
    And life's increase.

With flowers and song God opes our hearts
  To fill them with delight ;
He gives earth's treasures through the day,
  The quiet stars by night.

We list his messengers until we feel
We too are sent by Him, and bear His seal,
　　And should with joy respond unto
A healthy atmosphere with health ;
Gathering and giving truest wealth
From life's circumference to its core,
At one with Him for evermore.

TO MARY, WITH SNOWDROPS.

DEAR friend, we know the love that greets the
　　flowers
That grew by Hardenburn.　In the great city
These snowdrops, like some potent magic wand,
Do raise sweet memories that thronging come
With all the dear friend faces of the olden time,
When we would watch the small white tips that peered
Above the winter clod, and think upon
The gladsome time of leaves and birds and flowers ;
Then passing to your genial home, we'd draw
The sofa round, and look with glowing hearts
Into the glowing fire, and speak with free
And blessed unreserve because our trust was perfect.
　　And when the summer came
With all things beautiful, our hearts were filled
With summer gladness that shed o'er all a light
That made the green earth like the land of all
Our holiest dreams; while through the flowers
And grass we climbed the steep Grange brae, and then

Sat down to fill our souls with wealth of loveliness,
For O, the scene was lovely!   I wonder now
If the kind friend who shared our walks
Has in the Fatherland beheld a scene
More fair—hill and vale and wooded slope ;
The " fairy-haunted Lindeancleuch ;" the Ayle
Singing its ceaseless song through meadows green,
Like gentle maiden murmuring holy songs
Because her peaceful heart is pure and glad ;
The hedges high and white with bloom ; our own
Fair Lilliesleaf scattered along the ridge,
Calm in the holy Sabbath calm.   No wonder
That the scene remains on memory's whitest page—
That time's effacing finger dare not touch—
And ever with the lapse of years keeps growing
More dear and beautiful.   And when we've reached
The farther shore of this first scene of life,
We'll often think of " ancient Riddell's fair domain,"
Of Hardenburn, and all the walks we had
When life was young and all the world before us,
As all the summer lies before the snowdrops.

MARY.

I. KEN a winsome bit lassie
      That minds me o' rosebuds that lie
'Mang dewy leaves in the morning,
      A-wooin' the sun frae the sky.

An' I wish that her life may aye breathe
  An effluence as sweet as a rose,
An' as pure as the dews o' the morn
  That freshens the flower as it grows.

As the dewdrops kep and ensphere
  The rays frae the source o' oor licht,
E'en so may her pure soul ensphere
  The rays frae the centre o' richt.

An' when the lang years have woven
  Aboot her a mantle o' peace,
An' the angels are weary wi' waiting
  To crown her wi' life's grand increase;

When her heart is yearning for hame,
  An' her feet are sair wi' the road,
May shining ones waft her away
  To fulness of joy in God.

MUSINGS.

NAE doot the blackbird sings fu' sweet
    High on the auld aik tree,
But the whustle o' the whaup, I trow,
  Is fer mair dear to me.

O, weel I like the Ettrick hills
  Where I hae leeved sae lang,
Where a' the glens are glamoured ower
  Wi' auld romance and sang.

Amang the hills an' hopes an' holmes
  My thoughts fu' often daunder,
Like siller sangs frae siller rills
  That through the glens meander.

I enter in at open doors
  Where kindly welcome's gi'en,
An' where we crack the langsyne cracks
  An' see ilk langsyne scene.

But I carena to gang back to leeve,
  My hert wad be but wae
To miss the hert that made for me
  The bield below the brae.

I'm weel content to wait until
  The veil is drawn aside,
That hides the hert I leant on lang,
  Wi' muckle joy an' pride.

For where the hert is, there's the hame ;
  It's love that builds the nest ;
An' weel I ken love waits for me
  To hap me roond wi' rest.

Though then my thoughts may wander here
  To see ilk weel-kenned face,
I wadna come to leeve again,
  Though weel I like the place,

SWEET PEAS.

SOMEBODY aince walked into my heart,
    Wi' a posey o' flo'ers for a key ;
To other folks' een the flo'ers may fade,
    But they'll never fade wi' me.

Of course the sweet peas were sweet:
    Their sweetness scentit the air ;
But the sweetest thing about them
    Was the spirit sae leal and fair

That breathed through every blossom,
    Like words through a telephone,
In whispers that said kind things to me
    In a quiet undertone.

O' flo'ers are wonderfu' bonny !
    An' God speaks through them too ;
Oot o' the same earth, into the same licht,
    O' every description an' hue,

O' every form an' substance they come,
    Drinkin' the same rain an' dew,
Each wi' a word o' God in its heart,
    An' each to its mandate true.

An' now, my bonny wee woman,
    Your heart and mine should be
Like the clinging hands that twine
    Roond the stakes for the clinging pea.

Oor hands should cling to the steadfast laws
  That oor deeds may look to heaven,
Like flowers that sweeten all the air,
  With perfume freely given.

MORAL ATMOSPHERES.

WE a' evolve an atmosphere
    Roond us o' guid or ill—
An outer garment o' the soul
  Through which oor thochts distil
The spirit o' oor lives to shew
  Oor qualities o' hert an' will.

The cynic's atmosphere is ane
  That checks, an' numbs, an' freezes
Oor thochts ere they are coined to words;
  It fosters soul diseases,
Like snell east wunds that blaw aboot
  Rheumatics, coughs, and wheezes.

We feel as 'neath a Upas tree—
  The richt word wunna come ;
We stutter an' we warstle wi'
  A spirit halflins dumb ;
Oor thochts are a' astray ; oor heids
  Feel like an empty drum.

Frae his cauld unbelievin' gaze
  We shrink within oorsel's ;
Only what's warst in us he sees,
  An' what is guid repels ;
He judges most censoriously
  By ootsides o' the shells.

But kindliness roond kindliness,
  Like perfume roond the flo'ers,
Make thochts rin into fittest words,
  An' we could speak for 'oors
Bathed in a healthfu' atmosphere
  That fosters a' oor po'ers.

The man who takes the cynic's sword
  Shall perish by the same ;
Who wantonly his neighbour hurts,
  Writes on his own soul, " Shame ! "
But he is blest who kindly makes
  The golden rule his aim.

MOOTER.

LANGSYNE, when mills were few,
  The district roond
Was thirled to ane, an' a' within
  The legal boond
To it their corn bude take to grind,
Whether or no' they had a mind ;

An' for each lade
The miller made
He was paid weel
Wi' mootered meal.
But thirlage now has ceased to be,
  Wi' ane or twae exceptions
O' some deid hand's decree,
That like the ghosts that didna hear
  The morning cock craw in the day,
Still linger, unca deidly sweer
        To don their mantle grey,
        And gang away.

Now thirlage micht be wrang or richt
  When sic a law was made,
But wi' changed times an' clearer licht
  We a' maun hae free trade ;
When folk ootgrow their swaddlin' bands,
They tear them off wi' willing hands,
  So thirlage had to go.

But, oh ! I wonder sair to see,
  When wordly men do richt
They're wiser than the folk that think
  They're children o' the licht ;
An' there's the auld kirk mill,
  That grinds the breid o' life,
Thirles a' the parish to itsel'
  An' raises muckle strife ;

It's true they canna' make us bring oor corn,
Nor haul us in by lug an' horn,
But though we grind oor grain elsewhere,
  To their auld mill mooter maun gang ;
Now this, of course, is fer frae fair—
  Indeed its doonricht wrang,
An' mootered folk cry oot for richt—
  This state o' things they wunna stand,
An' auld kirk millers, filled wi' fricht,
  Wi' magic lanterns stump the land.

The watchmen on the sheelin' hill
May lift their voice wi' clamour shrill ;
The rank an' file rub stoorie een,
      An' a' concerned
    May greet an' grane
    An' make their mane,
    For they'll find oot,
    Withoot a doot,
    That nae lime licht
    Can make wrang richt.

THE DIFFERENCE.

SOME folk think to raise theirsel's up
  By pushin' other folk doon ;
It's a great mistake—they only show
  Theirsel's the pest o' the toon,
An' a' folk think they weel deserve
  To get a crack on the croon,

Others, again, forget theirsel's,
  Mindin' others to raise :
It wad be the last o' their actions
  Their kindness abroad to blaze,
But in the kingdom o' heaven
  It's written doon to their praise.

If a' folk wad only mind an' act
  On the golden rule o' life,
The diel could seldom raise a storm
  O' enmity and strife,
An' angels' visits, instead o' few,
  Wad be uncommonly rife.

We needna' think this rule is but
  For other folk to observe ;
It's for you, an' me, an' every ane,
  To quicken oor life wi' verve ;
The mair we help the helpless, the mair
  Oor ain guid we conserve.

Folk dinna lose by giein', if
  Their hearts are just an' richt ;
The man that scatters his seed abroad
  Get's harvest to gladden his sicht ;
But he that hoards the seed he has,
  Is a puir shortsichted wicht.

His barns are empty in autumn,
　When other folk's o'erflow ;
We get the seed frae oor Maister
　To scatter in fields below,
An' we'll reap oor harvest in heaven
　Accordin' as here we sow.

TO A. G. H.

O, ANDIE, ye're but a wee, wee chap,
　　Wi' the world a' afore ye ;
Yer ain route ye maun take on the map,
　An' write yer ain life's story ;
Yer wee, wee feet maun be weel shod
Wi' a firm trust in the love o' God.

Angels o' ill an' angels o' good
　Will gang wi' ye a' the way ;
The angels o' ill maun be withstood,
　But list what the good anes say ;
For the good an' the ill will strive to gain
The mastery ower yer heart an' brain.

Frae end to end o' the journey o' life
　Have a leal love o' the truth,
An' while weel prepared for jar or strife,
　In yer heart aye harbour ruth,
An' good shall be strewn along the road
That is lit up by the stars o' God.

Wisely walk in the light, that others may
　Safely in yer footsteps go ;
An' freely yer seed sow a' the way,
　An' gather where others strew ;
As pilgrim, sower, soldier, reaper,
Yer soul shall be its ain charter keeper.

Take truth for a sword an' right for a shield,
　When foes surround and assail :
The sword of the Lord shall win the field,
　An' make thine enemies quail ;
Aye move straight on, equip't, complete,
For onward march, but not for retreat.

An' a' on the way that ye subdue
　By effort of heart an' mind,
Shall render thee service, leal an' true,
　An' with kingliness enshrined
Within yer soul, kingly ye shall reign
Ower a' ye have won in life's campaign.

MAY BLOSSOM SUNBEAM CLUB.

(Rules to be Signed by the Members.)

I PROMISE to try to be true
　　In thought, in word, and in deed ;
To be modest and helpful and kind
　To each living thing that has need.
Never to listen to scandal,

Nor take pleasure in anything wrong ;
To be self-denying and punctual,
    To love what is good and be strong
To resist and conquer temptation ;
    To encourage each other in rightness,
By character and conversation.

OUR SUNBEAM CLUB.

I DREAMT that the angels abune
    Looked doon frae their spheres o' licht,
And saw the dear little Sunbeams here,
    Wi' faces a' shining bricht ;
And they danced and sang wi' perfect joy
    To see sic a bonny sicht.

Ane said to the rest " Let us each take ane,
    And tend her baith nicht and day,
We'll help them aye to be kind and true
    In a' that they think and say ;
We'll open their een to each wily snare,
    That wad lead their feet astray.

We'll make them see that the evil deed
    Grows oot o' the evil thocht ;
And every ten years we'll meet again
    To see what changes have wrought ;
Be glad wi' the guid and grieved wi' the ill
    That the years to them have brocht."

Then ane said " I'll have Fanny,"
  The next ane " I'll have Jane,"
The third said " Tiny Maggie
  I'll aye keep free frae stain ";
The fourth said " Isabella
  Shall be my very ain."

The fifth had een that shone like stars,
  O, she was wondrous bonny !
She said she thocht that I mysel'
  Had as muckle need as ony,
And she'd be mine to help me ower
  Paths thorny, steep, and stony.

So here, ower hill and dale, we journey on
  Wi' watchfu' angels by oor side,
That we should trust as pilgrims trust
  The knowledge of a trusty guide—
A kindly guide, whose love we know,
  Will lead us through the world wide
  Safe to our home at eventide.

THE SUNBEAM CLUB.

ALANE at the eventide I dreamt
  That fifty years had come an' gane,
An' the Sunbeams met in the same auld place,
  Each with the angel that was her ain,
An' a' were as leal as when they met
  Fifty years syne roond this hearthstane.

There was Fanny an' Tina, Maggie,
　　Jane, Esther, an' Isabella,
An' the licht that shone aboot them
　　Was genial, sweet, an' mellow,
The hair o' ane was as siller-white
　　As it aince was golden yellow.

An incorporeal Sunbeam cam'
　　An' sat in the auld airm chair,
The other Sunbeams smiled, weel pleased
　　To have their auld clubmate there,
Although she was as intangible
　　As the simmer evening air.

Wi' a licht like a smile frae Heaven,
　　Her voice said, soft and low,
" Let us a' gie thanks to the angels
　　That, wi' love that was aye aglow,
Strove weel to keep oor herts an' lives
　　As pure as the stainless snow.

An' Heaven's sweet benedictions
　　Dropt doon frae the angels' wings,
An' every clubmate's hert was filled
　　Wi' sangs that the glad hert sings,
While the sorrows o' earth for them
　　Nae langer had ony stings.

An' there they sat, the comely dames,
　　Each wi' her spectacles on ;
Wi' a far off look recounting by turns
　　Events that had come an' gone,

An' how through them a' a licht frae Heaven
　Had ever aboot her shone ;
An' the others listened wi' kindly grace
　To the quiet undertone.

Then said the voice frae the airm chair
　" I'm glad to be here this nicht,
An' pleased ower the lugs to ken
　How each Sunbeam has been a licht
That shone on the cluds o' the darkest day,
　Till the darkest cluds grew bricht.

I'm prood to think yer a credit
　To the guides ye've had sae lang—
That cheered yer journey through life
　Wi' mony a hertsome sang,
But dinna be pridefu', but gratefu'
　To ken ye've been keepit frae wrang.

An' now that the day's far spent,
　An' the shadows o' even grow dark,
Trust the love that has aye been aboot ye,
　An' leave to the world yer wark,
While loyalty writes on yer soul
　The word that is Heaven's hall mark."

Then there was a flutter o' unseen wings,
　An' a soond like the primrose rill,
Where ferns grow green in Lindeancleuch
　On the side o' Riddell Hill,
An' I wakened wide an' raxed mysel'
　In the nineteenth century still.

THE MONOLOGUISH MAN.

THE monologuish man wad sit
    An' drone eend on for ever ;
He loves his ain eternal voice
    That flows on like a river ;
Ye canna' get a shot at him
    However fu' yer quiver.

O' endless strings o' platitudes
    He will his soul deliver ;
If ye like ill to be repressed
    He'll speak ye in a fever,
For " men may come and men may go
    But he goes on for ever."

Ye listen, wait, and watch yer chance
    To get a word rushed in,
But on he goes until ye think
    His dronin' waur than sin,
An' wish to guidness he wad cease
    His unconvincing din.

A' conversation's at an end
    When he gets under weigh ;
Edgeways ye'll no get in a word
    Though ye should wait a day ;
He thinks yer charmed to side wi' him
    In a' ye hear him say.

An' if, by some unlooked-for luck,
  His tongue should cease to wag,
The subject's changed, it's oot o' time
  An' no worth while to drag
The dreary windbag back to licht
  It's blawn up sides to jag.

He is the greatest weariness
  Syne ever speech began ;
An', O, he very often is
  A holy clergyman ;
The guid forgie me if I wish
  He were ayont Japan.

For, wae is me, I dinna like
  The monologuish man ;
Oh ! had his harness ony joint,
  I'd drive through it a ban
Wad make him frame his future speech
  Upon another plan.

If there's a greater bore, it is
  The monologuish woman ;
She'll deave yer vera soul wi' din
  Till baith yer lugs are bummin' ;
Oh ! how ye wish for quietness,
  An' think it's never comin'.

Nae love is lost atween the twae
  Whenever they foregather ;
Ilk ane believes the other ane

A great lang-wundit blether,
An' like the man that couldna' speak
On onything but leather.

Were it no' for conceit, I trow,
    They'd baith say muckle less,
An' no' against a neebour's tongue
    Sae thoughtlessly transgress,
But let ilk ane that wants get room
    To speak' withoot excess.

THE GOLDEN WEDDING.

FIFTY years ago two pilgrims met
    When their lives were fresh and gay,
When the lily and the violet
    Strewed sweetness on their way ;
And love, like a priceless amulet,
    Their hearts made young for aye.

Hand clasp'd in hand, and with hearts a-wed,
    They tripp'd o'er hill and plain ;
While over their heads the fleet years sped,
    Doubling joy and halving pain,
With earth below and heaven o'erhead
    And sunshine in their train.

They were ever helpful, true, and kind
  To pilgrims travelling the road ;
For the love within their hearts enshrined
  Was love to mankind and God ;
And the kindly earth with heaven combined
  To smoothen the path they trod.

And all the way, as onward they went,
  There was neither jar nor strife ;
For trust and loyalty were so blent
  In their calm concordant life ;
Each was to each the complement—
  True husband and true wife.

When the day for the golden wedding came,
  A dark cloud hovered o'er ;
An angel through the dark cloud, cleft,
Came and bore one pilgrim through the rift—
One was taken, and the other left
  To wait until love restore
To the lonely heart, awhile bereft,
  Its mate for evermore.

Angels are hovering round the souls
  Whose eyes look up to the light,
Where their names are shining in the scrolls
  That the angels love to write,
And the pilgrim feet are led to goals
  Where the loved ones re-unite.

H. M. STANLEY.

METTLE, muscle, brain and will,
  Their unity in Stanley find,
And with his fearlessness combined
They level every hindering hill.

His eyes are quick as light to see ;
  His heart is wise ; his ready feet
  When duty calls know no defeat
In working out the head's decree.

Obstruction cannot bar his course ;
  It gives but token of his might ;
  It bows before his claim of right,
And owns the dominance of force.

Like all great souls, he seems to think
  Obstructions are but tests to try
  The strength we win our victories by,
From which no loyal heart should shrink.

The savage man with poisoned dart,
  The forest, dark, and damp, and drear ;
  And hunger, sickness, death austere,
Like hounds of hell growled round his heart.

But He who hears His children cry
  A father is in very deed,
  And help He sent for Stanley's need,
When he was in extremity.

And when the food his hunger sought
  Came from the stores of heaven direct,
  He felt a father's arms protect
His life with purpose high enwrought.

Some men in silence overcome—
  Not so Stanley—loud and clear
  His words direct fall on the ear,
And in the heart are driven home.

His two grand texts are true and good,
  " As thine own self thy neighbour love,"
  " Wish for best gifts," to be inwove
Within thy soul with brotherhood.

That wish, expressed in noble deeds,
  Like polished stones build up the life
  That turns aside besieger's strife
And foemen's swords like broken reeds.

Oh, fearful heart ! be strong and true,
  And know the help to Stanley sent
  When failure seemed so imminent
Was a grand guide post reared for you.

God sends his servants to his field
  To work, and till their task is done
  He keeps them safe—at setting sun
Their worth of work is signed and sealed.

None with His work to do can die
  Before his time ; no dart has power
  To pierce his heart before the hour
That brings permission from on high.

ISABELLA GERTRUDE.

YOU bonny wee blossom of love,
    Wi' a face like a pale pink rose,
  Where a pair of sweet violets lie
In holy and restful repose
As pure as the stars
    That look from the sky.

Surely your beautiful eyes
  Were kindled in Heaven
To shine on this world of ours,
  And to keep our hearts lovely
  Nae doot you are given,
As earth is made lovely with flowers.

We welcome thee nestling here,
  As we welcome the flowers in the spring,
When the buds and the blossoms appear,
  And the birds begin blithely to sing.

Oh, a' the hale way
  That your wee feet maun gang
May the angels lilt ower ye

Some heartsome bit sang ;
While guiding your steps
    Frae a' that is wrang.

May they love thee and shield thee,
And comfort and bield thee
    Frae sorrow and pain,
    Making rough places plain ;
While they bind thee to guidness
    Wi' love's daisy chain.
And 'mid a' temptations and jars
    May they keep thee for ever
As pure as the stars.

In the sweetness of morn,
    In the glow of noontide,
In the shadows of eve,
    May they keep by thy side.

And when at the close of the day
    Kind nature is hushed to a calm,
And the bonny rose petals decay,
From love to more love slip away
    Like the last holy line of a psalm.

HARRIET BEECHER STOWE.

"I feel about all things now as I do about the things that happen in a hotel after my trunk is packed to go home. I may be vexed and annoyed, but what of it, I am going home."

H. B. STOWE.

GOOD Harriet Beecher Stowe!
   In countless hearts the name lies sweet,
And countless heads with reverence bow,
   To know her round of life complete.

She lived in readiness to go;
   Death oped the door when God said, "Come,
Leave all thy hindrances below,
   Come up and rest a while at home."

And she passed through the open door
   Where loyal souls do enter in,
To share God's joy for evermore,
   In triumph over death and sin.

O, grand the crown that angels wait
   To place upon the victor's brow;
And bright the smiles that gratulate
   Brave Harriet Beecher Stowe.

While noble souls of every age—
   In Christlike deeds her own compeers—
Loyal in heart, the seer and sage
   Sing welcome to the higher spheres.

O, 'tis a blessed thing to sow
   The seed the Lord Himself hath given,
To see the harvest sheaves, and know
   Love garners them in heaven.

ST MARY'S KIRK AND ST MARY'S LOCH.

LONG years ago, within the mystic past,
    St Mary's fane was reared on the hillside,
And reverent feet went up to meet with God.
Chivalry and beauty have here ofttimes
Joined heart and hand for weal or woe ;
And here the warlike knight and humble herd
Laid down the sword and crook, and rested
Side by side ; while fairies flitted o'er
The rainbow's rim, and brownies hid
Within the deep ravine, and the clear
Gem-like lake claspt the calm hills in unity.
O, sweet St Mary's lake ! the past and present
Meet in thee—earth and heaven meet when thy
Pure loveliness draws down the enamoured sun
From shining steeps of light to lay
His rainbows on the heathy hills
That duplicate themselves at eventide
In thy calm depths.   No wonder
That the poet's heart has been so often
Raptured with thy queenliness, and quivered
Into song at sight of thee among thy hills.
My soul, too, has felt the mystic touch ;
And now, with trembling fingers, here I lay
One more poor tribute on thy rippling wave.

FORGET-ME-NOT.

DEAR friend, I thank thee for the sweet forget-me-
       not,
The fitting emblem of a sweet request;
But think not that I need its silent prayer.
Can I forget the love whose shining beams
Transformed whate'er they fell on,
Till everything looked up with gladsome eyes,
Responding to the bright congenial glow
That opened all the flowers to give them light,
While birds filled all the air with melody?
The love that lay like balm upon the bruised heart,
Made pain less sharp and toil less wearyful,
That gave a keener zest to all the good
That strewed the wayside of our pilgrim life,
While brightening hope for all the time to come?
No! your love is woven so into my life
That I must cease to live if I forget thee.
The flower that drinks fresh draughts of morning dew
Grows strong and beautiful—a pure delight:
Thy love has hung on me like morning dew,
And I have drunk it up as drinks the thirsty flower.
I've seen the light through all its lustrous shining,
Yea seen the sun itself reflected in each drop;
And if it hangs not now like crystal spheres
It lives in every fibre of my soul,
Calm eyed and deep, a true forget-me-not.
And in the higher life my heart shall call,
And thou shalt never choose but come to me,

For thou art mine ; and as thy love has slaked
My thirsty soul, e'en so my love has rained
Refreshment on thine own, and though dark clouds
May intervene, still come there must clear shining
When all the storms of life have wrecked themselves
Upon the hither shore of death's dark river.

MEMORIES.

I SIT alone and dream of walks
   Long past, but pleasant still—
Of walks we've had by wood and stream,
   By flowery vale and hill.

Of walks along the Riddell road
   Where trees their branches spread,
A living arch of greenest leaves
   That interlace o'erhead.

We've wandered up by Hardenburn,
   And to the muckle tree,
Or through the fairy-haunted glen
   And ower the daisied lea.

And memory loves to linger long
   By bonny Boosemill Haugh,
Where merrily the river glides
   Past clumps of stately saugh.

And sweeter walks ane canna get
    Than walks by fair Linthill,
Where murmuring soft the river sings
    To rose and daffodil.

And whiles we've daundered up the glen
    Where flowers nod by Shawburn,
And where the blossoms grow sae white
    On many an ancient thorn.

We'd cross the brig and thread the wood,
    And climb to Friarshaw,
Where we can see the Minto Hills
    And rugged Ruberslaw.

The uplands wi' their sportive lambs,
    The quiet sylvan vale,
Where birds sing in the summer morn
    That flushes hill and dale.

And where around lang Lilliesleaf
    With lavish hand is flung
A wealth of grace more dear to me
    Than aught that ere was sung.

I sit alone and dream, and dream
    Of friends that shared with me
The pleasures that have set their seal
    On gracious memory.

I know not if we'll meet again
  By glen and greenwood tree,
Or hear full-throated birds pour forth
  Their hearts in melody;

But in that lovelier land afar,
  Where all is dear and fair,
My heart shall call them unto me,
  And I shall meet them there.

ROBIN REDBREAST.

BRIGHT tints come ower the autumn leaves;
  The farmer garners in his sheaves;
The hip, the haw, the rowan red
Are sweet to see in dell and shaw—
I like to hear the vera craw
  Cawin' homeward overhead.

And robin, perched on yon tree tap,
Flings his rapt song in nature's lap;
  No happier bird than he, I ween;
His song is bliss without alloy,
Upspringing from a heart of joy
  As glad as when the leaves were green.

And not alone in springtime glades,
And not alone in autumn shades,
  But oftentimes in winter days

To some high leafless branch he'll come
When a' the other birds are dumb
    And cheer us wi' his blithesome lays.

O, robin! that my soul could sing
In winter of the coming spring
    From off some consecrated height
A song as true and glad as thine,
Then heaven should fill this heart of mine
    With like abandon of delight.

WRITTEN IN AN ALBUM.

IF thou would'st in thy heart
    Feel summer's balmy glow,
  "Forget last winter's snow,"
And read thou this suggestive book
In some reposeful nook
    Where dream-thoughts calmly flow,
As flows the rippling brook,
    Singing its quiet song
    The whole day long
To listening flowers that grow
    'Mong grass and sedge
    Fringing its edge.

The book's twice dear in friendship's eyes,
    For here high thoughts we find
    Of many a cultured mind
Traced on each page by friends we prize.

We read the lines, their thoughts we see
　Reflected well in what they write,
As in the lake each flower and tree
　Is duplicated to our sight.

Reading between the lines, we trace
Many a history, many a face ;
For memory reads distinct and clear
Many a thing not written here.

Here gathered flowers bloom sweet and fair
　As flowers bloom in a garden plot
And to the store I *dare* to add
　This small forget-me-not.

HOW NOT TO DO IT.

WHEN a man has gane a wee bit wrang
　　And his fauts ye need tae tell,
Mind and gie him nae hetter kail
　Than ye can sup yersel ;
For if ye do, it's ten to ane
　Ye'll only make him rebel.

Say naething to hurt his self-respec'
　If ye can help it ava,
An' when ye come to the sair bit
　Scartna the place that's raw,
To gratify yer ain puir spite
　Enlairging every flaw.

For guidsake pit on nae michty airs
   As nane were guid but yersel,
An' never forget the golden rule ;
   For it needs nae witch to tell
That naething is half sae like to succeed,
   For it acts on a man like a spell.

For ordinar, folk are easy led,
   But they're no sae easy driven;
Their legs and airms ye may sned,
   But ye wunna drive them, even
Wi' a' the force ye can muster,
   To sic a guid place as heaven.

SPECTACLES.

IN kindly conversation two divines
   Who serve the Lord on different lines
   Together sit at a soireé;
   A parish priest is Mr B.,
   And Mr Y. a staunch U.P.
Says Mr B. to Mr Y.—
   "Your spectacles I'd like to try."
   Says Mr Y. to Mr B.—
" By all means try you mine,
And I would like a look through thine."
   "Agreed, and we shall see
   If mine fit you or yours fit me."
So, as the gentlemen proposes,

The spectacles are soon transferred
To different noses.
    Says Mr B.—" I cannot see
    At all with yours."
Says Mr Y.—" No more can I
With yours.   But O, if you could only see with mine,
You'd see how all that's best in churches do combine
  To make the grand U.P. denomination
The very best church in the whole creation."
    " Hold, hold," says Mr B.,
    For sure am I, if you could see
As I can see through mine,
    You'd see that soon or late
    The church established by the State
    Shall every sect absorb and dominate."
O, gentlemen, I do suppose,
The spec's that do each reverend nose
So gracefully bestride fit different eyes,
To what each sees he testifies ;
    But truth has many sides,
And men from different points of view
    Look at one side that oft the other hides.
Then deem no side unseen untrue,
But both with me agree,
That blessed are the eyes that see
    All round the truth.
Their's is the light that fills
    The heart with ruth
And God-like charity.

HENRY'S BIRTHDAY.

AGAIN the year wi' noiseless feet
    Brings Henry's natal day ;
He cam' when the flowers cam'
    In the bonny month o' May,
When a' the woods were ringing
Wi' sangs the birds were singing ;
While the flowers looked up an' listened,
Through draps o' dew that glistened
    Fresh on every spray.

A wee bit mite o' life he was,
    Laid into open airms
That shield him yet wi' muckle care,
An' muckle love frae mony a snare
    That tempts wi' false unholy charms
The thochtless heart, the careless fit,
An' hurts the chaps that has nae wit
    Wi' mony griefs an' harms.

May wisdom licht the way he gangs,
    An' truth be his sure guide,
While courage keeps his leal heart strong
    Whatever fate betide,
Till at his journey's end he rests
    Wi' love on every side.

An' as wi' ready welcome love
    Was waitin' for him here,
Even so may love await him
    Within Heaven's higher sphere,

While angels roond aboot him crood,
  Wi' gladsome voices singing clear—
Welcome, brother, leal an' true,
We are waiting here for you,
  An' a' the wuds are ringing
  Wi' sangs the birds are singing,
An' fresh wi' draps o' dew
  The bonny flowers upspringing
  To thee their gifts are bringing
Aboot thy feet to strew ;
  All thy wants we'll gently tend.
Singing—Welcome, brother, leal an' true ;
  Welcome to our Fatherland.

THE BANE O' ST GILES.

O, THE bane o' St Giles,
    The bane o' St Giles,
Makes the face o' the faithless
  Runckled wi' smiles.
The great sea serpent may wallop away,
The papers aboot it have naething to say,
Nae maitter although its length
  Is a hunder miles,
Its place is ta'en up
  Wi' the bane o' St Giles.
O, the bane, the blessed bane,
That aince was a bit o' the saint that's gane
  To the dear kens where,

An' left this bane—worth every bane
    In a hale kirkyard.
Dear Jacob Primmer, ye whiles
Look in at St Giles
    To spy oot the images there ;
When ye gang in again
Ye may spy oot the bane,
    If its no' elsewhere.
The bent o' the times nae doot ye can read
In a bane that's been deid
A thousand years,
    An' something mair ;
But the worldly wise
    Will likely maintain
That some needy penscraper
    Has invented the bane
For the guid o' his paper.

FAULTFINDERS.

SOME folk take a wonderfu' pride
        In huntin' up other folk's flaws,
There's naething but guid escapes them—
        Even it they scart wi' their claws ;
Wi' smiles an' smirks, an' words like dirks,
They will scart yer hert on the raws,
An' expect folk tae gie them applause

APPLICATION.

YE may preach yer tongue into rheumatics
　　To gossiping Mistress Bain,
Exposing her fauts and her failings,
　　But ye'll preach to her in vain.
She'll think every word ye say applies
　　To tattling Jenny MacMain,
An' she'll haud up her hands in horror
　　At sins nae waur than her ain.

An' Jenny puir body is just as pleased,
　　An' as shure as shure can be,
That yer preaching was meant for the other,
　　In the vera first degree ;
For every ane sees their neebor's bit slips,
　　But their ain they dinna see ;
An' often ane sees ane's neebor's bit slips,
　　Wi' a certain kind o' glee.

But where we see in oor neebor a faut,
　　Or ony bit want o' grace,
We should honestly look to oorsel's an' see
　　What we might be in their place,
An' be ready to wipe frae body and soul,
　　Every uncomely trace
O' what we consider in other folk,
　　Folly or black disgrace.

ILL-USED FOLK.

WHEN folk are used wi' doing what's richt
   They think nae mair aboot it;
It never enters their honest heart,
   That ony ane will doot it;
They need nae brazen trumpet,
   Nor e'en a horn to toot it.

But if ever a body keeps herpin' on
   The way that folk takes him in,
Be shure he cheats when he gets the chance;
   An' aye the looder his din
Believe him the less, an' be
   The mair convinced o' his sin.

The folk that are heartless an' cruel,
   Ca' other folk for the same;
An' they that are greedy an' grasping
   Sic like are aye first to blame;
They ca' them at nae allowance,
   An' wonder they think nae shame.

If they have a richt to an inch,
   They groonge if ye gie na an ell;
But if *ye* have a richt to a yard,
   They'll thrimmel ye off an inch an' tell
To a' that it disna concern,
   How greedy ye are yersel'.

If ye should hauf yer kingdom wi' them,
  They'll think they deserve it a' ;
An' they'll rack their brains till they fancy,
  Somewhere or other a flaw ;
Then instead o' thanks for yer kindness,
  They'll ca' ye as black as a craw.

Their souls are lean and scraggy affairs—
  If souls they have ava ;
They think that a' things should fly to them,
  Whenever they like to ca' ;
An' if ony ane gets a share o' what's gaun,
  Ane hears nae end o' their jaw.

An' a' that's guid in themselves they see
  Through goggles that magnify,
Till mites look as big as camels,
  An' midges like guid milk kye ;
But your invisible fauts,
  They see with the naked eye.

A RHYME FOR A' CONCERNED.

THERE'S a wonderfu' ingenuity
  In finding roads to the deil,
An' a wonderfu' lot o' ways,
  In learning the way to steal ;
Ane wad think the chief end o' man,
Was to grab at a' that he can,
  An' wriggle through life like an eel.

Frae folk that have gathered siller
  Wi' brain, industry, an' thrift,
The brainless, the thriftless, an' idle
  Wad grab wi' organised theft ;
As if the chief end o' the bees,
Was to keep the drones at their ease—
  Nae wonder that honesty's glift.

The rich an' the puir are members
  O' the same body politic,
An' should leave thegether in peace ;
  But instead o' that they kick,
The donnert mortals never will learn,
That kicking the pricks can only earn,
  A jaggy road to Auld Nick.

It's a daft like thing for the heid
  To scorn the hands that toil ;
An' as daft like for the hands,
  The heid o' its richts to spoil ;
The hands o' toil an' the wheels o' wealth,
Are needit baith for the common health,
  An' shouldna each other foil.

The goose that lays the golden eggs,
  In puir folks pooch pits siller ;
They wad be daft to clip her wings,
  An' waur than daft to kill her ;
If ye have corn to grind for meal,
Water maun come to the water wheel,
  An' ye maun hae a miller.

Now, for the guid o' a' the race
    They absolutely need
To be upricht, aefauld an' straightforward
    In thought, in word, and in deed ;
An' kindly an' helpfu' an' true,
While wi' the golden rule they subdue
    A' selfishness an' greed.

MRS GRUNDY.

I'M shure sic tred as folk has
    To please Mrs Grundy,
She must be obeyed
    Baith week-day and Sunday ;
Against her behests
    They daurna play cheep,
An' wherever she gangs
    They follow like sheep ;
The question they ask is no
    "Is't richt or is't wrang?"
But " What wull she say?"
    Then at it slap bang.

To a' kinds o' extremes
Undreamt of in dreams,
    To please her they'll gang ;
In the warm days o' simmer
    They pit gloves on their hands,
    For sae she commands ;

They build theirsel's up like a rick,
Or tie theirsel's up like a stick,
  Contract or expand,
Or crumple their feet,
  Till they hardly can stand;
They wad swap their salvation
To be in the fashion
  An' please the auld kimmer.

But I think the unholiest thing o' a',
Is squeezing their waists unnaturally sma',
  It's the daftest like enormity,
  The pride they take in deformity ;
They grudge neither labour nor wealth,
They grudge neither reason nor health,
  In trying to please Mrs Grundy.

Then, if somebody dees
To enrich legatees,
  O sic a hurry and deavement
For black claes and crape
In the fashionable shape,
  To publish abroad their bereavement.

If their herts are laden wi' grief,
  If the gladness o' life has been chilled,
  Wi' a blank that canna be filled,
To the voice o' reason they're deaf—
  But they hear Mrs Grundy,
  An' they rig oot on Sunday
In black whatever the cost ;

Pay, or no pay,
They're bound to obey
For what wad folk say
Were she to be cros't ?
The debt they maun thole,
Hunger body and soul
To please Mrs Grundy.

'Twad be better I'm shure
For baith rich and puir
To try a' debateable things
By reason an' sense.
What's richt let us do,
What's wrong let's eschew,
An' carena a preen
What ony ane says
In blame or in praise
But calm and serene
Haud on oor ain ways.

GOSSIP.

WHEN neebor meets neebor they tatter
The neebor that isna there,
An' mirror themselves in every word
Mair truly I do declare,
Than the neebor they tatter sae sair.

They speak what their herts contain,
    An' mindna the golden law;
They gloat ower their neebor's fauts,
    An' blacken every flaw—
    They wad blacken the very snaw.

An' its less frae hardness o' hert
    Than for something else to say;
Still why should they feast on carrion,
    An' make sic a grand display
    O' a spirit that's better away.

An' maybe the neebor dissected
    Is doing the selfsame thing;
Tipping wi' gall an' venom
    Everybit as ruthless a sting.

Truly this world is bad eneuch,
    But oh! what a world it wad be
Did every ane hear what was said
    By the tongues that wag sae free;
I wat the licence they take
    They wad like gey ill to gie.

I rather think it wad be
    A jumble o' wrath and spite,
Wi' every ane ready to say
    It was a' their neebor's wite
    That life was mair black than white.

Oh! this wearyfu', wearyfu' wrangness ;
    That the time were here I wus,
When we'll think an' speak o' others
    As we'd like them to speak o' us;
When a' oor herts will be true as steel,
An' a' oor tongues kindly an' leal.

A GOWK'S DAY SONNET.

ONCE on a first of April, long ago,
    A troop of girls combining work with fun,
Resolved to make the day a jolly one,
And, slyly smiling, tripping to and fro,
"A Gowk" was written large by Jenny Crow,
    And pinned upon the dress of Betty Bun ;
    And Betty all unwitting what was done
Adornèd Jenny just exactly so ;
The rest, by Jenny's squints, were asked to jeer
    At "Gowk" on Betty's back; and quite as sly
    Did Betty squint, and as unconsciously;
And while the two, complacent smile and nod,
The rest with merriment at both explode—
    Alas! sic gowks are common all the year.

THE SNOWDROPS.

THE snowdrops know their time to come, and come
    Whatever the weather may be ;
First footprints they of the welcome spring,
    Bringing joy and gladness to me ;
The seasons come and the seasons go,
And here they are in spite of the snow.

However soundly the wee things sleep,
    They are quick to hear and obey
The Master's voice when He calls them forth
    To brighten our hearts with hopes of May ;
Brave, modest evangels, pure and still,
By shewing God's love they do his will,

And the royal seal of Heaven they bear
    When bringing God's message to me,
In the darkest hour He bids me trust
    His love, though the way I may not see—
He bids me trust with never a fear—
For Winter is past when Spring is here.

Our hearts too should be quick to know
    Where our helpfulness is needed ;
And ready to do what good we can,
    Though our help may pass unheeded ;
And if we do right because 'tis right,
Our spirits will halo our lives with light.

SUMMER IN THE SOUL.

OUR pleasures are enhanced by change,
  And this glad summer scene
That greets our eyes, could never fill
  Our hearts with joy as keen,
Did Winter not with stormy blast
  Make bare the dale and dean.

The earth is wrapt with loveliness
  In robes of Summer's weaving,
All speckled o'er with sunbright flowers
  The common green relieving.

Chewing their cuds, contented kine
  On buttercups and daisies lie :
The lambs frisk round the sober sheep,
  While roses hail the butterfly.

And mingling with the breeze
  That softly sighs
Through leafy trees,
  Where sing the birds,
Where hum the bees,
  The rippling streams
Enchant our ears
  Like music in sweet dreams.

All seem combined to gift
  Delights of sight and sound,
And pour on each responsive mind
  The love the flowers expound,

Even as the waters calm reflect
    Hill, flower and waving tree ;
Or as the morning dews ensphere
    The sun in gems of purity.

So from clear depths of love divine
    The pure in heart respond,
And mirror back from this life here,
    The higher life beyond.

Although our lips are dumb, oppressed
    With nebulous emotion—
Unformed thoughts, like drops that lie
    One with the restless ocean—

We know this loveliness contains
    A soul—a hidden power—
An effluence that constrains ·
    The heart to feel in every flower,
The love which every flower explains

To souls that are akin to God,
    Hearts touched with altar fire,
That thrill and glow by secret power
    Breathed through the living lyre.

LOUISA.

I KEN a wee bit lassie
  That I like wonderous weel,
Her face is unco bonny,
  An' her heart is unco leal ;
She loves the flowers that love doth strew
  Along the road to cheer her ;
At every step they sweetly shew
  That God is ever near her,
They wither in her tiny hand,
But in her heart they live and lend
  Their sweetness to endear her.

O, may her opening life unfold,
  As opes the daisy, with
A white fringed heart of gold ;
May a' her thoughts be growing seeds
O' kindly words an' helpfu' deeds,
  Her heart the home of purity,
    If pain and loss
    Must be her cross ;
May good grow out of pain,
And every loss be turned to gain,
  And every cross to victory.

HEART GIFTS.

"Do me justice always ! bid my heart—their shrine —
 Render back its store of gifts, old words and looks of thine ;
Oh ! so all unjust—the less deserved the more divine."

ROBERT BROWNING.

OH ! is it just, dear love, to ask
    My heart, that was their shrine,
To give thee back such store of gifts—
    Dear words and looks of thine ;
I tell thee nay, it cannot be,
    Through all my life they twine.

I cannot give them if I would,
    They're woven in my heart,
And I must cease to live ere aught
    Can tear the threads apart ;
Be just, nor ask a thing so wild,
    So full of pain and smart.

It cannot be, when least deserved
    Such gifts are most divine,
Like flowers whose rootlets clasp and pierce
    The heart, such gifts were thine ;
The life, the bloom, the fruit of them
    Now prove the gifts are mine.

JESSIE.

I LIKE the winsome wee Jessie,
  For she's guid, an' bonny an' clean,
An' I like the winsome bit smile
  That brichtens the look o' her een.

Her cheeks are far bonnier to me
  Than the first rose o' simmer sae fair,
An' her auld farrant heid is shining
  Wi' a treasure o' curly hair.

O, mony a ane wad be glad
  To ca' the bit lassie their ain,
An' there's few that have seen her aince
  But wad like to see her again.

If her wee bits o' feetie are spared
  To travel life's lang weary way,
May her life be mellow an' sweet
  When she rests at the close o' the day,

For the lot o' oor life is sorrow,
  An' it often seems to me
That the greatest favourites o' Heaven
  Have the heaviest weird to dree.

But the soul is strengthened by trial,
  An' the heart is sweetened by sorrow ;
The lowering clouds drop rain to-day
  That the flowers may bloom to-morrow.

An’ O, may the angels of God
　　Have the lassie aye in their care,
An’ fauld their wings round aboot her,
　　Stainless and sweet for evermair.

ROZINANTE.

THERE was a priest in Teriland,
　　An’ had he leeved lang syne
He’d been a brave Crusader,
　　An’ gaen to Palestine.

He was a keen equestrian,
　　An’ o’ his skeel was vaunty ;
An’ when he mounted his good steed—
　　His trusted Rozinante,

If e’er a gate stood in his way,
　　He stuck at nae sick straes,
But owre he flew, an’ ne’er thought on
　　The colour o’ his claes.

In coorse o’ time he thocht to gang
　　An’ see St James’ Fair ;
An’ maybe it might happen,
　　He’d sell or swap his mare.

An’ sae, wi’ bargains in his heid,
　　To do as he was thinking,
He mounted Rozi ae fine morn,
　　An’ off they went like winking.

He gaed aboot among the horse,
  An' men whose boast was cuteness,
To keep an even hand wi' them
  Wad need a like astuteness.

Soon Rozinante changed hands,
  Seller an' buyer pleased
To think how cleverly they had
  Each ane the other squeezed.

Then wand'ring up an' doon the fair,
  There, bye an' by he saw
A mare that seemed frae heid to tail
  Without a single flaw.

He looked its mooth, he looked its legs,
  Examined weel its feet;
An' then he tried its paces
  Alang a Kelso street.

An' efter prigging doon its price,
  A bargain forthwith made ;
Bestrode its back, an' homeward bound
  Wi' conscious pride he rade.

An' aye the nearer hame he got,
  The mare increased her paces ;
Blithely he hailed his man an' cried—
  " Will she win Teri races ? "

John clawed his heid an' took a snuff,
  Then said, " She's unco like the auld yin " ;
" O, John, she's clean a different colour,
  An' man, she is a yauld yin."

" Nae doot," said John, " she kens the road
  To her ain heck an' mainger ;
Light doon an' gie the beast its wull,
  We'll see if it's a stranger."

It went straight to the water trough,
  An' slaked its drooth wi' waitter ;
Then marched into its ain auld sta'
  As nocht had been the maitter.

They laughed ; but pride a wee
  The horseman's fun controlled ;
For he, like Rozinante,
  Had e'en himself been sold.

John said, when telling ower the tale
  As he clawed oot his bicker,
The look upon his maister's face
  Wad made an auld naig nicker.

LANGLANDS.

" OH, Langlands ye're a graceless man
    An' a graceless man are ye ;
If ye wunna pay the kirk its due
  The kirk's curse ye maun dree.

For first a Monk an' syne another
   The Abbot has sent to thee,
An' now the Abbot has come himsel
   Frae Melrose Monastrie."

When the Abbot met the perverse laird
   In his sanctity trusted he,
He ne'er thocht that a hand profane
   Dared touch the proud divinity
     That ruled the Melrose Monastrie.

He didna coont on the layman's sword
   That sprang frae its scabbard free,
An wi' ane swift an' deidly stroke
   Made his heid frae his body flee.

" There now, ye've raised a hornet's nest
   Aboot yer lugs I ween,
The Abbot's kain ye'd better paid -
   To the last bawbee yestreen."

Now Langlands sprang on his fleetest steed
   An' is off to Edinbro toon
To sue for pardon frae guid King James,
   For he was ane wily loon.

I wat he made the fire to fly
   Frae the strakes o' his horse's heels,
When by the Soutra hill he flew
   As he'd been chased by deils.

An' when he cam to Holyrood,
    I wat he didna tarry
Until he laid his case afore the King
    As cunning as auld Harry.

"Pardon, my liege, for a graceless deed ;
    I pray thee a pardon free,
For the insult I hae gien to the Abbot
    O' Melrose Monastrie.

"I couldna thole his priestly greed ;
    His threatening made me scoff ;
I gied my airm ane angry swing
    An' knockit his bonnet off."

The King he laughed ane gleesome laugh—
    Richt merrily laughed he ;
"If that's yer crime, yer prayer I grant,
    Ye shall hae ane pardon free."

Now Langlands was ane siccar man,
    An' ane siccar man was he,
He ne'er said a word until he got
    In his pooch his pardon free
    Sealed wi' the seal o' his Majesty.

Then thinking it time to finish off
    The story of the bonnet,
He said, wi' a twinkle in his een,
    "The Abbot's heid was in it."

A MAN SHOT.

JOCK had to gang through to the toon
    For things his mother needit ;
The road was past the bogly Howe—
    A place he sairly dreedit ;
An' efter he'd his shopping dune
    'Twas derk ere he wan there,
An' he, like Tam o' Shanter,
    Aboot him glowered wi' care
    Lest bogles catched him unaware.
He durstna even whustle
For fear it raised a rustle
    O' unseen wings o' fearsome things,
An' a' the weird an' eerie stories
    He'd ever heard cam in his mind ;
An' aye the thocht that ghosts or fairies
    Were closing roond, like souching wind,
Made his hert beat like ony drum,
An' his sweat reek like ony lum ;
An' duist when at the derkest spot
Oot o' the derkness cam a shot :
The bluid ran trickling doon his breeks,
The tears ran coorsing doon his cheeks.
His only trust was in his heels ;
He thocht a half a hunder deils
An' a' the horrors o' the Howe
Were gathering round about him now.
He ran, an' ran, an' ran
As never terror-stricken man

Had run afore ;
He ran, an' ran, until he wan
    In at an open door,
    An' there fell flat upon the floor ;
Faint wi the loss o' bluid he lay,
Wi' hardly pith eneuch to say,
    As tenderly he touched the spot,
What was the cause o' his alarm.
    True indeed he had been shot
    But wi' a cork, an' what he thought
His life bluid oozing warm,
Wasna bluid, but only barm.

LIFE.

LIFE is a scramel to find oor level,
    Which some never seem to do;
They grumel an' girn, an' greet an' cavil,
    An' keep theirsels in a stew ;
Like great big bairns they do nocht but snivel,
The length o' their fit they wadna travel
    To find what they're fit to pursue.

If ony roond man should happen to be
    Put into a four-square hole,
I think, if his heid an' his hands are free,
    An' if he has ocht o' a soul,
Some way or other he may surely see
The ill chance o' his life to modify,
    Or else he's as blind as a mole.

Of course we're no a' born into the place
　That we are the fittest for,
But it's nae use wearing a dolefu' face
　An' making oorsels a bore ;
Let us do oor best wi' oor best o' grace
To make hindrance only wi' mettle brace
　The nerves o' a conqueror.

An' the battle will make oor sinews strong ;
　The race make oor feet the fleeter;
If we shear away obstruction an' wrong
　Oor souls will be a' the meeter
For the place abune where we hope to gang,
The road will seem short we ance thocht sae lang,
　An' rest after toil will be sweeter.

AUTUMN LEAVES.

O, AUTUMN leaves! how beautiful
　Ye grow to die;
The gentle winds
　Breathe low and sigh
As ye rustle down from the trees
To rot under the feet
　Of the passer by.

I call to mind the sweet spring-time,
　When ye cast off your little hoods
　And clothed with green the gladsome woods
That merged into the summer prime.

The blithesome summer glows
  With life's perfumed breath,
But autumn fills our hands
With good, and shows
  The loveliness of death,

When death is but the casting off
The outer form that grows
  Around the living tree.
My heart is moved to upward thoughts,
  O withered leaves, by thee!
    Ye serve your end,
    And God's own hand
  Ripens and sets you free

So gently that you never know
  The sense of severance or pain ;
    Ye fall and die,
But year after year the trees still grow,
  And every year the boughs are clothed again
  With their own leaves, but not
    The leaves that lie
  Under the feet
    Of the passers by.

Even so do we cast off
  This mortal life ; and yet
The growing soul shall clothe itself
  Anew in raiment fit ;

> And by repeated change
>   Of vesture grow
> Strong as the light—
>   Pure as the snow.

AILIE AND ME.

OH, oor herts are heavy and sair!
    A' things are changed for evermair;
Twae o' oor bairnies are gane,
An' day an' nicht we make oor mane,
        Ailie an' me.

Johnnie scarce could stagger across the floor
    When his twae wee sisters cam,
He airtit aye for the open door
    To look for me, for he was his dada's lamb,
An' weel he likit to lie on my breast—
My wee lamb now is wi' God at rest.

We had oor hands weel filled wi' wark,
    But love made oor labour sweet,
    For we likit the patter o' little feet,
        Ailie an' me.
O, what planning we had for the bairns—
We were prood o' oor bairns,
        Ailie an' me.

Johnnie's queer bit says
An' his innerly ways
We'll mind a' oor days,
        Ailie an' me.

But now when we think on't, the angels
    Wad surely be near
Pitting the thochts in his heid
    That made him sae dear ;
For now that he's gane
    It a' seems sae clear
That ministering angels should like
    To be pettlin' him here.

Puir wee Jeanie, only fifteen months auld,
    Had to warstle for breath
        Ae lang weary nicht,
    Till the angel o' death
Took her and left a sair blank in oor fauld
        To Ailie an' me.

The vera next week the angel cam back
    For Johnnie, for Johnnie the licht o' my een ;
Oh, the cluds then grew starless an' black,
    An' my hert could do nocht but compleen !
I'll never forget his bits o' sensible says ;
I canna forget his kind bits o' ways,
    For he was the licht o' my een.

It's a comfort to ken they're but taen
  Oot o' ae faither's house to another's ;
The bairns were guid, an' the angels are guid,
  An' they'll tend them wi' care like a mother's.
We've but ae lamb left in oor fauld,
  An' we hap her at nicht wi' the tears in oor een,
To keep her wee feetie frae finding the cauld,
  For whae kens but the angels aboot her unseen
    May whisk her away
    Ere the break o' the day
      Frae Ailie an' me.

Little we ken what's afore us,
  And to kenna is maybe as weel ;
But the Faither that's taen them
Frae the faither that's haen them
  Oor herts will comfort an' heal
In His ain guid time an' way ;
  For His is a Faither's love sae leal,
  An' He kens a' that we feel,
    Ailie an' me.

Lang syne folk used to say
  When evil spirits were seen,
If ye named the name o' God
  They wad vanish frae fore yer een.
Sae the memory o' oor pet lambs shall lie
  In oor herts speaking His name for ever,
Keeping away ill thochts, bringing guid anes nigh,

Till we too cross the boundary river
To meet them again as angels bright
  In the green marged strand of oor Fatherland,
    Ailie an' me.

THE TWENTY-THIRD PSALM.

THE Lord's my herd, nae ill I'll fear,
    His lambs He cares for weel;
I'll thole nae wrang gif He is near
    To keep me bien and leal.

He'll lead me where the grass grows green
    Amang the daisied howes,
An' where atween its bonny banks
    The siller burnie rows.

An' gif I miss my road and gang
    Where prowling beasts o' prey
Are watching to devour the lambs
    That daunder far astray,

He'll bring me back wi' canny care
    To where I'm richt an' safe,
E'en though in wilfu' ignorance
    I murmur sair and chafe.

But for my sake and for His ain
    He'll gently bring me richt,
An open wide my wondering een
    Wi' touch o' heavenly licht.

Then though I gang the dreerest road—
    E'en through death's deep mirk vale—
I wunna fear, for weel I ken
    His love will never fail.

I ken it's aye a safe, safe lamp
    To licht the way I gang,
An' though the shadows flit aboot
    They canna do me wrang ;

For death is but a shadow made
    By licht that fa's on me
Frae my herd's lamp, that guides my feet
    To where nae shadows be.

Where'er I gang His hertsome love
    Will keep me aye frae ill;
His crook an' staff will keep me safe
    In every howe and hill.

My soul He'll feast wi' what is best,
    An' on my heid He'll pour
The oil o' grace ; afore my foes
    He'll make my cup run o'er.

Goodness an' mercy a' my life
    Shall free my soul frae care,
An' in my Faither's hoose at Hame
    I'll rest for evermair.

SABBATH BELLS.

RING out, sweet Sabbath bells!
          I love to hear
          Your voices clear
On the hushed air,
Calling to prayer.
The Father's voice ye seem to me,
Calling His children to His knee
          To rest awhile
          Under His smile
          From earthly care ;
          From muscle strain
          And aching brain,
          From toil and strife
          Of daily life,
          From wandering far
          'Mid hurtful jar.
O weary, weary children ! come
     As children come, with eager feet
     Unto their father's home to meet
Each other with fraternal love
     Beneath the father's eye ! O come !
          There's rest and peace
          And life's increase
With God " Who is our Home."

THE ANGELS.

AS we sat by the winter fire
    In converse free,
My friend, with quiet grace
    Addressing me,
Said, " If we resist an impulse to do right
We turn away an angel bright."
    " The thought is good," my heart
        Made quick reply,
    And angels in the air
        Seemed hovering nigh.
" Hell is paved with good intentions "
    And culpable delay.
Ah me ! how these intentions tell
    Of sorrowing angels turned away.
My soul is poor indeed
    If my best friends depart,
And leave me with a cold
    And withered heart ;
And yet how oft we lightly shut our eyes
    And will not see
Their shining wings, but rudely bid
    Them go away that we
Less holy guests may entertain,
    Thinking at some convenient time
The angels will come back again.
    Rather far, with open heart
        And shining face,
    Let's give them ready welcome
        To the highest place.

THE HIGHER SENSE.

THERE'S beauty here for common eyes,
   And beauty for the eyes that see
The soul of love that hidden lies
   Among the leaves of flower and tree.

The poet's soul is quick to hear
   Kind nature's never ceasing song ;
By heaven's concordances his ear
   Is soothed, his heart made leal and strong.

He sees the Father face to face,
   Lovely beyond our highest thought ;
The more his lineaments we trace,
   The more they are in us inwrought.

O, blessed gifts to poets given—
   The open eye, the holy light ;
The key that opes the gates of heaven,
   The love that robes the soul in white.

They see beyond the clouds of sorrow
   Into the Father's palace portal ;
If pain is here to-day, to-morrow
   Pain and grief like death are mortal.

A SONG FOR SOMEBODY.

OF a' the singers e'er I heard,
  There's nane can sing like thee, lassie;
Ye mind me o' the bird that sang
  High on the rowan tree, lassie,
  High on the rowan tree.

Wi' sic abandon o' delight
  He liltit up his sang, lassie;
The heavens abune were made mair bricht,
  The earth below less wrang, lassie,
  The earth below less wrang.

The thochts o' hills an' brattlin' burns
  Where grows the heather bell, lassie,
Made a' yer hert a thrill o' joy;
  The music was yersel', lassie,
  The music was yersel'.

O, had I but the whitest pen
  Taen frae an angel's wing, lassie,
I'd write a sang aboot yersel'
  An angel's sel' might sing, lassie,
  An angel's sel' might sing.

My thochts, as on some bonny flower,
  Wad shine like draps o' dew, lassie;
For heaven's ain licht wad make them bricht
  If they were sung by you, lassie,
  If they were sung by you.

"SOONER OR LATER."

A BRANCH all white with blossoms grew
    Upon a garden wall,
Love broke it from the parent tree
    To deck a lordly hall,
And all the hope of autumn fruit
    Seemed gone beyond recall.

Another branch beside it grew,
    In beauty's bloom its fellow,
It lived through all the summer till,
    When leaves were golden yellow,
It bent beneath a load of fruit,
    Luscious, ripe, and mellow.

Through light and shade, through toil and strife,
    We see an aged man
Has reached the eventide of life—
    His full allotted span,
While angels call away the youth
    That hope set in the van.

Lord Tennyson bore blessed fruit
    For all the coming years,
Till glory crowned a noble life
    Among the gifted seers,
While Arthur Hallam passed away
    Among a mist of tears.

But who can gauge the riches
  That came from grief's sad dower,
Unto the friend that loved him so
  When life was all in flower,
And Heaven-sent rains of sorrow
  Gave love its grandest power?

Our poor blind hearts arraign too oft
  The doings of the King,
When, were our vision clearer,
  We might see everything
Works out a higher good to make
  Our hearts with gladness sing.

MY LITTLE FREEND.

I HAVE a little freend,
  Her name I daurna tell;
But her witching, winsome ways,
Fer mair than what she says,
  Have ower me cast a spell,
  An' I canna help mysel'.

Nae wonder that I like
  The lassie wondrous weel,
For somehow or another
We're sae pleased when we foregather—
  O, her hert is true as steel,
  An' aye sae kind an' leal.

I micht rave a simmer day
  O' her mooth, her een, her brow,
But the graces o' her mind,
Wi' sic purity combined,
  Has set my hert alow
  Like a bleezing tap o' tow.

Now syne the lassie's mine
  The wunter wunds may blaw,
Oor herts shall intertwine
Wi' a love that's a' divine,
  An' warm eneuch to thaw
  The cauldest frost an' snaw.

FAITH AND ACTION.

THE acorn grows a tree,
  Faith of action is the seed,
And our lives, whate'er they be,
  Expound our faith in word and deed ;
Then let's be careful what we sow, for we know
  What we sow we reap, and what we reap we keep.

PRETTY NANCY.

NAE doot ye'll like fu' weel to ken
  Whae now has ta'en my fancy ;
I needna tell, for ye may guess
  It's nane but pretty Nancy.

O, life is oft a thorny road,
  But aye may luck unchancy
Gang scudding by the other side
  And never glower at Nancy.

As life is but a wairsh affair,
  Withoot a bit romancy,
May Love spread oot her whitest wings
  Aboot the heart o' Nancy.

May never one discordant note
  Disturb life's consonancy,
Till wi' a sang, swan-like, she'll gang
  Where angels wait for Nancy.

CONIE.

O, IF folk kenned whae I like weel
    They wadna wonder ony,
For a' folk kens how guid an' leal
  Is oor ain winsome Conie.

There's no' a ane in a' the land—
  At least there is na mony—
Sae clever baith wi' heid an' hand
  As oor ain lo'esome Conie.

The wushes guid I could indite
  To fill her life sae bonny,
Wad take a simmer day to write--
  Sae weel we like oor Conie.

O' a' the lassies that I ken
　　I'd choose for my life's crony,
To keep me tidy but an' ben,
　　Nane but my kindly Conie.

SPRING.

THE angels come down with harps of gold
　　And the flowers wake up to listen,
The trees their fresh green leaves unfold,
　　And the daisies with dewdrops glisten.
Our hearts are moved with the joyous strain,
And forced to join in the glad refrain.
O, the fair spring-time, the gay spring-time,
When heaven and earth so sweetly chime.

There's a rush of life-like eager feet
　　That hasten to hail the 'hest of spring,
When all things fair and all things sweet
　　Their gifts in nature's exchequer fling.
And leal hearts bathe in beauty and song,
Till every fibre grows fair and strong
As flowers that are fed by Heaven's own dew
When the old earth's garb for the year is new.

When beauty and song fill earth and air,
　　A thousand musical harps are strung
In oneness with all things good and fair,
　　And songs of gladness are gladly flung

From the hearts that see their home afar,
Through the gates the angels have left ajar,
When, with hearts attuned to choirs above,
They waken the earth with songs of love.

REFLECTION.

THE placid waters mirror back
   The shadows of the trees,
And in their depths we sometimes see
   Leaves rippled with the breeze.

The careless eye sees but the lake ;
   Beauty greets the artist's eye ;
When love looks thro' the shimmering leaves,
   There is a heaven of sky.

E'en so the common eye sees but
   The surface form of things ;
Beauty rewards the keener gaze,
   Love sees the angel's wings.

God sends his light to open eyes,
   The purest heart sees most of good,
The leal heart reads the law of love,
   By love the law is understood.

DESIGN.

IN these wise times our scientists do flout design,
    The plant brings forth the flower, the flower the
        seed,
    The seed the plant again, and so their creed
Revolves in endless circles fine.
If from nothing something was evolved
That caused everything, the myst'ry's solved,
And there's no need for an original overmind.
But if neatly folded up we find
In protoplasm all motion, soul and life,
And all the elements of internecine strife,
Where the strongest live and the weakest die,
Obeying a hidden law unconsciously ;
    Unless our souls are grossly blind,
All the more surely must we see
    The need of one all-comprehending overmind.

The power that fashions matter to its will
Is stronger than matter that exists but to fulfil
    The purpose of its unseen lord,
Whose power is hidden till revealed
    In outward deed or written word.
Matter is the kingdom of a king concealed ;.
    He apprehends and rules the laws
That cannot be repealed.
Holding the reins of force within His hand,
    He wills—temples and cities rise ;
    The lightnings serve Him from the skies ;

He drives His navies o'er the seas
From strand to strand ;
He crowns himself with knowledge grand,
For knowledge is the magic wand
    That with a master's hand He wields ;
        And nature hastens to obey
        The magic of its Master's sway,
    And gladly its allegiance yields.
If then in man this kingliness we find,
        Who shall be fool enough to say
There is for man no overmind ?

Link by link we trace the chain,
And every link may bear the strain
Of all, but who holds the first link in His hand,
Watching o'er all His mind has planned ?
The seed folds up the plant securely,
    Each one according to its kind,
And folded in its heart most surely
    Law and allegiance are combined ;
Who, in its bosom, wrapped potentiality,
And made earth, air, and sun to verify
The hidden word of prophecy ?

The organ planned with careful perspicuity
    Is dumb and answers not its end
Till breathed into by souls in unity
    With the designer, and who can apprehend
His purpose and work out his aim ;
Proving the nature of their minds the same.

'Tis thus we know we are the sons of God—
  By serving Him we apprehend His will,
By harmony our souls are overflowed
  When we, in love, His purposes fulfil.

A PARAPHRASE ON PAGE 234 OF " LATTER DAY PAMPHLETS," BY T. CARLYLE.

THE aim of all reformers is, or ought to be,
      Just laws, with this we humbly do agree.
To legislate for only one particular class
Is wrong, but legislate for all the mass,
And thus by lawful equity attain
For all mankind the truest, greatest gain.
For this we need the ablest man—a seer—
To make our laws a truthful transcript clear,
Of laws divine.   The fittest man to be
Our helmsman on the roaring sea of life
Is hard to find, and yet incessantly
The unseen powers admonish us to try.
Strict penalties o'ertake us if we stray,
And do not try to do the best we may,
To find and crown him king, and bow the knee
In offering him our hearts' best loyalty.
Only the honour worthy are of heaven
The aristocracy to whom is given
The government whereby the human race
Is raised by valour up to strength and grace.

For when the wisest, bravest, lealest, best
Bear rule, the land is prosperous and the people blest.
Then every popinjay and railway king
May on their well-earned gibbets writhe and swing,
To earth admonitory in heaven's name,
Showing the end of villainy is shame ;
The wretch that hungry Want goads on to steal
Is saintly to such traitors to the commonweal ;
Scoundrels supreme whose dark atrocity of greed
Insatiable the hoodwinked world did lead
In ways of gilded baseness seeking gain
Where nought was possible but loss and pain.
For scrip, claret, honour, and such small ware
They led their foolish dupes into a snare ;
Now all their speciosities unsealed,
And all their dark deformities revealed,
Proclaim aloud to all the world abroad
That not the devil is king, but God ;
Therefore be not scoundrels howe'er gilded o'er,
But honourable to life's inmost core.

THE SWORD OF TRUTH.

IF thy one aim be good and true,
    Hold on and have no fear ;
The stars of heaven shine out for you,
    To make thy pathway clear.

And all the angels of the Lord
  Watch thee with helping hand,
Let all thy ways with theirs accord,
  While ye for right contend.

If wrong and hind'rance bar thy path,
  Like ravening beasts of prey ;
The sword of truth all power hath
  To smite them from thy way.

Resistless as Excalibar,
  In hands by right made strong,
It mows down on the field of war
  All hinderance and wrong.

He fearless may his way pursue
  In spite of everything,
Who has the sword that can subdue
  The foes that flout the King.

MATTER AND SPIRIT.

THE poet said " The soul is form,
  And doth the body make " ;
And Stephen's soul shone bright as he
  Before the council spake ;
His seemed to be an angel's face—
So lovely and so full of grace.

For every thought, and word, and deed
  Do leave their true impress
Upon the soul, the face, the form
  Whatever tongues profess ;
The God-annointed eye can see
The truth in life's complexity.

In other lives our words are woven
  For good or ill, and we
Are answerable in part far what
  The true result may be ;
Then let no thought, false or unkind,
Within our hearts a harbour find.

MY BOOKS.

I'VE many friends ; I love them well,
  How well I have no words to tell,
Or even think in shapely thought,
But all the rich world's gold were vain
To what they give my soul of gain ;
  Within its finest fibre wrought.

That I exist they never knew,
Yet they are with me leal and true,
  And them I know and dearly see

Their inner thought, with watchful heed,
And feel them helpful in my need,
    With all their lore enlarging me.

They're with me in their highest mood,
To lead me to my highest good,
    They give to me their very best,
And fitly teach me how I may
Make beautiful my life each day ;
    They guide my feet in every quest.

They sing to me when I am glad,
They comfort me when I am sad ;
    I give to them my kindest looks,
For all the gifts their wisdom strews ;
I thank them with a heart that glows,
    For love has gilded all my books.

TRUE RELIGION.

IF we love God we will be like
    The flowers that breathe perfume,
And all around with kindliness
    Our hearts in deeds will bloom ;
A pleasant face, with goodness bright,
    Like sunshine chases gloom.

In giving joy to other souls,
　　Joy comes to us unsought ;
The cross is light that love shines on—
　　True love with love is bought ;
And round our souls a garment, white
　　With righteousness is wrought.

There's many a soul, like daisies shut
　　Beneath the gloom of night,
Spreads out in silence silver rays
　　To catch the rays of light ;
Their poor blind hearts will open eyes,
　　Glad to receive their sight.

And, as of old, the beacon's blaze
　　Flashed on from hill to hill,
So kindliness, from soul to soul,
　　Lights up the darkness still ;
While error flees before the force
　　Of consecrated will.

OUR EXEMPLAR.

JESUS, whose holy life has made
　　A ladder for our souls to rise
From earth to heaven with open eyes ;
A Priest, He on the altar laid
Himself, with holiness arrayed—
　　A spotless soul by love made wise—

A sacred life in God's emprise,
Upon whose life our life is stayed.
It shews what heights the race can reach
   Through abnegation and a cross,
In loving Him, whose life can teach
   That life is built on lower loss ;
The life we live for man and God
With good for self shall be o'erflowed.

The man with open eyes may well
   The unity of all things see,
   And from what is, what yet must be
May be well able to foretell ;
The pure in heart possess a spell
   That opens up, as with a key,
   The heart of many a mystery,
And many a truth within its shell.
And He, whose loyal life was true,
   Saw how the laws were made to serve,
And how obedience clears our views
   And fills our life with strength and verve,
His heart was pure, His eye was clear,
He is the star by which we steer.

VOICES AND ECHOES.

" There are many echoes in the world, and but few voices."
GœTHE.

THE prophet's voice with message clear
    Is heard above the wrangling rife
    Of mingling echoes in the strife,
By willing heart and open ear.

With heart on fire aloud he cries
    His message to the human race,
    But busy in the market place
Are men with neither ears nor eyes

For aught but what with using dies—
    Short-sighted folks who do not see
    The truth that makes the spirit free—
That makes the loyal-hearted wise.

Oh ! blest is he whose voice can bring
    A thousand echoes from the hills,
    That with responding echoes fills
The heart with all the verve of spring.

And happy he who opes his ears
    To hear the words that wisdom brings,
    And to their teaching wisely clings,
And by their shining wisely steers.

For wisdom's ways are safe and good,
    Even simple souls who walk therein
    Know that they walk with souls akin,
In true and kindly brotherhood.

KNOWLEDGE.

GOD gives us eyes to hail the light,
    He gives us hands to work his will ;
He gives us hearts to love the right
    And feet to climb up every hill.

Then lay aside each hindering weight,
    And run to gain the King's " Well done " !
Knowledge widens man's estate,
    And shews us what to choose and shun.

Knowledge is the rough material
    Placed by the toiling hand,
But wisdom must the soul build up,
    And brain with building blend.

For knowledge is as hands and feet,
    And wisdom as the overmind—
The flower of knowledge to complete
    Our fitness for each task assigned.

FATE.

HATE is a harp of many strings,
    That freewill fingers touch to strains
  Of tragic grief or sweet refrains,
Of songs like waft of angel wings.

Fate is the law—the stable rock
   That freewill, like the ivy plant
   With clinging tendrils consonant,
In mobile arms doth firmly lock.

Fate is the mill where we our corn
   Do grind of thought and word and deed,
   But fate grinds us if we impede
The wheels that nothing can subborn.

Revolving shaft and whirling wheel
   No favour show, for law is blind,
   And careless souls they catch and grind
Regardless of their woe or weal.

The laws of God like angels stand
   Ready to serve our every need,
   Responding with unerring speed
To the commanding Master's hand.

Fate is the warp wherein we weave
   The woof of charteréd freewill,
   That clothe with robes of good or ill
Our souls with what our souls believe.

We weave our lives into God's laws,
   And day by day the shuttle flies—
   With woof of right or wrong it plies,
With the result true to its cause.

We cannot hide the things we do,
   For all men see the robes we weave ;
   About our souls they firmly cleave,
As to the flower its native hue.

Death powerless is to separate
   The soul from character attained
   By deeds within the soul ingrained—
By freewill woven into fate.

THE PILGRIM.

O, PILGRIM on the world's highway,
   Be pure, and true and strong,
And have no fear of anything
   But fear of doing wrong,
   Keep marching-time with song.

Cast thou aside each hindering weight,
   And, with thy feet well shod,
Fix thou thy steadfast eye upon
   The guiding stars of God,
   That brighten all the road.

The way is often rough and steep,
   Through tangled flower and thorn ;
But on the steep hillsides the clouds
   With sunshine are o'erborne,
   And chased as if in scorn.

Gather into thy heart the flowers,
    And let their fragrance sweet
Adorn thy soul with grace, and make
    Thy life an offering meet
    To lay down at God's feet.

Fear not the clouds that hide from thee
    The sunshine for a while ;
They bring the showers that feed the flowers
    That by the wayside smile,
    And shorten many a mile.

Our souls were barren, did not God
    Send blessed showers of tears,
To sparkle in the kindly light,
    When sunshine reappears
    To chase away our fears.

We are but children looking up
    Into our Father's face ;
We walk by faith, as children do—
    God, give thy children grace
    To flee from all things base.

SPIRITUAL EVOLUTION.

TO-DAY is born of yesterday,
   And father of to-morrow ;
And if from rectitude we stray,
   Our children suffer sorrow—
We lengthen our account with theirs,
For all our sins have rightful heirs.

No man lives for himself alone—
   He sows his life within the race,
And he shall reap as he has sown
   Honour or deep disgrace.
Oh ! soul, in springtime, take good heed,
In furrows deep to sow good seed.

REGISTRATION.

LIKE automatic pens, our lives
   Record whate'er we think or do ;
What we avoid, what we pursue—
The soul stores all in its archives.

Though hid from every mortal eye,
   The evil thought is noted down,
   The hasty word, the angry frown,
The deed unkind, the false reply.

However false may be the soul,
  It keeps its record true as fate ;
  It cannot there equivocate,
But every word it must enroll.

Still we may hope to over-write,
  As palimpsests are written o'er,
  The past henceforth with holier lore,
As darkness is o'ercome with light.

LAW.

NATURE keeps a just account
    Of credit and debit ;
Every thought and deed is weighed,
    And in its place is writ.

Down it goes to curse or bless
    The heart from which it springs,
And we must reap with tears or joy
    The harvest that it brings.

We may not flout the smallest things—
    From small things great things grow ;
And reproduce for good or ill,
    Like seeds we careless strew.

A kindly deed may courage give
   To wanderers in the night,
A kindly word upon their path
   May prove a beacon light.

The deed unkind, the word untrue,
   Writes death upon the scroll ;
A just and kindly spirit writes
   Salvation on the soul.

Knowledge with love and loyalty,
   Grows in us stores of wealth ;
The more we give, the more we get
   Of larger life and health.

THOUGHTS.

THE builder builds with plumb and line :
   So may I build this life of mine.
The life that's built with leal heart stands
Like walls built up with honest hands.

Beyond the grave in other spheres
The true soul meets, and has no fears
To meet the holy eyes that see
How thought with word and deed agree.

When friend meets friend in Heaven's pure light
Some trait unknown may meet the sight
With which we cannot sympathise,
To fill the heart with strange surprise.

But, should we lack affinity
That may our friendship modify,
We may to other souls draw near,
Where heart reads heart with vision clear.

Where every heart is pure as snow
No hurt from heart to heart can flow,
For every heart will find a heart
That is its honest counterpart.

The friend I loved I shall not miss,
For her, there shall no lower bliss
Enfold her heart. We both shall know,
Without a pang, what hearts outgrow.

TRUE PRAYER.

OUR thoughts and deeds are prayers true,
　　That bring to us the answers due.
　Though we may not at once attain
What we, with earnest aim pursue,
　　God's angels whisper "Try again,"
　　No loyal effort is in vain.

The wingless word for ever fails,
But winged with love it aye prevails,
　And brings from God an answer meet.
For winds of Heaven fill outspread sails,
　And praying hands and praying feet
　Find welcome at the Mercy Seat.

Angels of God around us stand,
To strengthen every praying hand ;
　Swiftness they give to praying feet ;
Their aids with all our efforts blend
　To sow our fields and grind our wheat,
　And every want with promptness meet.

HIS WILL BE DONE.

" Fortunately for me, when I was very young I learned to repeat the Lord's prayer, and truly to mean it when I said 'Thy will be done,' and this I still say, and so nothing ever *really* troubles me."

BISMARCK.

HE who sits on high and reigns
　　Over all created things,
Knows all our errors, all our pains—
　The want that strives, the wrong that stings,
　The good that love from trouble wrings :
　　His will be done.

He knows the things we daily need—
　What's good to get or wise to shun ;
His angels teach our souls to read

How we may live in Him as one—
As loving Father, faithful son :
        His will be done.

We well may trust a Father's love--
  The love that has the power and will
To bless our lowness from above,
    The open hand with good to fill,
    And needed strength to combat ill :
        His will be done.

We trust Him in the darksome night :
  We trust Him in the dazzling day ;
The clouds may hide Him from our sight,
    And we may wander from the way—
    His rod will turn us when we stray :
        His will be done.

We ask His care, in thought and deed,
  With open heart and ready hand ;
Shut heart and hand do but impede
    The good, the good Lord wills to send,
    The light by which we understand
        His will be best.

We may with eager hands and cries
  Wish something that we have not won ;
There is no honour in the prize
    That's given for what we have not done—
    An earned crown for me or none :
        Nay, but His will be done.

Trials come our souls to test,
  And often what we deem our loss
Is but the love that doth arrest
  Our feet when hasting after dross ;
   'Tis then love lays on us the cross :
    His will be done.

When Heaven's own light shall round us glow,
  And angel hands clasp ours in Heaven,
Our souls, on looking back, shall know
  How we grew strong when we had striven
  Beneath the cross that love had given :
    His will be done.

THE MARTYRS.

WHEN darkness hides the pilgrim's way
  He leans upon his guide,
And in the battle with his foes
  He never quits his side ;
So clung the martyrs to their God
  When they for conscience died.

When all around is ease and calm
  We have no care or thought,
But highest life and strongest thew
  With toil and pain are bought,
And golden threads by trial oft
  Within our souls are wrought.

The noble men whose life-blood dyed
  Auld Scotland's hills and dales,
Had in their loyal hearts the love
  And light that never fails ;
They seemed to see the promised land
  Without dividing veils.

The glory to their souls revealed
  Expelled the thought of pain,
And persecution wrought for them
  And us an endless gain ;
The fiery tongues of flame but burned
  The chaff, the dross, the stain.

The loyal spirit triumphed o'er
  The flesh, the world, and wrong,
And striving with its foes but made
  The striving spirit strong,
And taught the soul called up to Heaven
  Exulting strains of song.

All men must die early or late,
  And suffering draws to God
The loyal heart, and it is well
  When we can kiss the rod,
And meekly follow in the steps
  Where holy men have trod.

A PRAYER.

O, FATHER, if it pleaseth Thee,
  In Thy great goodness send to me
An angel, musical and wise,
  To fill with light my inner eyes,
And teach my heart true loyalty ;
  To touch my lips with altar fire
  And give to me my heart's desire,
For what Thou givest I would give,
  That other souls may see,
And know, and love, and live.
Do Thou in Thy great love say " Come,"
  And I will answer, " Here am I,"
And my full heart, no longer dumb,
  Shall speak Thy words in glad reply.

O, Father, everywhere the weeds
  Usurp the goodly land,
While men are wrangling over creeds,
  Watchful of dogma, careless of deeds,
  Falsehood on every hand,
Rampant and brazen
  Like baleful clouds impend.
O, fill my hands with goodly seeds,
  That I may scatter wide and free ;
Give Thou the sunshine and the shower,
And all the land with plenty dower,
  That other hands may bring to Thee

The harvest sheaves with harvest glee,
And though I sow while others sleep,
  Joy shall be mine when they shall rise,
And my full harvest gladly reap.

THE MOTH.

POOR fluttering moth, your one desire
    Is to get near the burning flame ;
But know you not that you expire
Soon as you get at what you aim ?
The blaze consumes your fragile frame,
  But maybe life's small spark of fire
  Shall mingle with what you admire,
And that in thee we freely blame,
May be the power that overcame
  The lower life that clogged the higher.

I, too, fly from the outer night,
And flutter ronnd the fount of light ;
  I wonder if Heaven's central orb
  Shall in itself myself absorb—
Call home my soul to rest and live
In God, no longer fugitive.
  We do not know what yet may be,
But building on what we have learned,
  We trust the way we do not see,
And know we'll get what we have earned.

The law is just, and makes for good
When loved, obeyed, and understood ;
    Angels unseen may ope our eyes—
    May give us light and make us wise
To see and know and understand
    How 'tis obedience justifies :
And how a leal heart makes to bend
The laws, that we do apprehend,
To take our yoke and plough our land.

DAILY DUTY.

LET no needless fears for the morrow
    Hinder thy duty to-day ;
It's surely in vain that you borrow
    The fears that keep you at bay :
The future may have in it sorrow,
    But it need not the present dismay.

We live but a day at a time :
    Each day its own burden should bear :
Prematurely to take it's a crime ;
    Our strength we need not impair,
When hill after hill we should climb
    With limbs as free as the air.

Take the days one by one as they come :
    Forecast not the future with fears :
Why should we fret and look glum,

And drown the glad present in tears?
Because the dark future is dumb,
  Why people with goblins its years?

Live well in the present, and let
  The morrow take care of itself;
But never step o'er, nor forget,
  Nor carelessly lay on the shelf
The things to be loyally met,
  Though they bring neither praises nor pelf,

To-morrow grows out of to-day;
  And if its progenitor's good
The child is bound to display
  The likeness of filialhood;
And it on its offspring should lay
  Accumulant blessings accrued.

To-day we scatter our seed;
  To-morrow we gather and sow;
We sow and we reap the grain and the weed,
  Hind'ring and helping onward we go.
Hind'ring others ourselves we impede;
  By helping each other we grow.

THE DAISIES.

THE daisies by the dusty road
  Their dainty silver rays unfold,
To catch the sun in hearts of gold—
Evangels from the heart of God.

The hearts grow glad, the feet grow strong,
　　Of weary pilgrims as they pass
　　And read God's word among the grass,
While love flows through their lips in song.

The way were long for tired feet,
　　Were it not lighted with the glow
　　Of wayside flowers, that sweetly grow
Where God and man in Nature meet.

The love that meets our daily need
　　With flower, and fruit, and spirit light,
　　Opes the leal heart with love of right,
And, with the law, writes out our creed.

The hearing ear, the seeing eye,
　　In self and song and flower may read
　　The holiest bible, truest creed—
God's word to man, and man's reply.

God breathes His law through every place ;
　　Through flower and tree, through storm and calm
　　His laws are words in Nature's psalm,
Man, the refrain, with Godward face.

If, building on the stable law,
　　The faith that grasps the hand of God,
　　True love, the heart's divining rod,
Around his soul all good shall draw.

MY FIRST ACROSTIC.

GERTRUDE is a dear wee lass,
Elate with spirits all aglow,
Racing o'er the daisied grass,
Tripping light as falling snow.
Round and round she flits about,
Unfolding many a dainty grace ;
Defiance in her merry shout,
Excitement in her happy face.

Glad am I to see thee blithe,
Let come what will in after years ;
And now, with every limb so lithe,
Delight thyself with thy compeers ;
Young and bonny, bright and gay,
Sprite of gladness, romp away.

Violets ope their eyes in spring
In the garden and the glade,
Odours sweet they sweetly bring—
Largess to the little maid ;
Every bird its song will sing
To Violet from its leafy shade.

TRUST.

BE not afraid! above the storm
        Supreme God reigns ;
    His love ordains
The laws that help but do not harm
The souls that work with His right arm.

Be not afraid ! however dark
    May be the night,
    Dawn comes with light,
And at heaven's gate the singing lark.

Be not afraid nor cease to sing
    When winter raves
    O'er new made graves,
For love is over everything.

Be not not afraid, but keep in tune
    With laws that move
    In tuneful groove,
Through songs of May and flowers of June.

Be not afraid! all things rejoice
    In Nature's plan,
    And meant for man
The gladness of their varied voice.

Be not afraid! angels of God,
    From hill and dale
    And flowery vale,
Sing round thee love's divinest ode.

In cycles of eternal good
    Times come and go,
    And we shall grow
By laws we've served and understood.

Subdued and yoked to our leal will,
  Like music sweet,
  To words most meet,
For songs of praise on Zion hill.

THE KEY.

A HOLY spirit is the key
  That opes the gate of heaven,
And to the soul that seeks to see
  The Lord, 'tis freely given,

A holy spirit is the health
  Of every soul that's leal,
It sheds a kindly effluence
  Upon the common-weal.

A holy spirit oils the wheels
  That grind the bread of life ;
A holy spirit soothes and heals
  The hurts of toil and strife.

It is the breath of God, and brings
  To souls that yearn for right,
An atmosphere for angel wings
  To guard them day and night.

O, weary soul that blindly gropes,
    Pray thou for spirit grace
To lead thee through the maze of life,
    With light from God's own face.

O! blest are all to whom is given
    The key that opes the gates of heaven.

THE SEASONS.

WHEN Nature, rising from her sleep,
    Dons the green leaves of spring,
The daisies and the violets creep
About her feet, the young lambs leap,
    And birds wake up to sing.

The summer with its wealth of flowers
    Is flushed with loveliness;
The humming bees, the balmy showers,
The vocal woods at evening hours,
    Sing beauty's holiness.

But autumn crowns the glowing year
    With beauty all its own,
The heart of man with gifts to cheer,
And wisdom for the ears that hear
    God's voice in undertone.

CREEDS.

A THOUSAND loyal souls may have
   Each one a different creed,
And all, if held with hearts that serve
   With holy word and deed,
Converge in God, like different roads
   That to one centre lead.

'Tis well to walk with firm tread
   The way we've found most true ;
'Tis also well we should respect,
   With all forbearance due,
The path that other pilgrims may
   As honestly pursue.

It has been truly said of old
   That all roads lead to Rome,
And all the various Christian creeds
   Beneath Heaven's azure dome
Are but the tracks where pilgrim feet
   Are all night walking Home.

AFTER MANY YEARS.

IN the same old place
   Where his boyish face
I've seen so oft in the house of prayer,
   With father and mother,
   And sister and brother—
As they worshipped together there.

With a quick step back
O'er the beaten track,
Memory brings full many a scene
Of the long ago,
When youth was aglow,
With rosy sport on the village green ;

Or the time when he,
At his mother's knee,
Sang—"Here we suffer grief and pain ;"
The pain was brief,
And the swift relief
Was like the sunshine after the rain.

But since that day,
When, young and gay,
He lived in the light of love's own smile,
He has suffered loss,
And borne his cross,
Uphill o'er many a weary mile.

The same hymn now
He sings, I trow,
With a deeper sense and feeling,
And every word,
Has a memory stirred,
Some scene long past revealing.

Now father and mother,
Friend and brother,
Have through Death's mystic portal gone,

And o'er their dust,
To guard the trust,
He rears a memorial stone.

REVELATION.

GOD is not shut within the boards
      Of any book ;
We still can read His words
      In sea and brook ;
By hill, and vale, and forest glade—
In all things that His hand hath made—
In flowers that open to the light,
In stars that sparkle through the night ;
We see Him when the lightnings flash,
We hear Him when the thunders roll,
And in the deep recesses of the soul
      We feel Him near,
And to the pure in heart
      He giveth vision clear ;
The pure in heart of every age
      He still inspires,
And loyal lips He touches still
      With sacred fires ;
Knowledge and love
      Still draw aside
      The veils that hide
His glory from the eyes—
      And hearts that are too gross
      To see or feel their loss—

As holy men of old could read His will,
So holy men can read it still ;
For every eye by Him made reverent
Can see how earth with heaven is blent,
And write as true a revelation
As has been written since creation ;
   The pure in heart,
    The good and wise,
   Who read His will
    With reverent eyes,
Like priestly mediators stand
Interpreters at His right hand.

"MY BEAUTIFUL BOY."

[Perhaps the most beautiful thing that Emerson ever wrote was a threnody on the death of his little boy, Waldo, six years of age.

  " The gracious boy who did adorn
   The world whereinto he was born,

    . . . .

   Who gazed upon the sun and moon
   As if he came unto his own,

    . . . .

   And wandered backward as in scorn
   To wait an æon to be born."

His loss seems to have been the greatest trial of his life, and long years after, when he himself came to the boundary line that divides the seen from the Unseen, he took farewell of his friends and then smiled and said, " Oh ! my beautiful boy."]

YEAR after year had covered up
  Its heaps slain in the fight ;
The young grew old, the old stepped through
  The darkness into light.

Here eyes are dim with tears, our feet
  Are weary with the road,
But years may not their impress leave
  On cherubs dear to God.

And still within the father's heart
  His boy was young and bright
As when the cloud obscured the stars
  And hid him from his sight.

The pilgrim at his journey's end,
  Beneath the evening star,
Waits at his Father's door till Death
  The gates of life unbar.

He takes farewell of loved ones here,
  Then through the veil withdrawn,
He sees his boy all beautiful
  Wait for him in the dawn.

The gloom of death, the glow of life,
  The loveliness, the joy
Draw from his eager lips the cry,
  " O ! my beautiful boy."

Love welcomes here the helpless child,
  And in the realms above,
The one that draws aside the veil
  May not be Death, but Love.

PRAYER.

WE lift our eyes to Heaven and cry
    For gifts to fall in open hands :
God always hears, but what we ask
  Ofttimes withholds, and yet transcends
Our prayers ; we ask a gift, the power
  To win a higher good He sends.

He doth not put the bread into
  Our mouths ; He gives us fields to sow ;
He gives us heads, and hands, and seeds,
  To earn whate'er the laws bestow ;
And, if due service law receives,
  Our barns with good will overflow.

He does not grind our corn, but gives
  Us heads and hands to make our mills ;
He does not lift us up, but gives
  Us feet to climb life's highest hills :
We first must earn the things we want,
  And then our hands He freely fills.

Knowledge unlocks the hands of laws
  To do our will, when we know how
To give the homage they require :
  Like docile herds, they freely bow
Their trusty necks to take our yoke,
  For us the fields of fate to plough.

To earn the good that we receive
  Makes us both rich and strong,
And what we earn more surely doth
  Unto our earning souls belong ;
And strength accumulates to make
  A wall between our souls and wrong.

For gold and silver, land and sea,
  Our souls at death must leave behind,
But what we earn abides with us,
  And grows in heart, and hand, and mind ;
Such treasure, with God's help, we keep
  Against all enemies combined.

THE WORDS OF THE LORD.

THOUGHTFUL men of old imbibed
  The words of God through seeing eyes,
And with a pen of gold transcribed
  The words that make the world wise ;
So sure were they of what they saw,
They styled their transcript God's own law.

But what they read we still may read,
    Within, without, the wise decree—
A guide-book fit for every need,
    In mind and matter written free,
In all we see, and feel, and know
Of things above and things below.

To praying hearts the Lord gives love ;
    To praying eyes the Lord gives light ;
To souls that look beyond, above
    Material things, a sense of right
To love what's good, to hate what's wrong.
And gather strength by being strong.

God doth Himself to us reveal
    As freely as He did of old
To holy men whose hearts were leal,
    Who saw the only age of gold
Was in the kingdom of the Lord
For all who read and love His word.

" O, come, and let us worship Him "
    With truest love and service leal,
That our whole life may be a hymn
    That shall His love to man reveal ;
Come, lift the heart and bend the knee,
The bond of love shall make us free.

SONG FOR THE SEASON.

THE field and the forest
    Are dreary and bare ;
There's frost in the earth
    And frost in the air ;
The wee bits o' birds
    Seem niddert wi' care,
And the bleak auld year
    Now reaches the post,
    To gie up the ghost,
    Wi' the snaw in his hair.

He's been true as the sun :
Of all that's been done,
    An unbribeable registrar—
    Of peace and of war,
Of grief and of gladness,
Of wisdom and madness.
    Record and presage
      Has filled up his scroll,
    He has written a page
      For every soul.

Just and true every line :
    Every word that has jarred
On some good design ;
    Every deed that has marred
Some action divine,
    Goes down inexorably.
Nothing forgotten, nothing untrue ;

Nothing more, nothing less than is due ;
 And the tears of an angel
  No word can efface,
 But some holy evangel
  Good deeds may o'ertrace,
 And right may upgrow
  On the green grave of wrong ;
 What with sorrow we sow
  We may gather with song.

Now friend with friend is vieing
 With many a kindly greeting,
As thick as snow flakes flying,
 Like angels angels meeting,
From heaven above and earth below
 With prayers to love entreating,
That good each life may overflow,
And make it pure as falling snow.

May neither wrong nor jar
The young year's record mar ;
May heart, and mind, and hand
In holy effort blend,
To make each life an offering meet,
To lay down at the Master's feet ;
Then happiness, unsought, will come
With His well pleased encomium—
" Faithful one, well-done."

SOWING.

"Cast forth thy act, thy word into the ever-living, ever-working universe; it is a seed-grain that cannot die. Unnoticed to-day, it will be found flourishing a banyon grove—perhaps, alas! a hemlock forest—after a thousand years."   CARLYLE.

O SOWER, going forth to sow
    With thy compeers in life's wide field,
Think of the harvest that will grow,
    And what the ripened seeds will yield—
True bread of life, or only weeds
That bend their heads with baneful seeds.

'Tis not for one short year ye sow,
    But for all men and for all time;
Be wise and true, and good seed strew—
    Not poisonous seeds of grief and crime
That fill the sluggard's heart with woe,
And hem him round with many a foe.

To him who scatters precious seed
    A precious harvest shall be given,
And he men's hungry souls shall feed
    While storing compound gain in heaven;
He shall be blest who wisely spends
Himself in filling other's hands.

Who gives himself, himself shall gain
    Life's larger increment of good,
As he who scatters wide the grain
    Receives the harvest's plentitude;
With gifts and help all nature waits
For him whose life co-operates.

MEND THE BRUISED SHELL
WITH PEARL.

Suggested by Ralph Waldo Emerson.   He said he " could
mend his shell with pearl."

THE oyster, finding in its shell
   Some bruise, or grain of sand,
That it is powerless to expel,
   Can, with rich nacre, mend
The flaw, until it grows a gem
Fit for a queenly diadem.

Sometimes when laid aside by pain,
   We learn to sing a song
That overcomes our loss with gain,
   And makes the leal soul strong ;
With spirit nacre overlaid,
The pain a precious thing is made.

A bitter word, with malice spoken,
   Leaves on the soul a flaw :
Within the character a token
   That tells of broken law ;
What then can make the hurt soul well?
Mend with pearl the bruised shell.

For selfish ends, unkindly deeds,
   The soul doth wound and bruise,
But healing balm from love proceeds,
   That hearts from hearts transfuse.
True kindliness is like a spell
That mends with pearl the bruised shell.

Oh! happy he to whom is given
  Recuperative powers,
The baneful weeds, with seeds from heaven,
  To overgrow with flowers,
That do with rising incense tell
That love has healed the bruised shell.

SIGHT AND SOUND.

HE who from birth is deaf and blind,
  Imprisoned in the silent night,
  Can little know what sound and sight
Reveal to open heart and mind.

The green fields and the rolling seas,
The hills and vales and forest trees,
  The flowers below, the stars above,
The rills that down the hillside flow,
The sunsets with the skies aglow,
  The face and form of those we love.

The song of bird, the hum of bee,
The murmur of the restless sea,
  The west wind breathing summer air,
The organ's pealing notes of praise,
The songs that congregations raise,
  The voice of love, the words of prayer.

Unknown and unimagined all,
　For wrapt in silence dark and deep,
　No latent sense can vigil keep,
To guard the soul that is in thrall.

His joy and wonder who can tell,
When light the darkness shall dispel,
　While music fills new opened ears,
The lovely sights that meet his eyes
Shall fill his soul with wrapt surprise,
　As kings rejoice o'er new found spheres.

Even so, when this worn body dies,
God's hand may touch our ears and eyes,
　And give the soul unhindered sense,
When lovely things shall meet our view,
And music fill the senses new,
　With joy immeasurable, intense.

Ear hath not heard, eye hath not seen,
Nor thought conceived the joy, I ween,
　The pure in heart shall hear and see,
When every sense shall be unsealed,
And heaven around shall lie revealed
　To the leal heart by death made free.

PRAYING DEEDS.

THE Overmind our prayer hears
　　Expressed in feelings, thoughts, and deeds—
Exponents of our realest needs,

Realer than words ; as true as tears
  Of sorrow from a heart that bleeds
  For sin, that higher life impedes.

The evil thought, the shameful act,
  Pray for their due consequent meeds,
  Like seeds that grow to baneful weeds ;
And harboured hate doth hate attract,
  For every sin its name inscribes
  Within the soul that sin imbibes.

The upright aim, the kindly thought,
  The self-denial, and the grace
  That scorns to do aught mean or base,
Get answers in the soul inwrought
  That make it lovely as the light
  That shines on flowers with dewdrops bright.

There's no result without a cause ;
  We make or mar with our freewill ;
  We live our lives for good or ill,
According as we love God's laws.
  Environment may task our skill
  When adverse winds our sails do fill,

But we can signal in distress
  To One whose help is ever near—
  A Pilot who can safely steer
Into the port of righteousness,
  Where clouds disperse and stars appear,
  And songs of welcome fill the ear.

Maybe at death we'll leave below
    Entanglements that hinder here,
    And in a more congenial sphere,
With minds enlarged and hearts aglow,
    Beneath a sky serene and clear
    We'll find it joy our barks to steer.

Though in the land beyond the grave
    We still may err, and error leads
    Through ignorance to sinful deeds.
Well-balanced souls are strong to save,
    With wills made true and hearts made wise
    From death that under falsehood lies.

Sin from our system may be driven,
    As we from fevers here get free ;
    Our souls may gather health and be
Reclaimed, renewed, enlarged, forgiven,
    And with a cumulative grace
    Grow up from place to higher place.

IGDRASIL.

SYMBOLS are round us everywhere, and we
        Can read the unseen from the seen and bow
Before the majesty of Overmind
Transfusing law through all created things.
By Igdrasil—the Scandinavian tree—
Life, law, and fate are fully symbolised.

It binds in one the heaven, the earth, and hell,
Its roots deep down with Hela 'mong the dead ;
Its branches reaching up to highest heaven,
And spreading wide o'er all the Universe ;
The serpent gnawing at its roots, with all
Its dark unholy brood, at constant war
With life ; as constantly the Nornas, from
The Sacred Well, sprinkling its boughs until
They drop down honey dew from heaven
Among the sons of men, whose destinies
They grave on shields beneath the tree.
    They grave the destinies of men on *shields* :—
Law is a shield to every faithful soul ;
And law is fate wherein we weave freewill,
As woof is woven in warp, made fast from beam
To beam,
        Our thoughts, our deeds, are prayers that draw
The real consequent answers down from heaven.
And as the Jews raised up Jerusalem's walls
With sword in hand, so we, with hearts that pray
And hands that work do weave our lives into
The will of God.
        We are but viewless souls
That take material form for one brief day
Among the spreading bows of Igdrasil.
We work and sing, and laugh and weep, until
At eventide we lay aside our cross—
Our toilworn, workday dress, and rest all night
Till morning wake us up to other scenes.
    The ceaseless whirr of life is like the hum

Of bees on lindens that the summer lades
With flowers.
    The frost king comes when leaves are ripe
And at his icy breath they tremble down
Into the silent kingdom of the dead.
At times great gusts of passion pestilent
And helmless raves recklessly, like demons,
Through all the boughs of Igdrasil,
"Trailing its blossoms in the dust."
        There, too,
The righteous lightnings flash and quiver
Against unholy deeds ; the viewless air
Is lashed to fierce tempestuous storms as if
By deadly war of kings invisible ;
Till all the honey dews of heaven grow red
With blood, and fall, like molten lead, upon
The hearts of peaceful souls who mourn the dead.
  And there are soft and warm salubrious winds
Of grand enthusiasms that bend its branches
Down with gifts for men.
    Times, too, of holy calm,
When love spreads her white wings and sings her songs
With birds that perch upon its topmost boughs,
Sending heart lyrics into heaven, while men
Look up entranced to see the heavens bow down
To hear; friend grasps the hand of friend, they work
As brothers should, with one grand aim for good
To all. And as they work they sing. Strong men
Do bend the branches as they will, because their
    strength

Is one with law, and all the gods work with them.
Justice and Mercy meet and do not clash ;
Righteousness and Peace bind earth to heaven,
And all the chords of life are freely blent
In one most perfect harmony.

NANCIE.

MY heart keeps croonin' ower a sang,
　　For ane we a' like weel ;
Her he'rt doon to her finger tips
　　Is kind, an' true, an' leal.
　　　　An' blest be a',
　　　　Baith great an' sma',
That live to love my Nancie.

We like to pit oor money in
　　Banks where best interest's given ;
An' every blessing Nancie wins
　　Is bankit safe in Heaven.
　　　　Angels abune
　　　　Keep writing doon
The kindly deeds o' Nancie

But O, there never was a life
　　Where grief ne'er made inroad ;
But if grief come, may angels come
　　Alang wi' it frae God,
　　　　An' love be near
　　　　To dry the tear
That weets the cheek o' Nancie.

THE MESSAGE OF THE DAISY.

I LOVE the flowers by the wayside growing,
  And I stoop to hear what the daisies say,
When winter winds are rudely blowing
  The daisies alone by the wayside stay.
And there's never a day in all the year
    When we meet them not
    In some quiet spot,
When he that hath ears to hear may hear
  Holy hymns from their pure lips flowing,
  While all the time they keep on sowing
In the open heart through the open eye
The seeds of flowers that will never die.
Oh, fondly we call them the eye of day—
    They look to the sun with gold hearts glowing,
    Hearts of gold in white robes showing ;
But when laden clouds fill the dripping skies,
They fold up the gold with tears in their eyes.
    O, well may I learn from their quiet gaze,
    How as fitly to fill my lowly place,
    And as meekly to bear my quiet lot
    With a grateful heart that murmurs not ;
May my heart too be gold arrayed in white,
    Mine too a voice in nature's polyglot ;
And never a word may I speak or write
That may not stand in God's holy light.

THE SEASONS.

SPRING unfolds the fresh young leaves,
   And summer unfolds the flowers,
Autumn binds her heavy sheaves,
   And all are ours, all are ours.
The gifts of the year are manifold,
And the gifts of autumn are framed in gold.

When we have garnered our harvest gains,
   The wind may wail through the leafless trees,
And winter may soak the earth with rains,
   Or her silvery veins to crystal freeze,
And fold in snow the vale and the hill,
While sleeping nature is hushed and still.

When the nights are long, by our warm hearth
   We wait in hope for another spring,
When bud and blossom shall clothe the earth,
   And birds among the green leaves sing.
But all the seasons of all the years
Shew like a poesy besprent with tears.

And angel eyes from the stars look down
   On all the years of our life below,
And greet with a tear, a smile, or a frown,
   The growth of the seeds our thinkings sow.
Some seeds have wings and fly afar ;
Some words sow peace, and some sow jar.

For no man lives to himself alone,
  The air is impregned with what we think;
Oh, never a thought may our lives condone
  From which an angel of God might shrink.
O, pilgrim soul, by the wayside sow
Seeds that to flowers and fruits will grow.

Keep in thy heart the songs of spring;
  Let summer flowers in thy bosom blow;
For spring and summer to autumn bring
  All the gifts that from autumn flow.
Then store up the gifts of the whole round year,
For wintry times when the snows are here.

A PARAPHRASE OF THE FOLLOWING.

"Oh, unwise mortals that forever change and shift, and say 'yonder, not here.' Wealth, richer than both the Indies, lies everywhere for man, if he will endure. Not his oaks only and his fruit trees, his very heart roots itself wherever he will abide; roots itself, draws nourishment from the deep fountains of Universal Being. . . . . The wealth of a man is the number of things which he loves and blesses, which he is loved and blessed by."

THOMAS CARLYLE.

OH mortal, most unwise,
    Seeking change with restless eyes,
  Homeless, wandering here and there—
    What seekest thou?
  Rest from care?
  Scenes piquant and fair?

Foolish and blind canst thou not see
The blame of discontent abides with thee ?
  For round thee everywhere
Ready to fall into obedient hands
Is all you run to get in distant lands.
Be patient, loyal, ready to battle or·endure,
And daily sunrise is not more duly sure
  Than growth of sequent health and wealth
Into the heart that's pure.
  As fruit and forest trees
Strike deep their roots in earth
  And wave their branches in the breeze,
So be no more at strife
With laws that make for life.
But deep in Universal Being
  Take root and grow
Into the wiser seeing
  That makes thy heart to glow
With love to all ;
For all the love we get is wealth,
And all the love we give is health,
Even love for mountain streams
  And wild cascades,
For breezy woods
  And flowery glades.
Let man, and bird, and beast
  Find kindly home within thy breast ;
When love makes duty understood
  'Tis freely done, and open hands
  Are freely filled with good.

AUTUMN.

O, SOFTLY the autumn winds are sighing
    Like sylvan nymphs 'mong forest trees.
And gently the ripened leaves are dying
    And floating down the withering breeze.
Thickly they lie on the trodden road—
Leaves from the polyglot book of God.

The poplar leaves, like flakes of light
    That fall from heaven to earth in showers ;
The elms as golden are and bright
    As the glowing tints of summer flowers ;
The oak, the ash, and the rowantree,
The beech, the plane, and the pine are blent,
Sweet, picturesque, and opulent.

O brook that sings to the falling leaves,
    I fain would know the word of your song ;
The words of wisdom in Nature's book
    You sing so sweet as you glide along.
O leaves that fall by the flowing brook,
It is not the seeing heart that grieves
When garnering up its harvest sheaves.

The leaves are fresh in the dewy spring ;
    Flowers flush the fields in the summer time ;
On quivering wings the skylarks sing ;
    Bees gather sweets in the luscious lime ;
But autumn crowns the beautiful year,
Bringing her gifts when the leaves are sear.

Age·is a shedding of ripened leaves—
　The worn out leaves from our lives that fall ;
Age is a garnering up of sheaves,
　A storing up of our capital.
But all through the year our praying hands
Must work for the good the good Lord sends.

SUMMER.

IN grassy lanes when days are lang
　　I like to walk at even
Where roses blend with hawthorn bloom
　Till earth seems blent with Heaven.

God's angels shake the tree of life—
　It's blossoms fa' in showers
On open hearts that gather in
　The essence of the flowers.

·Laburnums hang their tasselled gold
　'Mang greenery fair to see,
An' mony a bonny bunch o' bloom
　Wechts doon the rowan tree.

The gleesome bairns gang oot to look
　For nests alang the hedge ;
They paidle barefit in the burn
　Beside the yellow sedge.

There's grace in every movement
  An' gladness in their een,
As buttercups an' daisies
  They gather off the green.

The birds sing oot sae blithely
  Frae every bush an' tree,
The flowers look up to listen
  To the heart melody.

O bonny birds, ye are sae glad,
  Nae wonder that ye sing ;
A' nature seems the harp o' love
  Wi' sangs on every string.

My heart absorbs respondingly
  Bird-like the joy o' living ;
The best o' life we freely get,
  The highest joy is giving.

There seems a sweeter stream o' love
  Through a' the leafy June,
To lift oor hearts through flowers and songs
  To Faither's love abune.

Why should we fear for anything
  When round us everywhere
The angels o' His love appear
  In a' that's gude an' fair.

VERSES.

BE honest, loyal, true, and kind
  In secret thought, in word and deeds;
The kindly heart, the honest mind,
  Like magnets draw life's truest meeds;
The soul that loves the right shall find
  That flowers grow from flower seeds.

The present, in the past surceased,
  Lives now to feed the coming day,
As flowers and fruits are all released
  From seeds we hide within the clay;
And growing souls by time increased
    Shall wider fields of good survey.

The laws of God like guide-posts stand;
  Obedience keeps us homeward bound;
Love is the spirit's magic wand
  That all the laws of life expound—
It gives a foretaste of the land
  Where the leal soul is robed and crowned.

The shadows lengthening eastward show,
  As hour by hour the day declines,
The way we've come, the way we go;
  And night hangs out her starry signs
That make the traveller's heart to glow
  While thinking of the light that shines
Where sweet home faces radiance flings
O'er all until the very silence sings.

CHANGE—NOT LOSS.

THE rill is lost in the river,
  The river is lost in the sea,
And heaven draws up the ocean
  To rain it again on the lea.

Is life no more than an ocean
  That falls on a thousand hills,
Refreshing the flowers as it flows
  To the river in murmuring rills?

If so, there is no great nor small,
  We are only parts of a whole,
And we lose ourselves when we die
  In the one imperial soul.

And though we may rise from the sea
  And be rained again on the hills,
We are not the self-same drops
  That flowed in the self-same rills.

I could not care for the bit of soul
  That walked beside me unseen
As I cared for the friend I loved
  And lost when the leaves were green.

Ourselves we do not lose, I ween,
  In the river or in the sea;
Two raindrops touch to one, but *we*
  Do keep our own identity.

And the soul that rose to Heaven
   When our hearts were torn with pain,
Will be the same that vanished
   If it comes to the earth again.

For life is not the revolution
   Of a ceaseless water-wheel,
But a growth of individual soul
   Within Heaven's commonweal.

The *spirit* of our lives aye falls
   Like mist and rain on the hills,
And flows to the heaving ocean
   In a thousand rivers and rills.

And as long as the hills endure
   It is caught in clouds from the sea,
And in ceaseless round is rained
   Again on the flowery lea.

A NEW VERSION OF AN OLD SOLILOQUY.

TO be or not to be ?   That is the question ;
   Whether 'tis nobler in the mind to suffer
The inconvenience of outrageous fashion,
Or to take up arms against the threatened
Crinoline, and by opposing end it ;

Banish it, we say ; and think to end with it
A thousand troubles that do, instead of
Natural ease and grace, make us like
Puppets above great overgrown umbrellas,
Truly this were a consummation
Devoutly to be wished !   But dare we
Take up arms against the gods of fashion
And all who bow the knee to graceless ugliness ?
There's the rub ; so few have grit enough
To brave the censorship of Mrs Grundy,
No matter what bears her imprimatur.
Then ever and anon bad dreams may come
Of her absurd ascendancy to break our rest,
After we've shuffled off the bars of steel
That bound our poor subservient souls
To huge balloons exposed to all the winds
That in a trice might blow us up
To fiery Mars or the cold sterile moon,
The thought's too horrible to entertain.
Shall we then bear the ills of crinoline
Lest otherwise we swing far past the golden mean ?
Nay!   Why should we grunt and sweat beneath
The hateful thing, when we might with a bodkin
End it ?   Still the dread that after it
The whipping-post, may stay our hands and make
Poor cowards of us all; and thus the native hue
Of resolution is sicklied o'er
With the pale cast of thought.   But are not angels
Our ideals of loveliness and grace,
And who ever saw angels in crinoline ?

Why then not openly rebel against
The tyranny of gracelessness in every form,
And with this enterprise of pith and moment
Turn the currents that run so much awry
Into channels of true grace and symmetry?

A SOWER WENT FORTH TO SOW.

IN every thought we think,
    In every word we say,
In every deed we do
    We very truly pray;
And whatsoe'er we wish or will
We get the fitting answer still.

    Our thoughts, our words, our deeds
        Go from us past recall
    To leave in other minds
        An influence for all;
In our own souls the wrong or right
Grows into weeds or blossoms bright.

    "Curses come home to roost,"
        Blessings come home to rest;
    And what we sow we reap—
        Harvest our seedtimes test;
If we sow nought the land grows weeds,
If we sow good we sow God's seeds.

His seeds are kindliness—
    The golden rule and true ;
Do ye to all as ye
    Wish all to do to you ;
And learn with meek and lowly mind
To be longsuffering and kind.

With charity that loves
    In truth a neighbour's name,
And hates to hear a word
    That blackens it with shame ;
With Christ-like self-forgetfulness
Be Christ-like in thy helpfulness.

Be pure in heart to catch
    The seeds that others strew,
That it an hundredfold
    Within thy heart may grow ;
Morn, noon, and night receive and sow
Good seed, and God the increase will bestow.

A HOLY SPIRIT.

A HOLY spirit is the sign and seal
    That makes us kin to all the Christs in God
Who bear the cross and trust his staff and rod,
And with true kingliness do set their heel
Upon the head of wrong. It doth reveal
    The Father's love on the·leal heart bestowed,
    While life with its sweet effluence is o'erflowed

With health that clears the air for common weal,
God breathes upon our souls and we do live ;
  We breathe God's breath and all the air is health,
The good we freely get we freely give—
  Unfailing kindliness and true soul wealth.
A holy spirit is the key to Heaven ;
Its want, the sin that cannot be forgiven.

THE BUILDERS.

ONE man with driftwood builds his house
    On heedlessness and lust ;
The shapeless thought, the careless word,
  The deed unkind, unjust ;
No matter how they fit the wall,
  He takes what comes on trust.

Another man with righteousness
    Builds life as on a rock ;
Each stone is made to fit its place,
  Wisdom guides each stroke ;
And when the floods and tempests come
  It braves the fiercest shock.

When troubles come the thoughtless man
    Drifts with the driving storm,
But he who builds on righteousness
  Need fear no loud alarm ;
The wrecks around may thickly lie,
  But him no storm can harm.

LIFE.

LIKE warp and woof our lives
    Are woven with our days ;
We clothe our growing souls
    With thoughts and words and ways.

No skill of man avails
    T'unweave the woven past ;
The word, the deed, the spirit
    Remain in colours fast.

The meanness that can stoop
    To call the aid, by malice driven,
Of falsehood, fraud, and guile
    To circumvent the will of Heaven.

The hurtful selfishness
    Of low sensual greed
Makes an ill woven web
    Of rotten word and deed.

And every thought that wrongs
    Another man with blame
The soul exudes, absorbs,
    And weaves to its own shame.

Then, O my soul, be strong !
    Arise and with firm will,
Scorn back each thought of wrong,
    And God's high hest fulfil.

The robe thy words and deeds
  Are ever weaving here
Shall indicate thy place
  Within the higher sphere.

Let every thread be strong
  And beautiful with truth,
And whiter than the snow
  With gentleness and ruth.

WATCHFULNESS.

" Guard well thy thoughts ; our thoughts are heard in Heaven."
YOUNG.

GUARD well thy thoughts, for, like winged seeds,
    They fly in words and grow in deeds,
  And ever reproduce their kinds
For good or ill ; and thou, their root
And source, may reap the gall or fruit
  That grow from them in other minds.

As ye would reptiles loathe and kill,
So loathe and scorn all thoughts of ill,
  Casting out the poisonous things,
Lest their vile progeny should claim
Descent from thee, and seal the blame
  With multiplicity of stings.

Nor only such dark demons exorcise,
But pray to God for open eyes
  And love for what is good and pure ;
Then shall thy thoughts, like white winged birds,
Bear strength and grace in saving words
  To every heart that harbours them.

PRAYING HANDS.

WORKING hands are praying hands,
  And to their prayer Heaven unbends,
Answering our best praying deeds
With what our soul and body needs.

Our prayers are different as our lives,
And only the Christ-like spirit thrives;
The heart that's black with malice nursing
Blindly prays for black self-cursing.

The heart that's white with love for all
Love answers to that spirit's call ;
The life that's spent for good to others
Is heard by finding all men brothers.

We know what plants will grow from certain seeds,
Even so the answer comes to praying deeds ;
For, what our lives do ask is given,
Then let us ask nought less than Heaven.

LET THE DEIL GET HIS DUE.

THERE'S some folk that's aye crying oot
    Wi' a tenderness really profane
For mercy; they wad droon the hale world
    Wi' mercy to save a sinner frae pain,
Although the sinner, I wot,
    Has neither heart, havins, nor brain.

They'd pit everything off the balance
    An' make life a jumble o' sweet,
Wi' nae distinction ava
    Saint and sinner alike they wad treat;
An' to speak o' hanging a murderer
    Is eneuch to make them greet.

For my pairt, I think it's fer better,
    When needfu', that justice should turn the screw,
An' let every sinner suffer
    By drinking the browst that they brew;
For however bad the deil may be,
    It's but richt he should get his due.

It's the height o' presumption to set
    Oorsels up abune the Lawgiver,
And tell Him what He shouldna do
    While we steal the shafts frae His quiver,
Pluming oorsels on a tender heart
    While deed frae desert we wad sever.

It's richt that the harvest should be
  The same as the seed that we saw,
If we saw nettle seed in the spring
  We'll have nae wheat harvest ava ;
There's truth and justice in nature,
  An' naething's mair helpfu' than law.

Nae doot there is plenty o' room for mercy
  If wedded to justice and truth,
But mercy that's aye ignoring
  Justice, is wanting in truest ruth,
While the mercy that draws the sinner frae sin
  Is a glory to baith age an' youth.

LAWS.

LAWS are like unseen angels
    Of God that work for good,
And we are safe and blest
    When they are understood ;
They ever stand and wait
To ope for us Heaven's pearly gate.

To him whose ears can hear,
    To him whose eyes can see,
All nature speaks in accents clear
    Words of calm veracity ;
The flowers that fringe the dusty road
Are each a written word of God.

The stars that sparkle in the sky,
  The eyes that meet them there
Fold in their light things deep and high
  That shall unfold elsewhere,
And every word of God is true
And claims from us the credence due.

Fools in their carnal hearts may say
  " There is no God, no Heaven,"
And thoughtless take their downward way;
  But to the pure in heart is given
Wisdom, to see and understand
The laws that have their source and end
In love, that all things comprehend.

MOVE FIRMLY ON.

MOVE firmly on and do what is right,
  No matter what others may say ;
The stars of Heaven shall guide thee by night
  And the blaze of the sun by day ;
For God shall be with thee wherever thou art
To bless thee in brain and bless thee in heart.

Shirk not the toil ; proudly scorn the scorn
  Of fools ; nay, if need be, fear not to die ;
From the death of the low the high is born,
  And the life so earned is pure and high ;
But long or short, may thy life in good
Be spent for the human brotherhood.

Our hearts are stirred by heroic deeds
  As was the pool by the angel of healing;
And actions grow from the living seeds
  That are fed by a flush of feeling.
'Tis good to have open hearts and eyes
To honour and love the brave and wise.

Hundreds may reap where one may sow;
  Freely we get, let us give as free;
For as we scatter our soul shall grow
  In health and in true nobility;
For unto the soul that gives is given,
And who sows on earth shall reap in Heaven.

THE LAWS OF GOD.

GOD'S laws are perfect and do good to all
  Who walk by law; they meet us everywhere
Like finger-posts that point to Heaven. We do not
    break
The laws, we break ourselves against their firm
Unerring sequence. The factory wheels do serve
Our needs; but if we thoughtlessly or heedlessly
Or wickedly permit these wheels to catch
Ourselves we are destroyed. Therefore let us
Beware lest we be drawn among the wheels
God made to grind for us the bread of life,
And crushed to death by unregarded laws.

The laws of man should be a close transcript
Of laws divine—relentlessly upright,
Divinely helpful to obedient souls,
Sure punishment to all who disobey.

When men begin to multiply and starve
On patches of ill-cultured soil as starved
As they are, God commands an exodus ;
And if they do not rise and go where there
Is room for all, 'tis only right they bear
The stern results of their shortsighted
Disobedience ; and it were spurious
Mercy and benevolence to feed them
With the pauper's dole, and for a time
Avert the curse that ought to fall upon
Material wants, only to let it fall
More surely on the pauperised soul.

True mercy, helpful and beneficent,
Will make men listen to the voice divine—
Send ships to take them to a wider land
And help them to subdue it, and to have
Dominion over all they do subdue ;
And thus, with willing hands and upright hearts
Become a strength, a glory to our own
United, duty-loving Fatherland.

There is no happiness for man apart
From duty to the perfect laws of God ;
They are not patriots who would feebly shirk
The stern responsibility of laws
That crush the guilty to protect the good.

Let the blow fall where 'tis earned, nor tax
The law-abiding man to pamper crime.
We do not want the tortuous tactics of
A party man.   We want a patriot
Strong, brave and true, who will not yield to noise
Nor turn aside from his straightforward course
To palter with a base expediency,
Or skin a sore that festers to the bone.

If Ireland's soul is sick with crime and shame
To give it sugar plums will only be
Encouragement to rank disease.   Rather
Give justice and a sword to shield the good,
To quell the bad and keep the peace ; and say—
"This is the way, walk ye in it," and thus
Your souls shall live, and only then by laws
Obeyed shall Ireland prosper and be blest.

A HOLY LIFE.

A HOLY life makes its own atmosphere,
    And every soul that cometh near
  Is softly blесséd unawares,
With incense on the altar stairs.
Our spirit is exponent of our creeds ;
Our prayers are expressed in deeds.

And whatsoe'er we ask is given,
And grows into our souls as hell or heaven
   In constant harvests that accumulate.
   Our freewill sows and reaps in fields of fate,
It may be worthless weeds or wheaten sheaves ;
It may be perfumed flowers or only leaves.

The life we get from God is our estate,
To keep, and dress, and cultivate :
   If we do well we eat the fruit
   That grows by faith from reason's root ;
The spirit of our lives is the sure test
If we have done or failed to do our best.

CONVICTION.

WE strive for victory, that flower which crowns
      The growth of earnest life ; our hands lay hold
On Heaven, and take by force the love of God,
Even as the plant uplifts its praying hands
And grasps a glory from the kindly sun :
God wills it so, and gladly gives to him who wins.
   The light of Heaven is round the pure in heart,
And they with open eyes behold their Lord.
The earnest will works out convictions ;
Doubts paralyse the feet, but we are free
And fleet and fearless by true-hearted, open-eyed
Conviction ; not mere sluggish, dark, unreasoning
Dogmatism, but that grand fruit which grows
Upon the tree of high endeavour.

We may delight in praise, and dread the blame
Of friends, and neighbours, and the race,
When on the land debateable, but when
Our open eyes have seen the Lord, and been
Within His holy place convinced of truth,
Then all denunciation or applause
Is no more heeded than the changeful wind
Upon an April day.   The seeing soul
Made wise by love is anchored firmly in
The gracious heart of the ALMIGHTY.

SILENT INFLUENCE.

'TIS not alone by word and deed
    Our lives spread good or ill ;
Our spirits make an atmosphere,
    The outcome of the inner will,
And all who come within this sphere
    Do feel its silent power ;
The silent light makes beautiful
    The silent growing flower.

But he who harbours evil thoughts
    Breathes out a pestilence ;
His eyes are dimmed with cherished sins
    That warp intelligence.
While he whose heart is clean and true,
    Who will not harbour ill,
Who every thought of wrong expels
    With salutory will,

Bears round himself an atmosphere
    Of health and gladsome peace,
That helps the souls drawn unto him
    To rise to life's increase.
The heart grows pure, the eyes grow clear
To see God everywhere,
    All robed in glowing spheres of light
    And Nature's vestments fair.

For He enspheres Himself in love,
    And laws magnificence
Breathed from His heart around Himself
    In true beneficence.

THE LILIES.

CONSIDER how the lilies grow—
    No rushing feet, no toiling hands,
But quietly, as flakes of snow
    From quiet clouds of heaven descend
    To clothe with white the winter lands.
God's voice is heard in Nature's laws—
    A still small voice but firm and strong,
And true and good ; it gently draws
    The heart that hears to right from wrong,
And turns the wail of woe to song.

And who hath ears to hear can hear
　　The flowers sing praises as they grow,
In tones that fall distinct and clear
　　Upon the heart that yearns to know
　　The love that makes the lilies blow.

TIME.

AS time moves on with steady pace,
　　We gather ill or good ;
The years to come grow from the past,
　　And all the past include.

And evermore our soul hands do
　　With thought, and word, and deed,
As woof weave in the warp of life,
　　Resulting blame and meed.
For all the faults I've woven in
　　My life I humbly grieve,
For not one thread of all the web
　　Can any power unweave.

But, like asbestos passed through fire,
　　My life shall come out pure
From death ; and all my soul has won
　　Shall in my soul endure.

THE WEB OF LIFE.

LIFE is a web we weave with woof
　　Of good and ill, of prayer and song ;
And oftentimes we feel reproof
　　And pain by what we've woven wrong.
The past we never can unweave,
However deeply we may grieve.

Life is a halting strain we draw
　　From God's grand harp of many a string—
Every string a perfect law,
　　From which imperfect fingers bring
Ill apprehended notes of sadness,
Blended with trustful peace and gladness.

Life's an Æolian harp played on
　　By winds of shifting circumstance—
Tempests that rage, and wreck, and moan—
　　Or gentle zephyrs that enhance
All life's best gifts and sweetest graces,
Wreathing with flowers the storm's rude traces.

Life, like the circling year goes round—
　　The bud and song in springtime sweet,
The summer with her garlands crowned,
　　And autumn with her golden feet ;
Then winter with his icy hand
Mows down the herbage of the land.

Life is a gathering up of wealth,
　　Enlarging all our inner store ;
Wise gathering keeps the soul in health,
　　And keeps it growing evermore.
There is no limit to the soul's expanse—
The growing soul rends circumstance.

When death comes with his golden key
　　To ope the golden gates of day,
Our eager souls shall struggle free
　　And fly to meet the dawning ray ;
And friends we loved while plodding here
Shall fold us in a sweeter love
Within a brighter sphere.

TRUTH.

"Little Jane will be beginning to have many notions of
things now.　Train her to this as the corner stone of all morality
—to stand by the truth, to abhor a lie as she does hell fire.
Actually the longer I live I see the greater cause to look on
falsehood with detestation, with terror, as the beginning of all
else that is of the devil."

THOMAS CARLYLE, to his brother.

STAND by the truth ; the truth is strong,
　　And all that's false is weak and wrong ;
Truth looks from the eyes and sets its seal
On every face that is true and leal.

All lovely things it makes cohere ;
Faith leans on it without a fear ;
'Tis the centre of all that's good in man ;
It guides the stars in the stellar plan.

Were truth withdrawn from God's creation,
All things would fall to swift negation ;
But He is love as well as truth,
And safely our hearts do rest in His ruth.

Then let our thoughts, like precious seed,
Spring into truth in word and deed ;
And ne'er may we seek to hide our blame
With a lie that doubles and blackens shame.

The wriggling soul that weaves deceit,
Like nets, around its wayward feet,
Is caught, and hindered, and disgraced,
By futile confidence misplaced.

Who lies must reap the fruit of lies—
A soul debased with darkened eyes ;
To those who love the truth reward is given,
Eyes open to the healthful light of Heaven.

The hateful things that shun the light
Crawl round the feet that love the night,
But beauty lines the Heavenward way
For feet that love the perfect day.

"WE SPEND OUR YEARS AS A TALE THAT IS TOLD."

TIME with his book beside us stands
    Turning the leaves with steady hands
  For us to write on as we go.
With ceaseless pen our lives note down,
Each thought, each deed, each passing frown
    Each weak resistance of the foe ;
    Each duty done with footsteps slow.

Down must go the false word spoken ;
Down must go the false love taken ;
  The work that cannot bear the light.
The skulking meanness hidden ;
The sneer by us unchidden ;
    The wish malign that fain would blight
    Whate'er is beautiful and right.

Thoughts and feelings leave their trace
On the soul and on the face ;
  The bent line, the deed unholy
Let not blur the daily page
That each must write from youth to age ;
    Let neither young nor wrinkled folly
    Fill the last page with melancholy.

But nobly live in word and deed,
So that our souls absorb the meed—
  Absorb the kindly, helpful spirit
That hopeth good, nor thinketh ill,

But fain would raise the downward will
  To reach up and inherit
  The guerdon that awaiteth merit.

And when the tale is fully told,
May it be every word in gold,
  That well the Master's eye may meet,
To whom may every page reveal
Some deed on which to set His seal—
  The whole a history complete,
  To lay with gladness at His feet.

"TO HIM THAT HATH SHALL BE GIVEN."

HE that hath soil can buy the seed:
    Seed cast in earth returns tenfold;
But he that hath the sorest need
  Hath neither land, nor seed, nor gold.
Labour is all his store, and that he'll give
To him that hath, that he may live.
For 'tis a law endorsed in Heaven,
That unto him that hath is given.

Wealth gathers wealth, draws more and more
  The poor man's toil into its net.
He that has wealth of learned lore
  With greater ease shall knowledge get.
And whoso hath a talent lying useless by
Must give to him that hath that it may multiply

And he who hath a cultured mind,
  Gathers from him with only hands;
The kingly man shall rule his kind,
  And homage get from all the lands.

But whoso harbours in his heart
  Curses, curses on himself shall draw
  With ruthless sting and greedy claw--
While round the man whose heart is full
Of blessing, angels shall flock to bless;
  They compass all his steps with peace;
  They crown his life with life's increase,
And all his boughs are bent with fruitfulness.

LINES FOR THE SEASON.

WITH firm resolve to do thy best,
  Begin the coming year;
The purpose high is helped by Heaven—
  Eyes that look up are clear.
The way is smooth for willing feet,
  The brave have least to fear.
On truth and right take thou thy stand
With honest heart and helpful hand.

Our lives are measured not by years,
  But by our fruitful deeds,
And by capacity of life
  To apprehend our needs,

And root from out our wayward hearts
  The overgrowing weeds.
The life that has but length alone
Is poor indeed when all is done.

Then live thy life wide, large, and full,
  And pure and high of mood ;
Let every day attest some gain,
  And every hour some good.
And though thy path be steep and rough,
  Still bravely bear thy rood—
It is the loom on which is woven
The robe that clothes the soul when proven.

OBEDIENCE.

OBEDIENCE in the hands of love
    Unlocks the gates of Heaven,
And what obedience asks in love
  Is freely, gladly given.
The laws like angels give their hands
  To help souls who have striven
To gain the heights where light appears
To make us wonder at our fears.

God's law is like an instrument
  That we must learn to know
Ere music of a noble life
  From its true keys can flow ;

It gives a voice to speak the love
    That in our bosoms glow,
And deftest fingers music brings
Most sweetly from the heart that sings.

The laws of God are foreordained—
    A warp in which we weave
Our own freewill, and from our heart
    We make a robe to cleave
Around our souls, that, by our dress
    Our lives men may perceive.
Into our robes we weave our creeds,
If honest hands weave honest deeds
Into God's warp, we get God-speeds.

The omnipresent laws of God
    Are His Almighty hands
That work together with the soul
    Whose will with His will blends ;
But fall with penal weight on him
    Who with the law contends.
Love stretches helping hands to draw
Our love within His helpful law.

The omnipresent laws of God
    Are his all-seeing eyes,
To Him our inmost thoughts in light
    For ever open lies.

The soul that from His presence flees
　In folly's meshes dies,
But whoso walks before His face
Grows beautiful with life's best grace.

EVOLUTION.

THE dark earth throbs with life
　Ere the green blade points to heaven,
And blossoms fill the land with joy
　Before the luscious fruit is given,
First the blade and then the ear
Ripening into plenteous cheer.
　Nature keeps her promise true
　And sends her gifts when they are due.
We watch and work and wait
　Through the life and bloom of living
Until we reach the further gate,
　Then crowd our life's best giving
Into the lap of those we leave,
　That they with God-magneted eyes
May our best autumn gifts receive,
　And learn to live and rise
　Strong, beautiful, and wise,
To bear whatever rood
The Father sends for good.

ONWARD.

EASY to man is paper goodness,
But hard the daily strain—
The blinding, grinding pain—
The self-denial evermore
From the outer gates of life
Even to its inmost core.
Not what we wish,
But what is right ;
Not the darkness,
But the light ;
Not ease and painless rest,
But what our Father deemeth best.
Courage, O tired heart,
With Godward eye press on ;
He'll give thee strength to totter to His feet,
And hear thy meed, " Well done."

DOING AND BEING.

WHAT must I do?   In distant lands
The heathen perish and my hands
Are idle.   At home the heathen in the street
With shrivelled heart and naked feet
To help I know not how.
The heathen, too, in highest places
With rotting core and many faces

Look for a smile and bow,
And none of them my help can reach ;
I cannot stop the blandly smiling face to preach.
O, troubled and perplexed heart,
  Love God and good shall grow from thee
Like boughs and blooms and seeds
  From out the living tree.
Thy life nurtured and hidden God shall teach
Where other teaching cannot reach.

WORK.

WORK and despair not
    Though the seed be thine
  And the harvest mine,
Still work and care not.

Your hand has gleaned the grain
    That grew from seed,
    Of word and deed,
Of other toiler's hand and brain.

Whether we sow or reap
    It matters not
    One single jot,
If in the Master's field we keep.

FRET NOT.

FRET not o'er thy sorrow,
　　Nor fear for the morrow ;
See sorrow and pain
Come laden with gain,
And the beautiful sunshine
　　Laughs after the rain.

We must have the rain ;
　　It wets us and frets us,
But we must have the rain ;
　　The green leaves,
The radiant flowers,
　　And the heavy sheaves
Come not without
　　The bountiful showers.

LIFE.

STRUGGLING and striving,
　　Drawing and driving,
Floating and diving,
　　Down the stream of time ;
In sorrow and gladness,
In wisdom and madness,
To the ocean of truth
　　Or the ocean of crime.

Away, away,
Day after day,
    To the gladsome light
Of our Father's home,
    Or the unblest night
Of a penal doom.
Souls of men bethink thee now,
While yet the cloud retains the bow.

VIA DOLOROSA.

WITH reverent steps and slow,
    With mourning heads bent low,
  Bear away, bear away
To earth all that can die.
  The soul no longer brooked delay,
Death oped the door that life might fly
  From the poor tenement of clay—
Dropping its heavy chains,
Its hindrances and pains,
  To grasp the Father's outstretched hand,
And rise above the jar and strife,
And weariness.of lower life,
  Into the peaceful Fatherland.

THE TRINITY.

LOVE is the spirit of God,
    The human race is His Son ;
The spirit, the race, and God are one,
    In Him we find our unity
    In infinite complexity.

ASPIRATION.

ASPIRE ! 'tis noble to aspire ;
    Only the chosen ones of God
Have hearts touched by His altar fire.

Aspiring, we most truly pray,
    Though oftentimes the answer comes
By starless night and stormy day.

But he who gets the highest place
    Must stand the hardest test,
And whoso hath is given grace.

Angels are with us in the night ;
    They may not bear our cross,
But their calm presence makes it light.

And when they flash their shining wings
    About us in the dark,
We see the wealth that trial brings.

THE COLLIE DOG.

A CROWD were gathered at a station,
	Each one self absorbed and silent,
The only sociable living thing, a dog—
A genial collie dog—that made himself
A friend for all disposed for friendship
His kindliness drew kindliness
From silent hearts, and for his kindliness
He got a smile, a pat, a kindly word.
The dog did good, and he by doing good
Got good, and every man a better man
Was made for feeling kindly. A woman
Cleaned the carriage windows, and as she cleaned
She sang ; her child ran here and there,
And toddled in before a coming train.
The mother sang and cleaned, the dog saw
And flew to save the frightened child
That started into safety ; the train crashed o'er
The noble self-forgetful friend of man,
And left it dead upon the rails.
But the fame of that good deed spread
O'er the world and made it better.

TRANSITION.

WHEN the ripe soul is ready to obey
	The homeward call, there is no need for fear
To guard the gates of death, for through the chill
And darkness God has stretched His hands and touched

The loyal eyes with light that shews the love
Beyond, and filled the soul that's homeward bound
With eagerness to go and leave behind
The dark and mystical perplexities
Of this uncomprehended life of hard
Probation, where all our energies are taxed
To learn the language of the higher sphere,
And speak it in our lives before the world.
When we have learned its grammar from the laws
Of God that make for good, we're ready with
Our harp-like souls to feel the breath of heaven
Make music in our hearts, and clothe us with
The pure white robes of songs that thrill and throb
Through every string of life ; while all the air
Is sweet with flower-like fragrance, and lovely
With a gladsome spontaneity.

"BE OF GOOD CHEER."

EVEN as the needle to the northern star,
        So turns our souls unto the perfect man
For guidance in the way of life.   His words
Breathe the sweet air of heaven ; above the din
Of lower life we hear them, " Be of good cheer
For I have overcome the world—
Poverty despite and cold indifference
I've overcome ; I fear not poverty :
'Tis nobler far to toil for bread than toil

To kill the time that hangs so heavy
On the idle hands of worldly wealth.
Hungry want has slain its thousands,
But overfulness lays its tens of thousands low.
What men call wealth I covet not ; why should
I hoard encumbrance by the way ?   Only
What grows into my soul by way of strength
I'll gladly, lightly, carry home with me ;
I envy not the rich bedazzlements
Of pride that do so needlessly exact
More irksome care than care of toil
For daily bread, and if some blameless cause
Hinder the daily toil and stop the daily bread
I can but die ; yet well I know that death
May wing his shafts in vain until the work
The Master puts into my hands is done.
Therefore I lean on God and have no care,
But how I best may weave His will into my life.
The foolish hate of men I also have
O'ercome ; it hurts me not, it but recoils
On their own heads.   Therefore I render not
Hate for their hate, nor spite for spite ;
I only pity them, they know not what they do ;
And what was hardest far to overcome
I overcame when I could tearless bear
The cold indifference or blame of those
Whom Nature linked to me with fleshly ties.
Their wide divergency of thought from mine
Seemed the result, in part, of organism,

Circumstance and different eyes
Perceiving differently.
                    Neither the cross
To live on, nor the cross to die on do I fear ;
Love lightens every cross, when I the world
Have overcome, with calm, clear eyes
Of reasonable trust in God.
Be ye also of good cheer, and even
As I have overcome do ye o'ercome,
With eyes made clear with a pure life,
And calm with well-established trust in God,
Built on the firm rock of law and reason.
Fear nothing, but do right and live your life
For good to those who thank thee not, not less
Than for all those who prize the gift."

A PARAPHRASE ON PAGE 78 OF "LATTER DAY PAMPHLETS," BY T. CARLYLE.

I'M sick, O friends, of all this jargon,
    Disastrous of philanthropy—
This universal brotherhood—
    This sugary reign of amity.

This paradise, not unto those alone,
    Of Heaven deserving well,
But paradise to all and sundry—
    Thus defrauding death and hell.

No doubt, most sugary friends, you'll think
    My language rather strong,
But your ideas of paradise
    Are altogether wrong.

No paradise for anyone I think,
    Who won't do right without it.
To such I say, "Just go your ways,
    And say no more about it."

Brethren distressed, 'tis all untrue
    This loathsome sugary nonsense,
There is no brotherhood for me,
    With such as have no conscience.

With base and foolish men I will
    Not live in any brotherhood ;
From such a baneful fellowship
    I never yet got any good.

I look on them with pity and some hope,
    Not yet absorbed in deep disgust ;
Otherwise in unappeasable aversion,
    And enmity most truly just.

Brotherhood ! the thought be far from me !
    Adam's children ? alas, no need
To call to mind the fact, and hence
    This rage against the perverse seed.

Gone over to the dragons vile—
　　The Father's house forsaken,
And the old serpent's slippery part
　　Against us they have taken.

Till they return from miry sloughs,
　　How can they ever brothers be?
They are enemies most deadly
　　To their own selves, to you and me.

But while hope lasts, them I will treat
　　As brothers fallen insane ;
But till they seek the Father's house,
　　A brother's love were vain.

When my small hope of them is lost,
　　I'll cut them off in God's own name,
With tears and wrath grown sacred,
　　And mixed with pitying blame.

I do not dare, with Satan's slaves
　　In partnership to stay,
Lest I become, as it is written,
　　Partakers of their plagues for aye.

PATIENCE.

PATIENCE, O fretful soul, so full
　　Of restless eagerness, thy cry for light
Is heard ; and though the shadows move
But slowly oft the bright sunshine,

Yet move they do most certainly.
Patience, O soul that darkly shivers
In the wintry blast ; the springtime comes
With all its fresh young life, praising the love
That never fails.   With trustful hope cast thou
Thy seed into the fertile furrows, nor think
The seasons lagg if all thy barns are not
Repletely full while yet the blade
Is green.   Wait patiently, nor thrust
The reaping hook among the grain before
The harvest sun has filled the growing ear.
Time moves along with steady pace, heedless
Of praise or blame, while love supreme
Impregns the clouds we dread with
Fruitful rain.   Nay, murmer not if harvests fail,
Or if they seem to lagg till other hands
Bring home thy sheaves : thou too dost reap
What other hands have sown, and if
The Master's work is done, be glad, nor vainly
Try to force the hand of God : we spoil the flower
If we unfold the bud before its time.
Good ripens slowly ; things most perishable
Grow quickest ; Jonah's gourd grew in a night,
And perished in a day ; the oak that grows
For centuries and serves the wants of man,
For centuries more is better than the gourd.
The soul that's ripened quickly serves
A poorer use than that which long years'
Training fits for kingly purposes.

Therefore be patient, doing each duty
As it rises, and be assured the time will come
When all the good that thou hast done
Shall ripen in thy soul to strength
And comeliness.   Then though the day
Of thy endeavour be long and wearisome
The eventide shall bring thee rest
Well earned and honourable.

A PARAPHRASE ON THE 116TH AND 117TH PAGES OF "SARTOR RESARTUS," BY T. CARLYLE.

THIS is how we put our claim for happiness,
    By certain averages and valuations,
Of our own striking we calculate
    What is by right our dues—not obligations,
If we get more than what we claim
The overplus we happiness may name,
    But deficit is misery
And some one is to blame,
Our own desserts we value thus:
    But then there is so much
Conceit in each of us,
No wonder if the balance dip
    The wrong way, and we feel abused ;
Many a blockhead crying loud—
    "Was every worthy gentleman so used ?"
Blockhead ! dost thou not see
It all comes of thy vanity,

And what thou fanciest thy desserts to be ?
 Fancy rather thy dessert is to be hanged
(Which is indeed most likely).
 Then would'st thou not
 Feel grateful to be shot ?
Or fancy thou deservest to be hanged in hair,
Then hemp would seem worth earnest prayer.
 The fraction of life, as such
Can be increased in value, not so much
 By increasing your numerator
As by lessening your denominator,
Unless my algebra prove false with me,
 Unity itself divided by zero
 Will give infinity.
If, then, thou wouldést have
 The world beneath thy feet,
.Make thy claim zero
 And thy victory is complete.

JACK THE GIANT QUELLER.

O, JACK was brave an' Jack was leal,
 He had a heart as true as steel,
An' a' that kenned him liked him weel.
 At nicht when he was at his play,
To lairn his tasks he was cried in,
 Then giant Pleasure blocked the way ;

Jack didna wait to hear his din,
　But turned aboot an' ran him doon,
　Tramping ower his vera croon—
He kenned defeat was in delay.

Next cam' to him in quick rotation
　A host o' giants clad in mail—
Addition and multiplication,
Subtraction an' division,
The whole tribe couldna make him quail ;
He took his slate wi' grand decision,
An' blattered doon his coonts like hail,
　An' sune he had them ane an' a'
Subdued by strength o' heid an' hand,
　Each ready at his lordly ca'
To wield for him a giant's brand.

Then giant Grammar dour appeared—
He thocht his look wad make Jack feared ;
　Jack cluffed his lugs wi' common sense,
　Subdued him in the present tense,
An' brought him to his bended knee
　And riped his pooch for recompense
An' chance o' war's indemnity.
Jack wasna like thae silly fules
That hate like soot a' kinds o' schules,
　An' nurse their indolence wi' sorrow,
　And pit off a' things till the morrow.

Then giant Letter cam', and Jack
  Thocht he, for size, was croonim,
He got a lot o' ink an' said
  He'd do his best to droon 'im.
He set to work wi' a' his micht,
As sune as he cam' hame at nicht,
  He tripp't him up, an' held him doon,
  An' wi' a steel pen nailed the loon.

Jack was a match for every ane—
He was determined he wad win ;
  At first he thocht them a' his foes,
  An' so it chanced they cam' to blows.
But when they saw his gallant deeds,
  They vowed that they wad serve him weel
  For a' their hearts were true an' leal,
An' they'll stand by him in his needs.

Now ower them a' supreme he reigns,
  Mair loyal subjects there are none,
  They make the kingdom he has won.
Lang may he rule wi' heart an' brain,
An' keep his kingdom free frae stain.

THE KINGDOM OF CHRIST.

" NEVER man spake like this man :
  This surely must be He
Who Israel shall redeem

And set our nation free ;
Come let us spurn the Roman yoke,
  And bow to Him the knee."

It was not as an earthly king
  That Jesus came to reign,
No ; earthly honours moved him not,
  Nor greed of earthly gain ;
And when He saw the mob's blind zeal,
  His soul was moved with pain,

And passing through their eager ranks
  He took himself away,
Up to a lonely mountain side
  To meditate and pray ;
And sent his followers o'er the lake
  That storms lashed into spray.

They also like the thoughtless throng,
  His mission did misdeem,
And wondered where their place would be
  When Israel he'd redeem ;
He'd surely keep them near himself
  And realise their dream.

But love denied their mute request,
  And kept them lowly still,
Nor set them where they could not stand,
  In spheres they could not fill,
To be dragged down with fickle fame
  And trampled on at will.

Better to breast the waves God sent
  That beat against our life,
Than to be hustled by the mob
  In ups and downs of strife,
With curses on incompetence,
  And self-abasements rife.

The kingly man is king o'er all
  The forces of his soul,
They to his will obedience yield,
  Bowing to his control ;
Such was the kingship Christ would have
  Them make their aim and goal.

When we subdue to heavenly rule
  Our passions and our wills,
The kingdom's built within our souls,
  And every fibre thrills,
With God who moves upon the sea,
  While life's rough storms He stills.

Ourselves must be the centre of
  Whate'er we rule as king ;
Our growing kingdom spreading out
  An ever widening ring.
While all the land with ready hand
  Allegiances bring.

For all that we subdue is ours
  In earth below, in heaven above ;
The earth we take by intellect,

N

And heaven we take by love :
Our title to the realm we rule
  Within our soul is wove.

We widen our inheritance
  By well directed force,
And what we take by force of arms
  The laws of heaven endorse ;
So under God we freely reign
  In law's benignant course.

We cannot all have earthly crowns,
  But every soul can gain
A crown of life with title clear
  Writ on our heart and brain,
In symbol true of golden deeds
  That ever shall remain.

SYMMETRY.

HEADS, hearts, and hands have each some one
    who pleads
  Their individual cause, nor understands
  That all the needful three in fitness blends
To show the manifolded man in deeds
That grow as flowers grow from the living seeds.
  Each in his triple unity of strands
  Has its own part in service, or commands
Earning consequent punishments or meeds.

Life should unfold itself and freely grow
  A perfect, well-concerted harmony ;
And all we do or feel or know
  Should tend to usefulness and dignity,
That over graceful lives shall sweetly throw
A robe of Christlike deeds as pure as snow.

JOHN HOWARD PAYNE.

THE beasts have lairs ; the birds have nests ;
    This man with feelings strong,
Homeless, at a stranger's door,
    Wrote a world-moving song.

He thought of all the thousand homes :
    Centres of Heaven on earth ;
Where love abides and labour rests
    Around the glowing hearth.

But yet for him 'mong all the homes
    Was none with homely cheer,
Where loved ones listened anxiously
    His welcome steps to hear.

Without a coin to buy a bed,
    He made a song of home—
The sweetest yearnings ever heard
    Beneath Heaven's azure dome.

MEDITATION.

THE well-known faces disappear in darkness,
    And never more do mortal eyes rest on
The forms we used to meet on life's highways ;
No more we raise our head to listen to
The well-known step ; their voice falls on our ear
No more, but in life's quiet hours they glide
From out the still recesses of the mind,
To fill once more the vacant chairs, and speak
As in the days that come no more ; again
The smile is lit and we respond with smiles.
But who knows if the dream is all a dream ?
Our eyes are holden with a veil of flesh
That separates soul from soul, and it may be
The body shields the growing soul until
The soul grows out of it into the light,
As the protecting calyx shields the flower,
And withers when the flower attains maturity.
The spirit of our lives, unseen but felt,
Is round us like an atmosphere
Of good and ill, and souls may fly as swift
As thought from star to star, all serving God
Like rays of light, that gather up our cries
And bless us in His name by night and day.
We do but dimly guess from what we know,
And this we know, goodness and power arc both—
Like God—invisible to mortal eyes,
And only are revealed to unseen soul
Suceptibilities by how they bend
Material to the unseen will.

O, blest is he whose memory recalls
With kindliness—with tears and smiles of love—
The kindliness of him who rayed his kindliness
O'er many a heart where his thoughts grew
To fragrant flowers that sweetened all the air.
How beautiful is kindliness ; how near akin
To good, the charity that shuts its eyes on sin,
And glorifies all nobleness and true endeavour
With smiles of glad recognizance—
That with vicarious tears would fain blot out
From every life the stains of evil deeds.,
How sweet the memory of the upright man !
Kind thoughts—like daisies—grow upon his grave
And open hearts of gold to golden light,
But wraps the gold in white robed purity
When darkness chills the tender heart of love.
O, Heavenly light come down on upturned eyes
And show how lovely all true wisdom is!
How peaceful all her ways ! that do converge
In God, the fountainhead of every good.

JUSTICE.

FOR all we get we surely pay,
    And promptly too, willing or not,
Who willing does his debts defray,
    Shall interest get on every jot;

But he who shuns, or seeks delay,
  No poor blind subterfuge nor plot
Avails him, nor shall shield his soul
That must disburse, with interest, the whole.
The giving soul aye gathers more ;
  While he, withholding more than meet,
Or giving grudgingly, his store
  Doth suffer loss and sore defeat,
With soul, too, sordid to deplore
  The loss that doth his soul deplete.
Fools try with wingless feet to scale the skies ;
The wise do preen their wings with fearless eyes.

GIVING AND GETTING.

IT'S no every ane that kens how to gie,
  And how to accept as few ;
Some gie wi' supreme condescension,
  As if they were better than you—
As if they were the cream o' creation,
  An' you but the bleared residue.

Some folk can gie the sma'est thing
  Wi' a grace that's worth fer mair
Than a costly gift by itsel' ;
  Some gie as if their hearts were sair
To pairt wi' the reek frae their kail ;
  An' some gie for vanity fair.

A gracious thing should be gracefully dune,
  An' promptness doubles the grace,
An' the pleasure we have in gieing
  Should shine on a kindly face,
An' make in the heart that gets the gift
  A holy and beautiful place.

It's never the gift's intrinsic worth
  Alane we should judge an' weigh,
But the kindliness roond aboot it,
  Like the gracious sun in May
That draws frae the throbbing heart o' earth
  The flowers in their sweet array.

B. thocht to gie hersel' pleasure ance,
  An' bocht for some fifteenpence
A sma' bit present to gie to C. ;
  C. took it wi' cauld indifference,
An' D., whose eggs have a' twae yowks,
  Remarked, with malice prepense,

" Sic things, for twae shillings a dizzen
  Are bocht ; that's duste the price."
B. felt baith anger, contempt, an' grief,
  For she thocht the thing vera nice ;
An' the speech was meant to annoy her
  An' make the speaker look wise.

I wadna like to have been the man
  Wi' the puir soul that said it ;
He lightly spoke o' a weel meant gift,

An' wi' false weights he weighed it,
An' the pleasure the saying gied him
  Was what the venom made it.

There's some puir mortals think they should be
  Like magnets ordained by law,
That whatever is guid or bonny
  They to their ain sel's should draw.
They take, but gie naething but grummells
  If the gifts ye gie are sma'.

But were a' the hale world to stick
  To their hurchin hides, 1 ween
The liberal soul wad be richer far
  Wi' a heart baith kind an' clean ;
For the man whose wealth is a' ootside
  Is no worth a pointless preen.

But the liberal soul devising good
  Shall be baith leal an' fair,
An' the blessed angels crood aroond
  The leal heart evermair.
For the best gifts in the sight of God
  Is love on the altar stair.

SYMBOLS.

THOUGHTS are revealed to souls in many ways ;
  In uttered words ; in symbols seen ;
Earth, air, and sea are full of them ;

The flowers that lift their heads to heaven
And ope their blossoms to the generous sun,
The trees with spreading boughs where birds build
    nests,
And sing glad songs of love that stir the heart
With thoughts of heaven ; the river with
Its ceaseless flow, never the same, and yet
Ever the same, like ceaseless generations
Of men that come and go in ceaseless flow ;
The stars above with quiet eyes and pure
That look down on the river and the race
Noting the changes that we do not see ;
All are the words of God—His book
That we are here to learn to read and love.
We stretch up praying hands to Him for light ;
For open eyes, for loving hearts to see
His will, and run with willing feet to do
His grand beneficent commands.
We, too, build up our thoughts in towns,
In cities ; in mills that grind out thoughts
Amid the whirr of wheels ; we make the wind,
The wave, the running stream, the lightning flash
Bow down and serve us ; we walk with God.
And elements that might devour us
We make to grind our corn.   Yea, and we build
Cathedrals where pillared aisle and fretted arch
Reveal our love with praying hands, and hearts
That cry for utterance in language known to God :
Where every part bears witness to a train
Of sequent thought ; doors for entrance,

Windows for light, and bells for invitation,
The whole surmounted by a cross, at once
A prayer and a symbol, a symbol
Of the lowly gate through which the highest
Life once passed to glory.   Symbols are words,
Jesus, the beloved of all the wise,
Was symbol and thing signified, a holy
Word of love made flesh, and holding in his bosom
The one divinest thought of God full of
The holy effluence of His holy spirit,
Showing thus the Father's image in the Son.
We too are sons bearing the same likeness,
But blurred, alas ! by error and by sin.

A HOLY LIFE.

A HOLY life has silent power to bless ;
  And sweetness giving, is not poorer made,
 But like the scented flowers whose fragrance lade
The air, and still the power to give possess,
Enriching souls that know with loveliness,
  And wooing them from husks that feed the swine,
  To higher thoughts that nourish souls divine.
Even so, an atmosphere of healthfulness
Is round the soul whose quiet life is spent
  In leal allegiance to the laws of God.

We, seeing, feeling, climb the steep ascent
  And scorn the roughness of the upward road,
If we but reach the heights where love awaits
To open wide for us Heaven's pearly gates.

LOYALTY.

IF sickness, pain, and poverty
  Quench not thy spirit's fire ;
If toil nor hindrance break the spell
  That bids thy soul aspire,
Obey the voice that bids thee rise,
And light shall meet thy praying eyes.

Be pure in heart and cast aside
  Freely each hindrance base :
The heart that harbours sin is not
  The heart that sees God's face.
With true obedience wash away.
The sins that stain thy soul with clay.

God's help is hindered and repelled
  By hearts that harbour wrong ;
The priest that feeds the flock should be
  By purity made strong.
And who would reign as kings must be
  Kingly with truth and purity.

HEZEKIAH, THE SON OF AHAZ,

Cut down the groves, and broke in pieces the brazen serpent
that Moses had made, for unto those days the children of Israel
did burn incense to it: and he called it Nehushtan (a piece of
brass).—2 Kings xviii. 4.

SYMBOLS are good when used to teach
　　Truth that our souls should know,
To raise them from the earth below,
And bring soul good within our reach
That we may understand the speech
　　Of angels, that shows us how to overgrow
　　The weeds that evil thoughts do sow,
While our whole lives the truth should preach.
But when the truth forgotten lies
　　Within the symbol that remains,
The symbol seals the thoughtless eyes—
　　Weaves round the soul relentless chains,
'Tis then a fetish that men bow before,
An empty husk for wise men to deplore.

REST AT LAST.

WHEN all the weary night we toss in pain,
　　From restless side to restless side, and wish
For morning light; and when day dawns to wish
Again for night; and fevered with the pain
We count the slow and weary hours until
The eventide, when pain and fever stayed,

We feel soft folds of sleep, sweeter than touch
Of mother's love, creep over every sense,
Till tired eyelids drop o'er weary eyes,
And we in calm oblivion sleep till morn ;
So, after all the tossing cares of life
We know the blessed eventide shall come,
When we shall see the watchful galaxies
Of Heaven crowd round our souls,
Singing dear songs of praise to him
" Who giveth His beloved sleep."

BEFORE AND AFTER.

THE old look back with wistful eyes
    To golden times long past,
Where discords in oblivion lies,
And memory sees but summer skies
    And scenes too bright to last
That glamour glorifies.

But youthful eyes look forward to .
    A golden age to be,
While, like the sun on morning dew
Hope gilds each day with brightness new,
    There is no storm to see,
No cloud to mar the view.

The golden age is only for
  A golden life of good ;
At God's right hand for evermore
There is of good a boundless store
  For such as have all wrong withstood
And loyal are to the heart's core.

THE WORDS OF THE LORD.

O, HAPPY is the man who has
      His soul attuned to hear
The harmonies that come from God
  Through all the rolling year.

Whose heart is thrilled with every word
  God-written here below,
Whose eyes are open to the light
  That life and health bestow.

O, blessed words of love we see,
  That makes our hearts attune
To all the gladness of the year
  In 'the gladsome month of June.

In every flower a Bible lies—
  God's law in living words—
The loveliness of bird and flower
  With law and life accords.

The laws of God are everywhere,
　Within, around they be,
God grant us open ears to hear,
　And open eyes to see.

REFLECTION.

THE sunshine on the drops of dew
　Mirror the source of day ;
So may the love of God in you
Give back His image pure and true,
　And all His light repay.

SMALL THINGS.

IN smallest things be faithful to
　The trust reposed in thee ;
The smallest things do indicate
　What kind of man you be,
And everywhere the Master's eye
　Our secret thoughts can see.

If ye are faithful over one
　Small province of the king,
He'll make thee ruler over ten,
　And tithes of everything.
Both small and great the faithful soul
　Shall to the Master bring.

And he who hath gets ever more
   For goodness crowds round good ;
The more we give the more we get
   The love of brotherhood.
By him alone whose heart is pure
   Is this truth understood.

A STRONG WILL.

THE strong will and the brave heart
   Are better than muscle and bone,
But muscle and bone do their part
Under the will that nought can thwart ;
   They lay obstructions prone
   And over them walk to a throne.

Kingdoms are for the brave and true,
   For they alone can reign ;
As every soul must first subdue
His kingdom ere its revenue
   Of honour he can gain
   For hand and heart and brain.

If we would reign with God we must
   Be fearless and upright,
And pure in heart with purpose just,
Allied to Him with holy trust,
   And round us clean and white
   A life that loves the light.

SEEDTIME AND HARVEST.

GOD gives to all seed-corn to sow,
    But we must till our field with care,
    And root out weeds that grow up there
If we glad harvest time would know.

And by the wayside 'mong the grass
    We may sow seeds that grow to flowers
    That catch the sunshine and the showers
To cheer the pilgrims as they pass.

For pilgrims weary and footsore,
    Waiting 'neath the evening stars
    Till death the Father's door unbars,
The rest is sweet when travel's o'er.

'Tis sweet within our hearts to feel
    Love waits for us with open arms
    At home with dear home charms,
To fold us in the love of all the leal.

WORK.

WHATE'ER you have a mind to do
    Bring to it mind,
For only he whose soul is true
    Success shall find.

In all your work, concentrate all
   Your forces
In harmony with law, then shall
The stars for thee reciprocal
   Fight in their courses.

And you with Him Who holds the reins
   Of every force
Take sides, and your obedience ordains
   Success of course.

'Tis love alone the law fulfils,
   For it compels
Obedience, that with eager wills
   All wrong repels.

For love meets love as magnets draw
   The grains of steel ;
Love is the starting-place of law,
   The God to Whom we kneel.

And thus our highest, only good
   Is unity
With Him Whom love makes understood
   In purity.

PSALM XV.

LORD, who shall dwell within Thy house,
   Upon Thy holy hill?
The man who walking uprightly
  Is eager to fulfil
The law of God with heart of ruth,
And spirit wise with heavenly truth;

Who speaketh not with double tongue
  Behind a neighbour's back,
Nor doth him harm in any way,
  Nor listens to the black
Reproach of enemies that do
With malice keen his soul pursue.

Who hates the ways of wicked men,
  But honours them that fear
The Lord ; who suffers loss for truth
  Because the truth is dear ;
Who will not take unholy gain
Nor pleasure from a neighbour's pain.

The man who thus controls his life
  Shall never more be moved ;
And he shall reign in heaven because
  On earth he hath been proved
And stood the test of truth, and won
The crown of life—the Lord's " Well done."

MALICE.

I THINK the deil's amang us enow,
　　The deil an' his angels baith ;
For ilk ane ca's anither I trow,
　　An' nane escapes without skaith.
Folk's aye ready eneuch to allow
　　They're sinners, but wi' the same braith
They will trail their neebour in through
Some dirty bottomless slough—-
　　It's eneuch to warrant an aith.

If ye've fauts ye canna weel kiver
　　Ye're a perfect deilsend o' delight ;
But O! if ye're guid or clever
　　Ye'll hear nae end o' their spite.
They'll pit theirsels in a fever
　　To make ye fer blacker than night,
　　An' bring ye doon frae yer height
Wi' a poisoned shaft frae their quiver,
　　An' a' the while they're polite.

They thinkna the measure they mete
　　Will be measured to them again,
Though they ken that slander's as sweet
　　An' gangs as weel wi' the grain
To others that like every treat
　　O' backbiting they can obtain
　　Though as black as the heart o' Cain,
Till every ane in the street
　　Is spotted wi' mony a stain.

Oh! if we'd but make it oor aim
  Oor neebour to love as oorsel,
An' assist them the vera same,
  Oor kindness wad act like a spell.
If we'd honour oor neebour's name,
  An' only wad strive to excel
In shielding each other frae blame,
An' having heart smiles for their fame,
  It needs na a wutch to tell
  How the blessing wad come to oorsel.

HEARTS OF GOLD.

THE daisy opes its heart of gold
    And spreads its silver rays
To gather light, and gladly hold
    The gifts the light conveys ;
It makes the most of what is given
To make the earth the gate of heaven.

We too should ope our hearts to good
    And love to feel the light,
Living in kindly brotherhood
With souls all gold and white,
Ready aye to catch the glow
Of light that shines on souls below.

Men may have loyal hearts of gold
  And dwell in lowly places,
And ray out blessings manifold
  With unpretending graces,
Enriching all who love to see
Heavenly coin in currency.

But it is good to climb the heights
  When called upon to rise ;
Our view is widened and requites
  The strain on eager eyes ;
The highest hill by man e'er trod
Gave largest life and nearest God.

HOPE OF SPRING.

WINTER is gone with his frozen breath,
    Life grows up from the grave of death ;
  The blithe birds sing
  To welcome the spring,
And every bud unfolds to hear.
  The trees hang out their bannerettes,
  The primrose follows the violets,
Each spear of grass holds a dewdrop clear
Over the rivulet singing near.
  In every breeze
  That stirs the trees

We hear the spring with glad young voice
Calling on nature to rise and rejoice.
We too are young while our hearts can sing,
Unfolding leaf and flower
    In the glorious spring.

THE LORD'S PRAYER.

FATHER, *our* Father ; dearest name ;
    The fountain-head of all that's good;
We come to Thee as children should,
In fearless confidence to claim
The love that blots out all our blame.

May true love hallow evermore
    The Name that binds with silken bands
    Our souls to Thee, while serving hands
And filial hearts yearn to adore
From life's circumference to its core.

Thy kingdom come ; come Thou and reign
    Within our eager hearts and give
    Us grace for Thee alone to live ;
Casting before Thy feet the gain
That grows from lealest heart and brain.

Our highest pleasure may it be
    To keep Thy law and do Thy will,
    And unto other souls instil
Thy love, that each pure heart may see
Thy face, and worship only Thee.

For daily bread we look to Thee ;
    Father, we will not look in vain,
    For Thou wilt give what shall sustain
This life, and bread of life that we
May love the truth that makes us free.

Oh! blot out with our contrite tears
    The sins we mourn before Thy shrine;
    Teach us with charity like Thine
Kindly to think of our compeers
And help them through the coming years.

Oh! give us strength in all temptation
    For our weak wills too subtly strong ;
    Deliver us from hindering wrong ;
And make our life in life's probation
A living, loving consecration.

Thine be the kingdom, Thine the might,
    In earth below, in heaven above ;
    Reign over all, O God of love ;
Dispel the darkness with Thy light,
Shine forth with all Thy glory bright.

THE CROSS.

THE noblest souls are ever driven
    Apart, into some desert place,
    Muscle and brain with nerve to brace
Ere they can reach the highest heaven.

Alone with God on Sinai's height
  Was Moses ; and hid by Cherith's brook
  Elijah was ; and John, with stern rebuke
To godless men, was lonely in the fight.

Jesus, of man the grandest type,
  Unfolded in the desert places
  His loyal soul's entrancing graces,
And made Himself our architype

Mahommed brooded in a cave ;
  In a Zambesian hut our own
  Brave David Livingstone
Returned the sword his Master gave.

Leal Livingstone the true and good
  Sowed wide and free the living seeds
  Among dark Afric's noxious weeds
Before the truth was understood.

From north to south, from east to west,
  With words of life in his crusade
  The symbol of the cross he made,
And now begins to manifest

The restlessness of wakening life;
  Now men begin to see the grain
  That soon will ripen into gain
Among the clinging weeds of strife.

But seed must in the furrows lie
    Long time, and many days be green,
    Before the harvest here is seen
The sower's faith to justify.

And Stanley told of one who sowed
    Nor saw result for six long years,
    But in a day his meed appears—
Nine hundred souls the truth avowed.

MRS GRUNDY IN PARLIAMENT.

IN the British House of Commons,
    With their noses all like gnomons
    Pointing to the Speaker's chair,
Sit the cream o' a' the race
Wi' what they can o' grace
    Of making laws to take a share.

There they sit in grand palaver
Each the other side to plague wi' claver;
    But the honourable of that place
Got a shock the other Monday,
When the mighty Mrs Grundy
    Was bearded to her face.

'Tis said that Britons rule the waves,
And they never, never can be slaves—
    Except to Mrs Grundy ;
So each noble British heart
Got an awfu', awfu' start
    At what happened there on Monday,

When Mr Radcliffe Cook sat down ;
Heedless he of Mrs Grundy's frown
    When she saw his billicock,
Though every startled eye
In that august assembly
    Felt an electric shock.

But he didna care a whustle
For a' the fearfu' bustle ;
    His homage he refuséd flat,
And in spite o' Mrs Grundy
On that memorable Monday
    Kept on the offending hat.

She micht rave till she was dumb,
He wadna wear a lum
    On his heid to please her ;
He thocht Britons werena free
That wad bend to her the knee,
    So he wore the billicock to tease her.

THE INDIAN CHIEF.

AFTER the man of God had told
　　The Indian chief his story,
The chief stepped from the listening throng,
　　Rugged with age and hoary.

" My hair," he said, " was once as black
　　As is the plumage of the crow,
And now grandchildren say it is
　　As white as winter snow.

" Did you not say that your God was
　　Our Father ? "　" I did," the white man said.
The chief replied—" 'Tis new and sweet,
　　We knew Him not and were afraid.

" We saw Him in the lightning's flash,
　　We heard Him speak in thunder ;
The tempest and the blizzard filled
　　Our hearts with fear and wonder.

" But now the Spirit that we feared
　　Our Father is, and this to know
Is very beautiful ; may I say more ? "
　　" Say on, I come the truth to show."

" You say *Our Father* ; He is yours, but
　　Does that mean He is mine ? "
" Yes, He is yours."　" Well then, He is
　　Poor Indian's and thine,

" Is that quite true ? "   " Yes, 'tis true."
  "Then we are brothers, aren't we ?"
"Yes, we are brothers."   " May I say more ?"
  "Speak on, you have a friend in me."

"Well then you have been long, white brother,
  In showing brotherhood
By bringing o'er the sea this Book
  To your red brother in the wood."

LIGHT AND LAW.

THE holy men of old whom love made wise
      Saw God, and walked with Him because their
          hearts
Were pure and loyal to His light and truth ;
While other men were blinded by gross lives,
And wandered, stumbling in the dark afar
From Him and light and happiness and peace.
  The Bible writ by holy men is but
A transcript of the Bible writ by God
In matter, mind, and heart ; in good and ill,
In life and death, reiterating evermore
The steadfastness of laws *ordained immutable*,
And man's *free-will* to choose security
By unison with law, or to be crushed

By disobedience.   We live by faith,
The disobedient die by faith misplaced.
There is no lack of faith, but lack of wisdom.
Men are so prone to follow wandering lights—
Prophets that lure unwary souls into
Forbidden ways where punishment awaits
The soul that sins against himself and God—
Rather than chosen sons of God—prophets
Who are like guiding stars for pilgrim feet.
  Oh! that all men were wise to choose the light
That shines from heaven above, rather than that
False ignis fatuus gleam that wanders o'er
The miry sloughs of sin, which fools do follow
Greedily to their own hurt, for lack of wisdom.
  The light of heaven shines for all, and he
Who loves it most can best transcribe
The laws of God ordained for men to walk
Therein with wise free-will.   Wise men and fools
Do prove themselves by whom they hang their trust
        upon.
  Were all men lovers of the wise whom they
Could safely trust and work with for one end,
Then would the light to open eyes unfold
The purposes of God, and we could write
Our name with His, endorsing all His will.
Knowing His will by reading His word, we then
Might freely say and truly of what we read—
  "THUS SAITH THE LORD."

BAIRNS AT PLAY.

PLAY on, O blithesome bairnies play !
   I'm glad to see ye a' sae gay ;
  This is the time for sport and glee.
When the young flowers are sweetly springing
An' birds abune their nests are singing,
   Be ye as glad an' blithe as they ;
An' dance an' sing as lithe an free,
   In a' yer movements there is grace,
Like lambs that gambol on the lea,
Or birds that flit frae tree to tree.

There's been nae time for cluds to trace
Wrinkles an' shadows on yer face,
An' oh ! may it be lang ere blame
Write wrinkly shadows on yer name ;
May never double face nor biting tongue
Leave some puir heart wi' sharpness stung.
May kindness keep yer hearts frae spite,
That love may keep yer hearts frae blight ;
In word an' deed be just an' good,
An leeve wi' a' in kindly brotherhood.

When e'ening brings the bairnies hame,
May nane hing doon his heid for shame ;
   Wi' fearless love may a' gang in,
After a faithfu' day's work done—

After a just day's wage is won,
  To rest among the near akin,
Wi' Faither's love fauldit as sweet
As mothers fauld .their bairnies' feet.

WHAT SHALL AVAIL?

WHAT shall it avail me
    Fifty years hence
If I lived and died in poverty
    Or opulence ?

Much it shall avail me
    If I lived true,
And gave to all in thought and deed
    What was their due ;

And if I used the talents given
    With purpose high,
And rendered back to God His own
    With usury.

God, help thou me to stand upright
    Before Thy face,
And claim a son's inheritance
    By doing nothing base.

THE SEASONS AGAIN.

EACH springtime clothes the forest trees
    With fresh green leaves
That make sweet music in the breeze,
    And interweaves
With song of birds the hum of bees.

The summer comes with shine and showers
    And dews at morn
That deck with gems the blushing flowers,
    The scented thorn,
And all the earth with beauty dowers.

The autumn comes with heavy sheaves—
    The crown of hope—
The trees let fall their yellow leaves
    Like words that drop
From weary men on harvest eves.

We too, by change, do live and grow,
    And should expand
And ripen in the summer glow,
    While all the land
We, with autumnal goodness strow.

FORWARD.

I SEE the mark aimed at afar,
    Above the world's loud hum,
Between me and the lovely star

P

I count not on the strife and jar
  That must be overcome.

With wings half fledged I fain would fly
  Where I must climb and creep,
Still, evermore with upturned eye,
Heedless of hindrances that lie,
  I would, at one fell sweep
  Surmount the giddy steep.

I wonder if I ever will
  Learn patience and restraint,
And be content to climb uphill
Till I have gained the higher skill,
  Without sigh or complaint.

I cannot keep from looking up ;
  I stumble on in pain,
While disappointment's bitter cup
I constantly am made to sup ;
  I fall, but rise again.

With aching heart and bruised feet,
  I climb with progress slow;
I never will admit defeat,
Nor turn away in weak retreat,
  I'll reach the goal although

My path by thorns be overgrown ;
  Through frost and fire I'll go ;
Though hindrances be thickly strewn
I'll fearless throw the gauntlet down,
  Defying every foe.

Though here I fail to reach the mark
  Before I reach the grave.
I struggle on however dark
Until on life's rough sea my bark
  Surmounts the highest wave

And leaves me on the golden shore
  Where I with opened eyes
May see true effort evermore
Kept laying up a secret store,
  While angels in disguise

Kept warding off a poor success,
  That effort might attain
A higher, grander usefulness,
And evermore get new access
  Of muscle, nerve, and brain.

I then may see success was reared
  On failures hard to bear,
And that the very things I feared
Were angels of the Lord that steered
  My bark past every snare.

MY WORK.

I FEEL impelled to write, but what
  If some rude hand—
Some careless soul that does
  Not understand

The work I do, the path I tread,
  The battle that I fight
  With darkness through the night,
  That I may ray God's light—
Shall come when I am dead
  And cast aside or burn
    As worthless things
The children of my brain ;
  Some cloven foot may spurn
    My work and be
Too gross to feel the pain
Made by the brand of Cain.
Deep in my heart a voice I hear
Speaking to me in accents clear.

" Thy life is larger than material wants
  Can satisfy,
Receive Heaven's holy visitants,
  They shall indemnify
Thee largely for the lack of earthly good
  With higher wealth to be attained
Mayhap by poverty, and understood
  When in a higher sphere 'tis gained.

Learn thou as birds
  Do learn to sing
In darkened cages,
  And freely fling
Thy songs to coming ages.

Trust thou the love that made
  Thee coin thy heart in words.
Trust thou nor be afraid,
  They yet like tempered swords
Shall mingle in the strife
Of onward striving life.

In faith cast thou thy seed
  In the cold ground,
And in due time
  The harvest will come round ;
Thy work belongs to God, and He
  Will care for it, and give
Its increase unto thee.
  Have thou no fear
    For soon or late
  There must appear
    At Heaven's own gate
The harvest of divine co-operation
In all its grand accumulation."

I dare not, cannot disobey
  The Heavenly call
In God's own field to work all day ;
  And when the evening shadows fall
I'll homeward turn my tired feet,
  And rest, till I, mayhap, with sleep
Refreshed shall rise up strong to greet
  The rising of a grander sun
And grander work in higher spheres
  With new life to be done.

GOD'S TREASURE-HOUSE.

LAWS lock the treasure-house of God,
　And knowledge is the master-key
To every seeking soul bestowed
　With benedictions full and free.

Law, like the strong and docile ox,
　Receives the yoke from knowing hands,
And patiently the field unlocks
　For harvests that the good Lord sends.

The laws of God, like angels, wait
　To do the will of him who knows
How he their powers can subjugate,
　And get the good their work bestows.

Knowledge is the rough material
　Placed in the toiling hand ;
But wisdom must the soul build up
　And brain with building blend.

CLOTHES.

IF we sow chaff we reap no grain ;
　If we sow death no life we reap,
The husk shall never rise again
　To clothe the soul it could not keep.
At death we rise from death as from
A chrysalistic state to God, our home.

The body's but the pilgrim's gabardine
When travelling eastward to the holy shrine.
　　But when the gates of life death doth unbar
We lay aside the soiled and worn out rags
That to the winged soul would be but drags
　　And fly to meet the morning star.
Maybe our friends who have their home
　　With God will watch our coming from afar,
And hail with songs of love and joy
　　The victor from the field of war
　　Where we have won with many a scar
The trophies that we gladly yield
To God, who is our strength and shield.

Mayhap, within the higher sphere
　　A body round the soul shall grow ;
　　We may but hope, we do not know,
But building on our knowledge here
We " greet the unseen with a cheer."

But there as here our spirits weave
　　The robe of character to show
The status that our souls achieve.
　　Be true and make them pure as snow.

CRACKS.

WHEN dusting the things in my room,
　　If onything there has a crack,
I hide it as weel as I can
　　By turning it roond to the back.

But the seamy side o' oor nature
  In fiction is turned to the licht,
Till earth seems peopled wi' demons
  That jumble up wrang wi' richt.

I doot it's a notable instance
  O' demand that's made by supply :
Oh, folk will do muckle for siller
  In pandering to what is awry.

The ten commandments for pleasure
  Are broken ; e'en love is draggled through
Alang wi' fraud an' murder,
  The deadly disgusting slough.

Sic prurient exhibitions
  Only pits wrang in folk's heid,
An' they eat the bait o' the deil
  Wi' thochtless hunger an greed.

" Dinna pit him below the pump,"
  Said ane when he meant the reverse,
So sic fiction teaches a lesson
  Just as completely perverse.

Oh ! why do folk fill up their hearts
  Wi' sic dirty, rubbishy things
Like serpents ta'en into their bosoms
  To poison their lives wi' their stings.

I dinna condemn a' fiction,
    It has its legitimate place ;
But I'd like to see the best side o' life
    Instead o' the ugly an' base.

The best an' the highest guid in life
    Is gi'en to the pure in heart,
An' why wi' a' abominations
    God's purpose in life pervert.

THE POLE STAR.

SHINE out, O bright pole star ;
        Hindrance my way may mar
    But cannot hide thy light ;
My eyes with steadfast gaze
Hang on thy kindly rays
    That brighten all the night.

Earth's treasures are but dust—
Corrupting moth and rust ; ·
    Where thieves with greed made blind—
Foes to the common weal,
Break through God's laws and steal,
    Poor fools ! an empty rind.

We're here for one short day
To learn, but not to stay ;
    We seek another land.

Why, then, impede our way
With burdens that decay
  And that is contraband.

Wisdom bids lay aside
Avarice, malice, pride,
  And every hindering weight,
And with a Heavenward face
Step out with easy grace
  And heart inviolate
  The earth to subjugate.

ANOTHER CARLYLE PARAPHRASE.

I LOOK from my tower
  On that monster hive
Where wasps and bees
  Promiscuous strive,
And I see their wax and honey making,
Their poison brewing and sweet cake baking.
From the palace, music
  While pomp' is pleased to eat.
Down the low lane
  To the door-sill seat
Where the widow knits
  For a livelihood,
While palace inferiors fare
  On better food.

Yes ; I see it all, for there's none so high
  As the Schlosskirche weathercock and I.
Booted and strapped the courier comes
    With joy and sorrow in leather bags
To the king in purple
    And the man in rags.
The sybarite baron with velvet palms
And the soldier with timber leg begging alms.

UNEQUAL DEVELOPMENT.

SOME souls there are who cease to grow
    When they have reached the body's prime ;
And other souls who yearn to know
    The open secrets of all time ;
They flourish in perpetual blow
In summer's heat, in winter's snow.

They reach out to a larger life ;
    They read the living words of God ;
They may look backward in the strife
    To draw the laggards on the road,
Who have no restless fluttering wings,
And no response for higher things.

But the dear love of long ago
    To pity in the larger soul,
Has grown for want of kindred glow

In him who yearns for no high goal—
Who little thinks of wrong or right,
And breathes no prayer for more light.

So high, so low, so far apart ;
  No point where they can meet as one ;
A coolness grows within the heart
  When all the early bonds are gone.
The richer soul can only sigh
For loss of what was doomed to die.

" Love is love for evermore," said one,
  Perhaps when he was young,
Maybe the springtime love of yore
  When friends about my young life clung
Has been my own reflected back
And shedding light along its track.

Alas, alas ! the larger light
  Reveals, sometimes, repellant traits ;
The poorness of the parasite
  That hinders with unholy weights—
With no response for higher moods—
No loyalty for brotherhoods.

The plant that sends its tender shoots
  Through the dark earth into the light
Can have no fellowship with roots
  That have no heart for sunshine bright.
O soul ! communion keep with such
As with thee God's bright garments touch.

It seems to me that all the way
  We must step out with equal pace,
If love would live with no decay
  Until we reach the resting place,
And are at one with Christ in God
Where life with love is overflowed.

SABBATH.

WITH joy we hail this Sabbath day
    That brings the weary toiler rest ;
When jar and strife are overborne,
  And in God's house each welcome guest
May freely take the bread of life
To fit him for the week-day strife.

This day is like a wayside inn
  Where weary travellers rest awhile,
And shut their ears to worldly din
  To lean their hearts on Heaven's sweet smile
Reflected bright from flower and tree,
From hill and vale and silver sea.

As children in the house of God,
  We wait to hear our Father's will,
Having our feet with courage shod

Ready to climb life's rugged hill.
Our hand in His we have no fear
In darkest night or sunshine clear.

FEAR NOT.

WE are too prone
    To fear and moan
And live the coming day
    Before it come.
We wonder where
    The way will lead,
And where the store
    For all our need.

But dark and dumb
    To all our fears
The coming days,
    The coming years,
Before they come.

Live well to-day
    And let the morrow bring
Whate'er it may ;
    Be loyal to the king,
And be it understood

From angel wings
Helpful things
Are scattered for our good.
   And He who clothes the lilies, feeds the birds,
Shall give both soul and body food.

JESUS.

THE noblest words that man ere spoke
      Enchained the wondering throng,
Who hung upon the lips that woke
   The slumbering echoes into song.
They trusted this was He
Would set their kingdom free,
   He was so good and strong ;
And unto Him the power was given
To open wide the gates of Heaven.

Their hopes clung round Him night and day;
They strow palm branches in His way ;
   With regal pomp and loud acclaim
   They lavish blessings on His name ;
Their garments on His path they fling,
And hail the Son of David king ;
   Only the learned and reputed wise
View him with fear and scorn,
   And the illiterate herd despise.

Wisdom may come in other ways
    Than by the learning of the schools,
For erudition often makes
    Of shallow men but learned fools,
    Mechanic slaves of lifeless tools.

Unlettered toilers may have more
    Of loyalty for what is right
Than men who sit on heaps of gold
    With telescopes to aid their sight
    When peering into the dark night.

Knowledge is good when light from Heaven
    Illumes and hallows all we know ;
The more we have the more we get;
    The more about our way we strow
    The more our stores shall overflow.

And he who patient vigil keeps
    And dares the conflict with strong will—
Who working with the laws of God
    Can set his cross on life's high hill,
Has won his crown and reigns by right
O'er all he has subdued by might.

We have not talents all alike,
    But whether we have one or ten
We'll get the King's " Well done " if we
    Are loyal to His trust, and when
We lay our earnings at His feet
Our happiness will be complete.

SIN.

SIN with his left hand offers gain ;
  Hid in his right he bears a scourge ;
And he will make you pay in pain,
  All he on your acceptance urge.

Gold oft he liberally giveth
  To him who stains his soul with crime ;
As he giveth so his victim liveth,
  Wasting eternity for time.

Oh ! why make loads that none can bear
  Through the strait way—the narrow gate ?
Nude souls alone can climb the stair
  Where crowns the noblest souls await.

A ROSE.

A ROSE grows at my window pane,
    And all the day
  It seems to say :
"You do ; I be ;
  I am beautiful for thee."
And the dear words
  Of a flower so fair
Filleth my heart
  With psalms of prayer.

And I heed far less
  The thorns of life
When the roses bless
  Me in the strife ;
And I feel around me everywhere
Father's love and Father's care.
    Rose after rose comes and goes,
    And leaves a sweetness of repose
    In the heart that loves and knows
The beauty of completeness.
Blessed are the ears that hear
    What the dear flowers say ;
And blessed are the hearts that open
    To their message night and day.

EACH.

OUT of the same earth,
    Into the same blue
Light of heaven grow trees of every form
    And flowers of every hue ;
And every kind of fruit,
    Good for food or pleasant to the eye,
For man and bird and brute,
    Within man's reach doth lie.
And all according to God's law
Their own constituents draw
    From elements around,
  In the light and in the ground ;

And over each created thing
Is man—the crown and king—
To learn the laws,
Their aim and cause,
  That he with knowledge true
  May bridle and subdue,
As willing subjects to his reign,
The laws that to his heart and brain
  Do yield a revenue.

A PARAPHRASE.

ALTHOUGH I speak like angels singing,
  And have not love, I only am
As sounding brass—an empty ringing ;
  A senseless, soulless, brazen sham ;
I have not yet the key to heaven—
No loveless soul can be forgiven.

If I could tell of things to be,
  And mysteries read of all below ;
'Tis only love can wisely see,
  'Tis only love can wisely know
The soul of knowledge deep and true,
Refreshing life with heavenly dew.

Had I the faith that could remove
  Mountains, it were but work in vain,
And Heavenly sonship could not prove ;

The heart is better than the brain ;
Out of the heart the spirit flows
    That lights the way the pilgrim goes.

And though I give my goods to feed
    The poor, and build up fanes of prayer,
Sowing my wealth abroad like seed,
    To make the earth more sweet and fair,
Yet without love no harvest home
Unto my loveless soul will come.

Although the labour of my life
    I give for some most righteous cause ;
Yea, die upon the field of strife
    For truer, wiser, better laws,
Yet loving not the true and good
My life and work were one falsehood.

Love is the atmosphere of God,
    Which, if we breathe, we live,
And all our life is overflowed
    With health that love alone can give ;
It is the very God in whom
We live like flowers that breathe perfume.

It bears itself with seemliness ;
    Grieves not for self, but evil done
That renders poor souls Fatherless
    And blind beneath the shining sun ;
At wrong and shame it will not smile,
Nor gloat o'er aught that's mean or vile.

Though feeling much, love suffers long—
   Though suffering much is always kind,
Nor feels revenge, enduring wrong ;
   It looks below the priskly rind ;
It vaunts not vainly of itself,
Nor stretches greedy hands for pelf.

The right that's hid by seeming wrong
   It sees, rejoicing in the truth ;
It never fails, but grows more strong
   By the calm exercise of ruth ;
Though grace and strength abide above,
The heart and crown of life is Love.

LOVE.

FOR love to our Father in heaven,
   And love to our brother below,
Is the one great good that is given,
   The one great debt that we owe.
It steers us safe to the golden shore,
'Tis the key that opens our Father's door.

We trust that our hope is not vain,
   And that e'en deeds with a crooked aim,
That are the fruit of the toiling brain,
   May be rooted in love, and thus may claim
The good that to love is surely given—
The key that can open the Kingdom of Heaven.

CREEDS.

GOOD friends whose lives are better than the
  creeds
They do profess with easy prejudice,
Have never tried to square their practice with
The creed they have, it may be, never read ;
And cornered with a creed untenable,
They draw false inference from premises
As false, and claim a victory o'er men
Who build upon the rock impregnable
Of truth. The blind, well-meaning fools
Do urge the wise to shut their eyes and walk
By faith, ignoring reason and the light.
The foolish with their one poor talent hid
Urge him with ten to hide his too, nor give
His Master gain when he accounts with Him.
We must be true unto our trust whate'er it be—
One talent or ten. If we do hide what we
Are given to trade with for our Master,
'Tis at our peril. We cannot shut our eyes
To that. As well expect the mighty oak
To squeeze itself into the small acorn
From which it sprang, as think to stay the soul
From Godward evolution. In vain
The lowly daisy counsels the tall oak
To have humility and dwell among
The grass like it. It cannot be. It must
Obey the law within itself and rear
Its branches to the sun, and clasp the light

Of heaven.   It must be true unto itself.
'Tis false humility, and false to God,
And to ourselves 'tis false, to lower ourselves
Below the truth and stay our upward growth
To please the foolish pride of lowliness.

PRAYER.

WE lift our hands to Heaven and cry for light,
    For open eyes, and hearts made wise to love
The truth ; but scarcely realize that we,
Like our Exemplar, must receive the gifts
We crave in husk of trial hard to bear.
All that we get we must, by help of God,
Earn for ourselves, nor be like men whose souls
Exist, but do not grow, upon the pauper's dole.
Take courage, O my soul; know thou that help
From Heaven shall never fail the loyal soul
That strives for good.   The praying hands of men
Are ever met by helping hands from God.

HOLY SPIRIT.

SOMETIMES when God breathes on our hearts
    and we
Receive the inspiration of His love,
We speak some common words, but fill them with
The verve of our own spirit caught warm and true

From God's own heart; and they, like live coals from
The altar, make the hearts of other men
To burn with love.　'Tis good that intellect
Should flash its light before our eyes, and claim
And get its due of admiration ; but
Holy spirit breathed through holy men gives life
Unto the poorest words that man can speak.
For God is love, and love is crown supreme
Of life.　As flowers do wreathe with finished grace
The plant, so love doth wreathe with beauty's dower
The finished grace of life.

TRUST.

POWER, wisdom, and beneficence
　　Everywhere I see,
Like angels of the Lord that bring
　　My Father's gifts to me.

My Father knows what things I need,
　　And with a father's hands
Freely my every want supplies—
　　Yea! all my needs transcends.

Then why should over-anxious thoughts
　　My days with fears o'ercast ?
I'm safe within my Father's love
　　Till every cloud is past.

There free from care I'll rest, and trust
    The love that might be veiled
By passing clouds from weary eyes,
    But *never, never* failed.

THOU IN ME AND I IN THEE.

O LORD of all, O Love divine,
    My soul cleaves fast to Thee ;
The angels everywhere are Thine ;
I too am Thine and Thou are mine.
    I need not troubled be,
For as the living branches grow
    Out of the living tree,
Even so, O Father, Source of all,
    My soul abides in Thee.
And if a withered leaf should fall,
Or if some sin like insect small
Should gnaw the young and tender shoot
Or eat the bud and spoil the fruit,
Not mine alone the hurt and loss,
For I am Thine and Thine my cross.
    Together we do grow as one ;
    Together sit on the same throne
Of knowledge, love, and loyalty—
    Thou crowned with the excellency of right,
        I lowly at Thy feet,
    And living in Thy perfect light,
        In Thee my live complete.

SENTIMENTAL GRUMBLERS.

THINK ye that it pleases God to say
    That ye are weary with the strife,
    And all the toilsome cares of life,
And fain would cast your cross away.

Weary of the strife, faint heart ?
    Unworthy thou to bear a sword,
    If in the battles of thy Lord
Ye shrink to take a soldier's part.

Weary art thou of earthly care ?
    Unworthy labourer in the field
    That thou should'st till and make to yield
A harvest with thy Lord to share.

The way is long, thy burden great
    Ye say, and dost thou grudge to bear
    Thy load, yielding to weak despair,
Would'st thou with wrong capitulate ?

Be brave, be true, thy sword belongs
    To God, ask Him, He'll give thee strength to hew
    Down hindrances ; thy way pursue
Till victory crown thy life with songs.

Work thou for good and have no fear ;
    God gives to all true work increase ;
    And in true work alone is peace ;
Service shall make thy pathway clear.

And if thy way be long, lean thou
   Upon thy strong and willing Guide,
   Nor vainly wander from His side,
To His mild yoke be wise and bow.

He sees the eyes that intercede,
   He helps the hands that do His will ;
   To feet that fly from doing ill
He gives the swiftness that they need.

He gathers not the harvest where
   No seed His gracious hand has sown ;
   Seedtime and harvest are His own,
We too are His and own His care.

If we have only one poor pound,
   We must not hide but use it well
   And make its wise increase fortell
The servant's work approved and crowned.

ARGUMENT.

SOME folk that canna argue say—
   " Nae maitter how wise an' expert
Ye may be, ye may argue a' day
   An' never a man ye'll convert."

But weel ken I, ye canna get
   A loaf frae the wheat until
It's shorn, an' thrashed, an' dichted,
   An' ground to meal in a mill.

FALSEHOOD.

FALSEHOOD baits its hook with truth,
      And cruelty with words of ruth,
We need a holy spirit to divine
The false beneath its lying hood—
The poison wrapt in seeming good,
      O Father, may the gift be mine.

HOMEWARD BOUND.

"It matters not to us who are immortal,
    Which side of the grave we stand on."
                              J. B. SELKIRK.

TRUE indeed, what matters it
      When we have friends on either side,
And we as pilgrims walk through life
      With all the stars of Heaven to guide
Us homeward bound, homeward bound.

Absurd it were to linger here
At eventide when home is near
      And we are homeward bound.

Why fear to step across the grave ?
      'Tis but the place where we disrobe,
To dress again for what we crave.
Then let our heart's last feeble throb
      With joyful hope all fear confound
      When we are homeward bound.

The flowers shoot through the cold dark ground
   And have no doubt, no shrinking fear ;
So may we rise and feel around
   Expanding souls, Heaven shining clear,
As we are homeward bound.

Or like the chrysalis that wakes
From its long sleep and gladly breaks
   Its prison walls to feel its wings
   And all the joy that freedom brings,
Why then should we, the children of the King,
   Bewail our lot when homeward bound ?
Nay, rather let our glad hearts sing
   As we step o'er the grassy mound,
Homeward bound, homeward bound.

A BLUE-BOTTLE FLY.

YOU'VE been buzzing about all day
   With musical wings, blue-bottle fly,
Shall I kill you ?   No indeed, not I,
I'll list your song ; so buzz away.

Between my finger and my thumb
   'Twere easy for me to destroy
   Your life, and every sound of joy
In one brief moment render dumb.

But the wisest man with all his art
   Could never make a form so true ;
   Nor could he that small form endue
With life, and glad songs in its heart.

It's all very well when you come alone,
   You jolly old blue-bottle fly,
   But coming in scores you should die,
Every one of you, skin, wing, and bone.

For I'm not a Brahmin, you see ;
   I'm not afraid to kill a fly
   Lest the ghost of my grandma occupy
Its form, and be trampled out by me.

You are all alone, blue-bottle fly,
   And yet you are happy, and sing
   As a sprite of joy were in your wing,
You fear no morrow, though when you die

No comrade will care ; no heart will break,
   No small fly tear for you be shed ;
   No doggerel dirge of rhyme be read
Above your grave for your dear sake.

Never mind, old fly, you are safe to-day ;
   I'm glad you have such a flow
   Of spirits, and I like to know
Your life was meant to be glad and gay.

Still I wonder if your gladness
  Has no dark undertone—no strain
  Of half remembered grief or pain—
No counterfoil of hidden sadness.

No, there seems to be no sign
  Suggesting aught but good intention ;
  Or even of life's extention
Beyond death's dark dividing line.

A spark of life by law impressed
  Ye seem, with gladness printed there ;
  No wearing toil, no seeming care
The joy of living to molest.

As dies the spark, do you e'en die ?
  Or does your life at death return
  To life's great sea, through death's dark bourne,
And the occult mists that wander by,

As the river, the lake, the sea
  Are upward drawn to Heaven
  To be to the earth regiven
In cycles large and good and free ?

Surely the king is a kindly king
  Who has, for thee fitted so well
  Thy house of life, where thou dost dwell,
And given thee glad songs to sing.

There now, I've wondered much of thee
  You old blue-bottle corpulent ;
  But have you ever one moment spent
In wondering aught about me ?

———

TRUE LIFE.

THE poet's words of truth will live
    All down far distant ages,
And evermore true largess give
    Of wisdom from his pages.
Many a poet is forgotten
Yet lives in thoughts by him begotten.

Surely the man can never die
    As long as his true thoughts live on
As vestures round the soul do lie
    That from his inner life have grown :
Like light that robes the sun of day,
Or stars that gem the evening grey.

And while his thoughts give spirit fare
    For hunger to assimilate,
He lives, though men know not nor care
    Who did their food predestinate.
The present time grows from the past
And doth the coming time forecast.

BUILDING.

$\mathfrak{A}$ND evermore the rising walls
    Are builded up on our beliefs,
With porticos and capitals—
    Outstanding sorrows and reliefs,
Till we our trowels lay aside
And from our labours softly glide.

And other men do take our place
    And build on what our souls have built—
True work the rising walls to grace,
    Or only shams with falsehoods gilt,
Then feeble hands do limply drop
And night's dark gates for them do ope.

So on, and on, forever on—
    Relays of workers evermore ;
Each soul must be, builder or stone,
    And happy he who makes a door
For souls at night to enter in
To life, and rest with souls akin.

SHINING SOULS.

$\mathfrak{T}$HE heart that can throw a halo of light
    On whatever it deigns to fall,
Can love the stars in the depth of night
And make them appear more pure and bright
    With a magic as true as 'tis mystical.

R

O, great is the gift of a heart that dowers
The earth with its spirit leal and sweet ;
Better it is than princedoms and powers ;
　Like sunbeams it falls in golden showers
Unfolding the fairest of earthly flowers—
　A carpet of beauty for angels' feet.

Or like sunbeams shining on drops of rain
　That make bright bows on the leaden sky ;
So love that shines on sorrow and pain
Binds earth to Heaven with a silver chain
　That doth the darkness glorify.

As magnets draw from heaps of dust
　The smallest particles of steel,
So the Overlove ever true and just
The best of us and the truest must
　Draw to itself for the common weal.

DETRACTION.

THERE'S folk that grab at every flaw
　　Detracting frae their neebor's merit,
Wi' malice black as ony craw ;
　They show a mean, ungenerous spirit.

They like to draw folk doon below
　Their ain low and unholy grade ;
Nae maitter whether freend or foe,
　They probe the sairs wi' poisoned blade.

An' if a faut they canna find,
   They gie a vague an' general sneer ;
To a' that's guid they're deef an' blind,
   They only like to stab an' teer.

Detraction seems the meat an' drink
   They feed their guidless souls upon,
An' wanting words they smile an' wink
   An' gloat on rotten carrion.

But though they dearly like to breathe
   The poison o' detraction,
An' in yer hert their swords to sheathe,
   They beat a' for exaction.

They think that ye should bend the knee
   In humble adulation—
Praise a' they say an' a' they be
   Wi' self depreciation.

Oucht else they wunna tolerate,
   Nae maitter if it's richt or wrang,
Theirsels maun aye predominate—
   The hero o' a flattering sang.

Alas ! if they sow nettle seeds
   Nettles will surely grow and sting ;
Just retribution for their deeds
   To their malicious souls will cling.

CONCEIT.

SOME folk think a' other folk gowks,
 And loodly their trumpet they blaw;
They think their ain eggs have a' twae yowks,
 An' other folk's nane ava.
O, sic wonderfu' stories they tell,
 An' sic wonderfu' things they hev dune,
That nae ane else could do but theirsels.
 Self is the keynote o' every tune.

When they meet their dooble they canna bear
 To hear frae another mooth
Their ain kind o' cracks; they declare
 The half o' them's no the truth.
When we find in another a failing,
 We should look to oorsels an' see
If we're no in another assailing
 Fauts we have in a waur degree.

LIVE TRUE.

FROM God's own treasure-house is lent
 To us, for usury, a day;
When evening comes and all is spent
 Our thoughts and deeds we should survey
And shew to Him what we retain
Within our souls of loss or gain.

For every moment that we spend
  We backward step, or forward go—
With life or death ourselves we blend
  And make the law our friend or foe.
Only the soul at one with God
Makes progress on the Heavenward road.

The bow unbent its spring retains—
  The soul must have its times of rest
When recreative power it gains
  To live its life with truer zest
Lest the monotony of toil
The sunshine of our lives should spoil.

We need not rush with heedless feet
  On work we are not fit to do,
But every task we duly meet
  Let's meet with ready will and true.
God's laws, like angels, ever wait
All efforts true to consecrate.

The crown we win ourselves must make,
  The help of Heaven is freely given;
And we the higher life partake
  If we for it have toiled and striven.
We reach a heritage divine
By climbing up with God's design.

"HE WHO TILLETH HIS LAND SHALL HAVE PLENTY OF BREAD."

THE untilled land produces weeds
        That mock the sluggard's sorest needs ;
The soul with faculties unused
Is self-defrauded, self-abused.

When fields with weeds are overgrown,
And souls to evil deeds are prone,
The weeds must be eradicated,
The soul with right be penetrated.

On land and life we must bestow
True labour and right seed to grow,
Until the harvest wealth accrue
To the clear eye and the strong thew.

When we can find a fitting sphere
To work therein is life's best cheer,
But if, with high endeavour we
From base environment can struggle free

The joy of strength attained may crown
More fully us who trample down
The hindrances that bar our way
Through the lone night till dawn of day.

ANALOGY.

THE plant that has no budding eyes
　　For the warm sunlight dies.
The man whose heart is never drawn
Outside himself for love of man,
Or bird, or beast, or humble plant
Suffers an eternal want,
　　And dies conserving self.

If thou would'st live let budding loves
　　Grow from thee into light
Till kindly thoughts and helpful deeds
　　Make all around thee bright.

CAUSE AND EFFECT.

" FICKLE fortune,"—sair misnamed—
　　By feckless souls is often blamed
For gieing some folk golden store
An' leaving others bare and puir,
But I o' this am certain shure
　　There's nae result withoot a cause ;
　　The idle scholar gets the tawse.

True some seem born for easy chairs,
An' some for worry, work, an' cares ;
But folk that are the maist to blame
Are aye the first wi' greedy claim ;

Howe'er it be it's true the same,
Where there's a sequence there's a cause
As shure as thorns are grown frae haws. ·

Frae honest labour, lowest doon,
There is a road to life's best croon ;
An' a' may rise in some degree
If they will stir their fins an' be
Like men that wunna turn agee,
For very shurely what ye saw
Shall grow the same by Nature's law.

An' he that thinks that guid things a'
Into his open mooth should fa'
While he lies listlessly below
The tree o' life where guid things grow,
Expecting what he didna sow
Will find where he has naething sawn
That weeds will grow on field an' lawn.

But let the man be up an' doing,
Some lawfu' guid intent pursuing ;
If he his work can understand,
An' freely ply his heart an' hand
Heaven its best gifts will freely send,
For he that seeks shall shurely find
The guerdon for the earnest mind.

Then let oor hearts be leal an' strong
To tackle life with sword and song,
And we may get the prize in wealth,

Or better still in true soul health,
A treasure free frae fear o' stealth.
Oor ain soul is oor safest bank,
An' as oor wealth, so is oor rank.

DO RIGHT.

LOVE God, and do what's right
    E'en though the priest on Sunday,
The world on Monday,
  Wi' meddling Mrs Grundy
Should disapprove ye quite
And sweer that black is white.
    Be true to your ain sel,
    Believe your inner light,
    In spite o' earth and hell.

Believe in God, the apex of perfection,
Your loyalty insures protection.
    Whoso is on His side
Shall all things overcome—
    Flesh, greed, indifference, pride—
And get His true encomium,
    " Good and faithful one,
    Well done, well done,
    Reign over all that thou hast won."

THE WAR.

NO promise trust for the downward race
That leads from the sunlit height ;
Nor ever trust captain in the war
That fights not for truth and right.
There is no gain
For souls insane
That fight on the lawless side,
Or who shirk the campaign
For fear of the pain,
To sail with the flowing tide.

If thou would'st win in the race of life
With truth let thy feet be shod.
If thou would'st win in the battle of life
Fight under the banner of God.
There is no loss
Of aught but dross
If we bear the cross
Where the sons of light have trod.

WEAVING.

WE'RE here the laws of life to learn,
And weave within their warp our weft.
As we their secret ways discern
We'll weave our web with fingers deft,
And so the Master's meed will earn
Within our souls, by Him, infeft.

God's truth is stamped on all His laws
  Where we conforming lives should weave
And strive to make them free from flaws
  Of guileful deeds meant to deceive
The world, to gain the world's applause—
  A poor ambition to achieve.

The soul that yields to falsehood's sway
  Can never weave to stand the test ;
It blindly gropes in twilight grey
  And weaves a robe by self impressed
That cleaves around it with dismay
  To advertise the laws transgressed.

Within the heart God's laws demand
  The love of kindliness and truth
That makes the loyal understand
  The soul of law is kindly ruth,
Service that holds by God's right hand
  By holding claims eternal youth.

O, love the truth ; the truth is strong
  And beautiful, it brings us near
To Him to Whom our souls belong ;
  We see His face ; His voice we hear,
Our loyal hearts are filled with song
  And we can see with vision clear
Angels of God about us throng.

TOIL.

A YEAR of toil is worth an age
    Of listless idleness with household fires ;
Better the field where hosts opposing rage
    Than peace where all the nobleness of life expires.

SEMBLANCE.

MAIST folk are apt to keep in shoals,
    An' thochtlessly sail wi' the stream ;
For if they're only *like other folk*,
    They think they're a' that they seem ;
But think for yersel an' they'll say yer wrang,
    For ye mauna disturb their dream.

They think if they're only fauldit up
    In the empty husk o' a creed—
If they gang to the kirk on Sunday
    That's a' that they want or need,
They dinna think to control their thochts—
    The untrue word, the unkind deed.

But had they to risk their life wi' a rope,
    They'd examine every strand ;
Or if they wanted some work to do
    They wad train baith heid an' hand ;
Nor wad they expect a crop to grow
    If they didna sow the land.

Now I think its every ane's interest
  To see that their creed is true ;
An' to see that God's holy spirit
  With holiness their's imbue ;
An' that to baith God an' Cæsar
  They render a' that is due.

For a' oor thochts are written doon,
  An' the spirit root o' oor thocht ;
An' the white robes o' the risen soul
  By the loyal life is wroucht ;
'An' Heaven is freely gi'en to a'
  That Heaven have truly soucht.

KIN.

IN those we love, 'tis qualities we love,
    A subtle spirit inspires the moral principles
Of truest men, and gives life's common-places
A beauty that love alone can apprehend.
    Sometimes our friend is but a mirror
Wherein we see reflections of ourselves,
And the deluded heart goes out
As unto one akin, when suddenly
The native soul takes its own hue
And stricken love recoils and dies,
While o'er its grave we weep regretful tears :
Nay ! love never dies ; one channel is but found

Disqualified and frozen, but it will find
Mayhap, a worthier, where it may bring
Refreshment to some heart more truly kin.
  Let us thank God for His benignant hindrances,
His revelations of the truths o'er which
Our purblind souls may sometimes grieve,
Love finds its level ; God's will be done.

EVENTIDE.

THE pilgrim at the gloaming grey,
    Weary and worn and footsore,
    Drops down at his Father's door,
Tired with the long and toilsome day.

And ever 'mong the shadows deep
    A muffled sentinel awaits
    To open wide the ponderous gates
For weary pilgrims fallen asleep,

That angels with white robes may come
    To clothe the soul all shriven,
    And waken it in Heaven
With restful songs of home, sweet home.

THE GATES.

TWELVE gates into the city of God,
   There's no night there and no decay ;
Twelve gates into the beautiful city
  That are never shut at all by day.
And angels at every portal stand
To welcome pilgrims from every land—
From every land and from every creed ;
All are welcome who feel their need.
   Whoso is athirst may come.

OUR ALPHABET.

GOD'S effluence in Nature's laws
   We see in adumbration ;
And there we learn the alphabet
  That spells his revelation,
And in the higher life of man
  We read His incarnation.

In Him we live and move,
  In Him we have our being ;
We live in Him and He in us,
  The laws of life decreeing.
We are responsible as sons
  With wills as free and eyes as seeing.

Rightness upward draws
　The soul that's pure and leal ;
But he whose soul is full of flaws
　On death has set his seal.
Still pardon waits within the laws
　The penitent's appeal.

VESPERS.

THE night cometh ; the toilsome day
　Draws to a close, and one by one
The stars come out with evening grey,
　And vesper bells ring out the sun.

The angels from the heavens inlaid
　With spheres of light at evensong
Come down, the soul to serenade,
　Till sleep blot out all sense of wrong.

When we awake beyond death's portal
　With every sense enlarged and clear
We shall be clothed with life immortal,
　And perfect love shall banish fear.

For purest, lealest love is given
　Where all are pure and leal and good,
For God is there and God is Heaven,
　And Father of the brotherhood.

NATURE IS QUIET CREATING; LOUD IN DESTROYING.

SILENTLY the sweet flowers grow
　　Unfolding all their quiet grace,
And silently their odours flow
　　Around them in their quiet place.
There is no noise, no jar, no strife,
They live to God their quiet life,
　　Nor wake a thought of aught that's base.

The earthquake rends the hills asunder ;
　　The wind lays mighty forests low ;
　　The flaming fires flash to and fro :
God speaks from Heaven to earth in thunder ;
　　When host meets host with cannon's roar
　　Earth trembles to its utmost core ;
The sons of peace look on in wonder

And wish the glory of the true—
　　The glad millenial time were here
　　When men shall beat the sword, the spear
To implements that do subdue
　　The quiet laws that wait to be
　　The slaves of sons the truth makes free
To recreate the world anew.

NOISE AND SILENCE.

THE winds with loud and rushing gusts
    Crash through the startled air ;
And earthquakes shake destruction round,
    While beasts are startled from their lair,
And sleep that thoughtless eyes have bound
    Is driven from eyelids everywhere,
    Then men are driven to cries of prayer.

And then the still small voice of God
    Whispers to the soul's deep core
The words that it may coin in deeds
And make its practice living creeds,
    And Heaven to earth again restore,
While law and love supply our needs
    That look to Him for evermore.

Like wind and earthquake, fire and flame,
With trumpet voice the Baptist came ;
    Gentle and still, with quiet deeds,
    Jesus brought balm for all our needs ;
Thunder and lightning clear the air,
The gentle rain makes all things fair.

OPEN EYES.

O MAN, with eyes God made to see,
    Look through the flowers that gem the grass
To make the old earth dear for thee,

Look through them as you look through glass,
And read words writ by God's own hand
If thou hast love to understand.

All through the songs that nature sings
  A grander song for open ears
Comes from the heights of Heaven and brings
  A blessing to the soul that hears.
To ears that love has oped is given
The soul of songs they sing in Heaven.

FOR GOD.

GIVE thy best thought
    And look for nought
  From thy compeers.
  The seed may lie for years
Ere it grow green with leaves,
Then come the blades, the ears, the sheaves
    With harvest blessings fraught.
Do good because 'tis right,
    And not for praise ;
    Nor grudge if after many days
Other hands
Shall reap thy lands.
    Work thou for God—
Be thou with Him at one ;

Whoever does His work,
Rejoice if it is done.
His perfect law
Shall upward draw
The soul that grasps His hand
Into the Fatherland.

STEERING HOME.

CAST on an island of the sea
  Of dark and deep eternity,
A compass I have found
And I am homeward bound.

My bark is frail
And scant of sail,
My faith round God is wound
And I am homeward bound.

Storms oft arise
When threatening skies
Lower all around,
But I am homeward bound.

The sea is wide,
Yet ships collide ;
But my small boat
Keeps still afloat,
And I am homeward bound.

However dark the night,
Like sweet home-light
Shines overhead the stars
Beyond life's frets and jars—
   They guide me home.

The gates fly wide,
When on the tide
My boat a triumph car
Shall clear the harbour bar,
   Bearing me home.

And there in Heaven
My friends all shriven
My soul absolved shall greet
With gladness made complete
   By love at Home.

REVELATION IN MAN.

GOD'S highest revelation is
   The noblest of the human race,
  The man who harbours nothing base,
Whose life is his propitiation.

Christ our ideal is—the highest
   In wisdom, justice, truth, and power,
   And every grace in sweetest flower,
The likest God and nighest.

In loving Him we love the Lord—
Our brother He ; our Father's son ;
So near to God in purpose one,
Adoring Him, God is adored.

MATTER AND SPIRIT.

MATTER and spirit robe the mind
Of God, who is the inner soul—
The over-Lord whose written scroll
The coming ages will unfold.

The green earth and the mighty sea;
The stars above, the flowers below ;
The seasons as they come and go—
All, all are sacred unto me.

And man, the son of God, with brain
Annihilating space and time,
With God unfolding powers sublime,
With works that earn eternal gain.

And love evolving spirit leal—
The highest good the crowning grace,
The light that shines from God's own face,
That doth Himself to us reveal.

For spirit is the highest test—
The hall-mark to the true soul given ;
The key that opes the gates of Heaven,
The garment of the wedding guest.

SONS OF GOD.

OUR souls, unseen, are known by what we do;
  The sun afar is by his affluence known;
And God, prime mover over all, by His
Transcendence seen in nature and the souls
Of many-sided man, and known by His
Sublime self-monograph writ over all.
And we can touch the hand that writes in prayer;
Our heads can plan a sequence to His plan—
For He has planned our souls with such a power,
Our hearts can throb with His; and shall we then
Despise our prospects high, nor care to know
That we descend from Him who crowned creation
With the soul of man? And shall we speak
Of "death" and "grave" as terms of final doom?
True sons of God can never die; they share
The Father's immortality. From time to time
They shed their withered leaves that they
Be clothed upon with robes that better suit
Their growing life. And who shall rashly doubt
The evidence so clear that presses *round*
The soul on every side, while *in* the soul
A still sweet voice whispers conviction?
Shall the ethereal soul die when its clothes
Are laid aside? And shall it have no power
To don the wedding robe when passing through
The vestibule into the palace of the King?
Is it not meet that we should lay aside
Our poor attire, and don our best when we
Attend the King? Yea, and I think we make

Our own admission robe, weaving each day
The woof into the warp of life. O soul !
See to it that thy robe be rentless, stainless,
Strong in its texture and graceful in its folds.

SONNET.

WHERE leal hearts live by God's own law 'tis well;
    Peace and prosperity to them are given,
And all things smile beneath the smile of Heaven,
While anarchy is but another name for hell
In which foul sphere accursed spirits dwell
    Who charge the clouds with wrong till they are riven
    By Heaven's avenging wrath ; they are self-driven
Against the laws that crush the infidel.
O God, Thy laws are just, make thou us strong
    And quick to do Thy will when Thou dost call
To rise and smite the upas tree of wrong,
    Where men, whom ignorance and sin enthral,
Do wilful crouch beneath its deadly shade.
    O with Thy healing touch make all men sane ;
By wisdom let the surging plague be stayed,
    And all the race freed from the curse of Cain.

SONNETS—HINDRANCE.

MY eyes are fixed upon the guiding star
    That shines in heaven, and leads me ever on;
And will lead me until the night is gone.

Onward I keenly press through strife and jar—
Nearer I press, yet still it seems afar ;
  And oftentimes I feel so much alone,
  And all my life with hindrances o'ergrown,
That were not life a pilgrim's holy war
That lies between me and my Father's home
  I would lie down and die outside the gate—
Careless to live, careless to overcome—
  Till dreamless sleep my life should dissipate.
Courage, I say ; that star must surely be
The eye of God that lights the way for me.
     *   *   *   *
Ofttimes we aim at bronze, and fret
  When turned aside for gold. Our souls are blind ;
  And when we grope about and only find
Hindrances that hindrances beget,
Each hindrance seems an angel to beset
  The tree of life. Not so. They bar the way
  Where our unwary souls would blindly stray ;
Each hindering angel with his sword of flame
Hinders only to help us to our aim—
  Helps us to hew down hindrances that bar
  Our homeward way, and foes that try to mar
Our life with suicidal deeds of shame
When we God's love with deeds of love should claim ;
  And fearlessly and wisely brush aside
  Each hindrance that the face of God doth hide.
     *   *   *   *
Sometimes we ask a gift with clamorous prayer—
  Our prayer is heard, and yet the gift refused ;

But in our souls instead there is infused
Nerve health—gifts oft with hindrances ensnare,
And feeble souls with nervelessness impair.
　Better it is to work for strong soul thews,
　And justly earn the strong soul's revenues.
Better to earn a title than to heir
　An empty name with soul corrosive rust;
Better the heaviest cross that man can bear
　Than grovelling cry for gifts that are but dust.
The prize by effort won grows in the soul;
　To take an unearned gift is scarcely just;
The man is poor that needs the pauper's dole,
　But he is rich that earns his honest wealth,
　And strong in muscle, brain, and heart with health.

THREE SONNETS.

I.

WHILE looking back through all the golden haze
　　Beyond the weary space that intervenes,
We give the past more than its due of praise,
　And clothe with rosy grace life's youthful scenes.
In music heard o'er hills and vales and streams
　The false notes die, the true are borne along;
So die the jars in retrospective dreams,
　And springtime sweetness swells life's evening song.
If there was aught of bitterness or pain,
　'Tis but remembered with a wistful smile,

While all the joy brings cent. per cent. of gain—
　　Blest heritage for souls that have no guile.
Oh, happy he "who leaning on his guide,"
Rests in an afterglow at eventide.

II.

Two souls, like seedling plants, together grow,
　　And to the common eye seem much the same ;
But they take diffcrent courses when they go
　　Into the crush, with each a different aim.
Each one develops his particular powers
　　Until the difference is as great as is
The different colours of two different flowers ;
　　Some traits seem new, while other traits we miss.
When first they meet, after long years of change,
　　When youth has faded into hoary age—
Gone the old buoyancy—each to each seems strange :
　　Two weary pilgrims nearing their last stage.
At scenes of long ago they both unbend,
But that's the only theme where they can blend.

III.

'Tis qualities we love, and they may change
　　With changing years : the plastic soul may take
Another hue from sources new and strange,
　　And of itself another self may make—
Another changed self that may but be
　　A feeble paraphrase of someone near,
As long ago it was but that of me,
　　Now blotted out without a sigh or tear.

The change may be for better or for worse,
　But leaves no likeness of the friend of yore.
Oh, weary change, with nought to reimburse
　The debt of love that nothing can restore.
We meet—I cannot grasp an empty glove ;
Of all I loved there's nothing left to love.

SONNETS.

ONCE I imagined that to squeeze a thought
　　Into the rigid space of fourteen lines
　Was much like cutting yews into designs
Elaborately ugly, resembling nought
In earth or air or sea by nature wrought.
　Or like the slender tendrils of the vines
　Forced into most unnatural confines ;
Or caging the lark that high in heaven ought,
On quivering wing, to fill with overflow
　Of its own joy the palpitating air,
While all the leafy summer scene below
　Felt the sweet largess on its bosom fair.
I thought form should not mould the mind's warm
　　　glow ;
Better far that mind should make the form grow.

*　　*　　*　　*

But now I think 'tis nice to have a plot—
　A diamond or a star of sweet heart's ease,
　Where art and nature harmonise to please

The heart attuned to chord with such a spot,
That seems a sonnet in God's polyglot ;
  Where the pure heart with purest vision sees
  How pliant nature with true art agrees
In harmony, without a jarring note ;
For nature when idealised by art
Sends finer thrills through every cultured heart.
  So a good thought may fitly find a place
  Within the sonnet's fourteen lines of space,
As in a setting fit and opulent—
The setting of the set the complement.

UNPUNCTUALITY.

PUNCTUAL yourself, you do sincerely hate
  A dawdling want of punctuality
In others.   A certain time you specify
To go somewhere ; you're up to time and wait,
  And wait, and wait to see your friend appear—
  Your temper's going—gone, that's very clear ;
You ban the selfishness that's always late;
  Your friend's worst failings crowd into your mind,
  And imperfections by the score you find
On which with irritation you dilate.
  At last, in wrath, you do resolve to go
  And leave the selfish soul that tries you so
With thoughtless carelessness that arrogates
A right that wantonly exasperates,
When up he turns all smiles and perspiration,

Unconscious he of doing aught that's wrong ;
Takes no account of having kept you long ;
Begins his chronic explanation.
He never sees the frown upon your brow,
And never dreams that you will disallow
His right to give you provocation.
Someone he met, that spoke and spoke till he
Forgot the hidden wings of time could flee
Far, far beyond his calculation,
And then he said " Goodbye " and fled in haste—
Ran every blessed step as he'd been chased ;
Now here he is with late precipitation,
The sweet disciple of procrastination.

SWEET VIOLETS.

THE violets in the verdant lap of spring
Flaunt no aggressive colours on the eye,
But, meekly, on the soft winds lingering nigh
Breathe out their hearts when birds begin to sing.
O violets, that heart to heart hath given,
Your odours fan the soul with breath from Heaven,
While thoughts, like fays from every petal peering,
Whisper spirit words in spirit hearing.
The blent aroma silently enspheres
A power that smoothes the crumpled cares of life ;
That mingles balm with sorrow's burning tears,
Pours sacred oil on stormy waves of strife ;
And all the atmosphere is fragrant made
With violets in the heart that never fade.

SUNSETS.

O BLESSED sun ! before thee darkness fled
  When, like the benedictions of a king,
 Thy light fell down to fructify the spring ;
Earth smiled, with all her fairest flowers outspread,
  Responding to thy splendours far above,
  As souls respond to God's far-shining love.
Man toiled, joyed, wept beneath the blessings shed
On him by thy beneficence o'erhead,
Careless, until beyond the western hills
  Thy passing left such afterglow of light
He felt the pressure of the infinite that fills
  The heart with thoughts as with bright stars the
      night ;
Unmindful was he of the noonday sun,
But moved to rapture when the day was done.

O soul that walked with God ! in high degree
  Evolving good for all in words and deeds ;
  Training to sweet content our hungry needs ;
Pure as the dawn, and strong in purity,
  And wisely good in sowing precious seeds
  To crowd from out our heart the baneful weeds.
Thy course was like the sun's, straight on and free,
Thy spirit like the light made darkness flee.
  We did not gauge thy worth until the night
  When thy calm light shone on our cloudy grief,
Making the atmosphere around us bright
  With such an all-entrancing afterglow

From the unseen shore, enlarging our belief,
Transforming all our pain and all our woe,
Till faith was sight and we could let thee go.

MUSIC.

THE streams, the winds, the birds, the trees,
　　The lowing kine, the bleating sheep,
The rolling thunder and the roaring seas
　　Touch soul and sense with music deep—
A-wed to thoughts that sweetly please,
　　Like words enfolded in the sweep
Of melody that flows from fingers deft
　　That on some perfect instrument
Weaves thought with sound as warp with weft.

Simple strains do charm the ear,
But higher moods demand to hear
True rhythmic wisdom clothed in words
　　That speak in music fit and clear ;
That touch like dreams; that strike like swords;
　　That lift the arm ; that wake the tear ;
That bind the soul with silken cords
　　To lawful liberty, which is
The music of the higher life
Where is no jarring note of strife.
　　Our lives, with willing hearts, should be
　　Like songs of perfect harmony,
　　Attuned, O God, to love of Thee.

THE UNSEEN SOUL.

MUSCLE, sinew, brain, and motor nerve
    Are but the wondrous tools we touch and see
  Created by the Overmind to be
Revealers of the unseen mind and verve;
And well the purpose of the soul they serve.
    They yoke the lightning to his kingly car,
    And bring him knowledge from the morning star.
They sound the sea and gauge the restless storm,
And all the master's messages perform ;
And if from their ordainéd use they swerve,
    Too oft the unseen master is to blame
For misdirection culpable and wrong
    That weaves around himself a net of shame
That, as his will grows weak, grows gross and strong.
    O unseen lord of many slaves, be kind
    To them and loyal to the Overmind.

THE RAINBOW.

A CLOUD was by a lovely rainbow spanned,
    And every several drop that helped to form
  The coronet upon the passing storm
Of its own brilliancy felt proud and grand
In binding earth to heaven with such a band,
    As if some sweet inherent merit
    Made lovely all its soul and spirit.
When lo ! a higher cloud obscured the sun,

T

And every raindrop lost its radiant hue,
And fell from heaven feeling itself undone.
  The glad earth caught them in its bosom true,
And all the flowers spread out their leaves to greet
The downcast rain with benedictions sweet.
    Sunshine and rain spanned heaven with a bow,
    Sunshine and rain were woven in the flowers below:
All things combine to make God's laws complete.

When from some dark-browed cloud our tears, like
          rain,
    Troubles with stormy thoughts our atmosphere,
    Full oftentimes we feel a glory near
That tempers all our bitter grief and pain
With soul-ennobling loveliness and gain.
    'Tis God's own smile on every trembling tear
    That makes our sorrows beautiful appear.
We lift the heaviest cross with ready grace
    And bear it up life's steepest roughest hill ;
If thus we may but see His gracious face
    And feel His peaceful presence with us still.
Love binds the soul to God with sorrow's chain
    As earth is bound to heaven with drops of rain.

Upon the falling rain the sun shone bright,
    Spanning the heavens with a resplendent bow
    That made the dull grey cloud with glory glow.
So shines upon our souls God's gracious light,

And is refracted and reflected so
To all the many coloured creeds we know
That bind the heaven above to earth below.
We vainly think of all the various creeds
    That ours alone is adequate and true,
Nor see refracted in our thoughts and deeds
    The light that shines upon our cloudy view.
Oh ! that by us 'twas clearly understood
That every creed that loves the light is good.

LIGHT.

WHEN weary with the strife my tired eyes
        Looked up to God through all the silent night,
    Waiting for Him to touch the east with light,
His heedful love heard all my moaning cries
And shewed me how on hindrances to rise,
    And view all round from such a vantage height,
While His own hand touched my poor eyes with sight ;
And the wide prospect made my spirit wise—
I saw the way He led me by the hand
    Through thorny paths, up rugged heights and steep.
He gave the seed I scatter o'er the land—
    The harvest in my soul I keep ;
And now I know the toil, the grief, the pain
Are slaves of God that lade my soul with gain.

When, in the night, beneath the starry heaven,
  Where, through the clouds, moonbeams uncertain
      quiver
Among the boughs that span Life's flowing river,
With praying hands, like Jacob, I have striven
  With Jacob's God to be all purely shriven :
  That wisdom, grace and strength, and truth might
      ever
Bind my poor life unto the great Lifegiver :
That all the gifts for which my soul has striven
Might be returned to Him with usury.
  I stumbling strove with toil and weariness,
  With pain and sore heart dreariness ;
God touched my eyes with light, and I could see
These were His angels sent to answer me :
  Who strive to overcome them is full wise—
  The vanquished angels freely give the prize.

TRIED.

FULL many a time my heart was sorely tried
    When cherished hopes, like morning drops of
      dew,
  Glistened and dried, or, like grey phantoms, flew
Before my face with promises that lied,
Though for the promises I could have died.
  I felt that where a shadow was a true
  Substance must most surely be, which to pursue

Was worth all effort.   All hindrance I defied
  And marched straight to the goal heedless of pain,
  Of toil, of hopes, like withered leaves that fell
  Around some lonely hermit's desert cell,
And all inducements to relax the strain
  To win, I heard God say unto my soul, " Repell
All whispers that would clog thy life with sin,
Then shall the pearly gates fly wide to let thee in."

LAW.

PLEASURES are ever found at God's right hand ;
    No matter in what place or world we be,
  The loyal soul at God's right hand is free ;
For God's right hand is law that cannot bend
To wrong, but will service with service blend.
  The restless wheels go round by wise decree
  In grooves that only serving souls can see,
And he alone, who best can understand
  The law, giving heart service leal and true,
  Is safe and helped—service for service due ;
But he whose life runs counter to the law
  Is caught within the wheels' unceasing round—
  Is crushed, and round the whirling shaft is wound
And cast from life into the arms of death
  By wheels where healthful bread of life is ground.

IMMORTAL DEATH.

IMMORTAL death! 'tis terrible to think
    How men, from eastern figures, understood
    Eternal torment : holy men who could
Boldly declaim on such a theme, nor shrink,
But rather gloatingly o'erlook the brink
    Of deep despair, nor see the magnitude
    Of woe that never found an interlude—
A depth of woe that could no lower sink.

Better to look on sin as that which makes
The soul a rotten branch, that pure wind shakes
    From off the living tree into the mire—
    Gathered by death and cast into the fire,
And there consumed to all unconscious dross,
This is eternal death—eternal loss.

EXPRESSION.

LABOUR to give thy thought the best expression
    In fittest words that may take root and grow
In other minds until it overflow
And find embodiment and full possession
In noble deeds, stamped with its own impression,
    That, like bright suns that shed a kindly glow
    All round, on hearts above and needs below,
To foster kindly deeds in long succession.
We have no happiness unless we toil
    In labour hard, or sweat, for some good end ;

'Tis then we plant our seed in fruitful soil
   And our will with the will of Heaven blend ;
Then increase comes, with Heaven's anointing oil,
   In harvest of good that all our thoughts transend.   ·

DO RIGHT.

LET no weak wavering mar a good resolve,
   But fearlessly and firmly do the right
 With willing promptness and with all thy might ;
To fear and hesitate is to involve
The soul in obstacles that do revolve
   And twine themselves around thee in despite
   Of thy poor wavering attempts to fight.
Firm purposed effort shall alone absolve
Whoever turns from wrong resolved to win
   Release from bonds that do the soul disgrace—
From false and wily blandishments of sin,
   To freedom in the light of God's own face.
Kingship is never won by soft content,
But by resolve with truest effort blent.

KINGDOM.

WE only reign o'er what we can subdue
   By brain and hand to freely gladly give
Allegience we can claim as justly due,
   By bond of ableness most positive.

And we shall surely reign at God's right hand
By right of laws we serve and understand.
　　The wider that our kingdom is we rise
　　The nearer God, with purer, opener eyes,
Laying our gifts upon the altar stair
With bended knee before the absolutely fair,
　　Claiming with all the fearlessness of love
　　The right to reign, as sons of God, above
The clouds of ignorance and wilful wrong,
By right of His inherent self making us strong.

WORK.

WORK is the nutriment on which we grow,
　　That man is poor who has no aptitude or will
　For work that waits for his particular skill ;
The work we're fittest for, that best we know
Is work that shall with good our life o'erflow,
　　When we in it God's purposes fulfil.
　For work unfit the primal curse is still
To toil with sweat writ sorrow on our brow.
The work that's done with a complying heart
　For God is good, and brings sweet peace and light.
In idleness the soul remains apart
　From God, and only earns the curse of blight.
O, soul, with all thy powers be quick to serve
Thy Master well, with willing heart and nerve.

THE SPIRIT OF OUR DAYS.

" THE spirit walks of every day deceased
          And smiles an angel or a fury frowns,"
     The spirit of to-day to-morrow crowns
With life and health, and store of good increased,
Or makes us foes that will not be appeased ;
     Then make each thought, each word, each deed
     A helpful angel for the next day's need ;
Build thou an altar on the past surceased
Where thou may'st lay thy life, with God at one,
     And feel in every nerve salubrity
And power to trample all obstructions down,
     When this day's soul the next shall sanctify,
While all the tempter's darts, pointless and light,
Do fall upon the loyal shield of *right*.

RETROSPECT.

" 'TIS greatly wise to talk with our past hours
          And ask them what report they bore to
          Heaven,"
     'Tis wise to use the hours as they are given
In freely consecrating all our powers
To Him who sends His grace in growthy showers ;
     And every soul that hath with evil striven
     Shall be with help and pardon shriven.
And far above earth's brawls, and pomps, and towers,
His soul shall grow with upward growing things,
     For all our days are steps on which we rise

To thrones, where we shall sit and reign as kings,
  According as our hearts are leal and wise.
So live that every hour's report shall be
Of coming good a certain prophecy.

OBSTRUCTIONS.

OBSTRUCTIONS are as angels that we meet
    On life's low hollows, and on life's high hills ;
  We wrestle with them till our higher wills
Gain over them a victory complete.
  By right of strength we take their secret skill
  And bid them all our purposes fulfil ;
They watch our eye, our lordship they entreat,
They run our messages with willing feet ;
We wrestle with them at the gates of life,
  With all the promised land spread out before,
When we subdue them in the friendly strife
  Their faces shine with service evermore.
Kings are no kings unless while here they do
A kingdom from the wilderness subdue.

THE LAKE.

THE lake beneath the moon is calm and clear
    As if it held in store the light of all the day,
And here and there are clumps of sallow willows
Like ships in miniature on some small inland sea,

And every twig is mirrored faithfully
In the still waters, as if the bush were double—
The bush above, its duplicate below. Speak loud,
Echo reflects your words as if the dead
Within the lone churchyard were mocking you.
  Reflection sees the long procession
Moving slowly east from village homes
Left desolate, to this still congregation.
Of the dead, where weary pilgrims
At the door of God's own house cast off
Their dusty robes to enter into rest.
  O living soul make thy life beautiful,
For every word and deed, is mirrored in
The inland lake of life, and makes for good
Or ill, in the great sea of universal being.

TRUTH.

THE man who stands upon the truth is strong;
    All stable things and right are on his side,
  And will the final victory decide
For him, though falsehood with her brazen throng
Of ugly, slimy things, that crawl among
    The dust and dirt of life, and, fearful, hide
    In unclean corners, may the truth deride,
And slander souls that fight against all wrong,
As Luther did at Worms, when priest and prince
    Assembled were the fearless man to crush:

Firm as a rock he met the impetuous rush,
And made the fiercest of his foes to wince,
  "So help me God," he said in word and act,
  "I cannot, and I never will retract."

TIME.

TIME moves along with sure and steady pace,
    Heedless ; nor stays for joy ; nor hastes for
        grief ;
When coming seems so long, when past so brief ;
Youth, fearless, hails it with a glowing face,
Girding itself as one that runs a race ;
  Sees but the summer flower, the autumn sheaf ;
  But age, with pensive thought in the sear leaf
Doth read a thousand memories that retrace
The steps of time—the wise man's heritage.
Youth's rosy cheeks and heart that brims with glee
And pride of strength so lithe and blithe and free
Should weave white robes for honourable age.
The weary pilgrim nearing his last stage,
  In sight of home, laden with gathered store,
  Would not be wise to ask for one mile more.

TEMPTATION.

SOULS balanced true in ever part are strong ;
  Efficiently they keep the capitol
With all their vassals under wise control,
Nought tempts the tempter to entice to wrong ;
But round ill-balanced souls temptations throng,
  And where the walls are weak their arts employ
  To weaken weakness and what's good destroy.
O soul ; though sweet may seem the syren's song,
Ope not the gates but throw the gauntlet down,
  Defying treachery with noble scorn.
Be brave, fight well and win the victor's crown,
  Having no fear but to be overborne,
Then shall thy scars attest the title given
To such as win by force the right to Heaven.

GOD'S LAWS.

THE laws of God in everything inhere—
  The will of God is everywhere enshrined
  And to the open eye reveals the Master's mind,
  Like songs that thrill the heart and please the
      ear,
But wait within the instrument till he appears
  Whose hand is trained to loose the strains
      confined

And silent, until they are with soul combined ;
Then the dumb organ speaks in accents clear.
All nature is an instrument that's made
   With laws, and keys that do the laws unlock,
To set the singing angels free to aid
   The knowing hearts that can their aid invoke.

The Oversoul has breathed law,
   Through all we feel and see and know ;
   Through birds that fly and flowers that blow;
Through " Nature red in tooth and claw " ;
In earth and air and forest shaw,
   In stars that shine, in suns that glow,
   In brooks that murmer as they flow,
In everything that man ere saw,
Is folded up a steadfast law,
   And everything the eye can see
Is printed by God's holy hand,
   And full of wisdom strong and free,
That we must toil to understand
How soul with law may sweetly blend.

Nature is God's teaching book,
   It lies before us open wide
   Ready to be the leal soul's guide,
And give its gifts to such as look
For them, with hearts that will not, brook
   To be denied whate'er betide,

To fools it doth its wisdom hide,
For they run counter to its law
  In wilful ignorance that must
Most surely on their folly draw
  The sequent punishment that's just.
But he who reads with heart on fire
  Shall see the angels waiting, stand
  Ready to serve at God's right hand—
Shall hear them say, "Come up higher
And get from God thine heart's desire."

LEADERS.

SOMETIMES a giant of the human race—
    A son of God, appears to guide and lead
  To higher planes of onward word and deed
The sons of men ; with steadfast soul to chase
The darkness from the land, and in its place
  To flood with light the truths that pilgrims need ;
  Heedless he is of blame, acclaim, or meed,
Intent alone to lead men to the Father's face :
How gladly should we hail the kingly man—
  How gladly should assenting reason run
  Loyal as light is to the lordly sun—
With eager feet to follow near the van ;
  And when the clouds receive him from our sight,
  Let's write his eulogy in deeds of light.

KEYS.

MASTERS of song arise who take the keys,
     And with strong hands unlock the thunder
          cloud,
And from its bosom helpful angels crowd
Eager the master mind to serve and please,
Bearing his messages o'er land and seas.
     They do his battles with the night, dark browed,
     And drive it to the jungle disendowed.
When the strong man the willing angels seize
Heaven smiles, the young earth wonders at each act,
And marks with sweet completeness their compact.
     When man subdues, with love, the angel band
They blend with concrete service thoughts abstract,
     Swift to obey the master's magic wand
Of knowledge, that proves his lordship over all
That answers freely to his lordly call.

SABBATH.

THE Sabbath morn fills all the Sabbath air
     With a sweet restfulness and heavenly calm—
     To earthly care a blessed and welcome balm.
Within ourselves, without, and everywhere
The soul of sacred peace broods calm and fair,
     As if creation sang her holiest psalm,
     While all the way for pilgrim feet the palm
Branches are strewn up to the altar stair,

Where we our lives a willing offering lay
With hearts that yearn to be at one with God,
And walk with fearless feet within his way,
As pilgrims walk along a pleasant road,
Knowing that home and love are at the end,
Where love with love shall sweetly blend
With love that doth all other love transcend.

LEAVES.

WHEN autumn leaves grow ripe they die,
They have gathered the light, the heat, and the
rain,
And stored them up to make leaves again ;
They have lived their life, and now they lie
A carpet of death for the passer by.
In their fresh young life they made a fane
That quivered with many a gladsome strain ;
But now they rot 'neath a leaden sky.
But death shall transmute them to life once more,
For life is nourished by death and change ;
Waves come and go by the lone sea shore ;
Leaves come and go by the forest grange ;
The trees live on in the ebb and flow,
As the tide of life swells to and fro.

So the soul shall live while the form dies,
And draw round itself a raiment meet,
With room for the large heart's larger beat,
In a higher sphere, where clearer eyes

Shall see how the pure heart wins the prize ;
  While angels of love shall hasten to greet
  Life emerged from wraps grown obsolete—
Wraps forgot by the soul grown wise.
Why should we cling to rags outworn
  When the Master calls us home from pain,
From a prison dark to freedom's morn,
  From needful loss to eternal gain ?
If the soul would live the form must die—
" Dust to dust, the soul to its home on high."

EVIL.

" Evil is seen ' as cloud across God's orb ; no orb itself.' "

ROBERT BROWNING.

SATAN is wrong personified and should
    Not as a person worsting the Most High
  Be understood, but as reeking to the sky
A foul miasma, clouding over good,
Obscuring truth with sin's falsehood.
    Truth is an orb ; sins are clouds that fly
    'Tween us and it to blur and mystify,
And wandering fools with vain pretence delude.
Sin is disease that fastens on the life,
    And we must overcome the festering sore
By a wise watchfulness and constant strife,
    Till we are sound and whole to our hearts' core,
And victors stand before the King all shriven,
And hear Him say, " Well done, ye have won Heaven."

CHARITY.

THE weakness of our will when trials test
    Our loyalty to what is good and right
   Should teach us charity when we would smite
With scorn a fallen brother, or would jest
At wrong, enjoying with malicious zest
    His downward plunge from some high height—
    Bright promise lost in dark temptations night,
Where talents meant for good are grown a pest.
May we walk warily, for who can tell
    But he, the man whom we so much deride,
Was strong where we are weak, and might excel
    Where we could gain no foothold by his side.
O, let our weakness teach us to be strong,
To succour weakness when assailed by wrong.

LIMITATION.

THE water from the fountainhead may be
    Fresh drawn and pure, and clear as morning
        light ;
But yet ye cannot fill with all your might
Pitchers beyond their own capacity.
And there are minds whose hard rigidity
    Have no expansion for new views of right,
    And eyes that seem to have no power of sight.
In vain the light to truth doth testify.

Eyes have they, but they neither see nor know
　What larger, more elastic minds perceive ;
They have no hunger for the ceaseless flow
　Of dignity that loyal souls achieve.
O, shall we blame the ignorant content
Only less than we do a life ill spent ?

RICHES.

THY barns may burst with hoarded heaps of grain
　　And coin thy coffers fill like flakes of snow,
　All earthly good to theeward ceaseless flow,
Thy body never feel a moment's pain,
Thy strength no needful labour's overstrain ;
　Still he whose task it is to till and sow
　Thy fields, and must each day some want forego,
May have a richer soul and kinglier reign,
O'er wider regions that his power subdues.
　For that alone is to be counted wealth
That with true nutriment the soul imbues
　With wisdom, nobleness, and vigorous health.
It matters not the want or have of gold,
The test of kingliness is life controlled.

That man is rich who has the blessed gift
　Of drawing to himself true, loving friends,
　Whose helpfulness around him binds
Love's silken bonds.　No winds can turn adrift,

No current sweep away, however swift,
  The soul that anchorage securely finds
  In sweet community of hearts and minds,
Where clouds are rent, and love looks through the rift.
O, blessed gift to see with friendship's eyes
  The beauty and the blessing everywhere !
The sweetness and the light that charm the wise
  When shared with friendship's eyes are doubly fair.
Love is the golden key that opes the heart ;
Hate bids the helpful ones of God depart.

"GREET THE UNSEEN WITH A CHEER."

ROBERT BROWNING.

YES, we may "greet the unseen with a cheer,"
    For all the way our eyes have seen afar
  The steady light in heaven of our pole star
By which our onward course we steer.
Though rough and steep the way we have no fear,
  But trample o'er whate'er our way would bar,
  And all that we subdue in peace or war
Shall make the light of heaven more sweet and clear ;
And each accession of new strength we find
  Shall be a key to ope another door
That shall disclose new glories to our mind,
  And riches that we keep for evermore ;
And when the morning star shall disappear
In light, we'll greet the dayspring with a cheer.

CONSUMING FIRES.

" God, who is a consuming fire for all evil ;
Tophet, which is a consuming fire for all good."

OFTTIMES when hearts grow poor and cold,
  God heats affliction's sacred fire,
To burn the dross of vain desire
And leave more pure and bright the gold.
We cry in pain when flames enfold
  The soul as on a funeral pyre ;
  They burn the dross to bring us nigher
The love that shall no good withhold.
Then let us kiss the chastening rod,
  It saves us from the fires of hell
That burn up every trace of God.
  Better the fire that burns the shell
Than fire that burns the image and the name
Of God out of the soul with ruthless flame.

THE RACE.

LIFE is a race ; we see the goal afar ;
  Obstructions hem us in on every side—
Temptations, waywardness, and worldly pride ;
With these our souls must wage a constant war,
Trampling them down where'er they rise to bar
  Our onward course. By what impedes we're tried,
  And he who wills to win must lay aside
Each hindering weight and keep on life's pole star

A watchful eye, nor turn aside for aught—
  Heedless alike for idle praise or blame,
Careful alone to do the thing he ought.
  For him there is no failure and no shame,
For he runs well who runs with all his might
And keeps the course according to his light.

SOWING.

O SOWER going forth to sow thy seeds!
  'Tis for eternal harvests that ye sow ;
As is the seed, so shall the harvests grow.
Watch well thy thoughts, they are the germs of deeds;
Cast out the thoughts that are the germs of weeds
  As ye would drive away a deadly foe
  That would with withering blight thy field o'erflow,
And leave unsatisfied man's hungry needs.
Sow thou thy seeds with the first dawn of day,
  When evening comes withhold not thou thy hand ;
Sow thou from rosy morn till evening grey,
  And as ye sow let prayers to Heaven ascend,
Nor grudge that other hands shall reap thy field—
Seedtime can give what harvests cannot yield.

MIRACLES.

MEN vaguely speak of miracles, and say
  They prove the Bible is God's word direct
  From Heaven, inspired, infallibly correct;
And if our souls refuse the vague array

Of words that come between our eyes and day,
  We're branded infidels that do infect
  Our sphere with heresies that do reject
The word of God, whose kingship we betray.
While we do claim to see a clearer light
  And know in miracles a higher law,
We see God's words in letters shining bright
  Everywhere, and bow in love and holy awe.
The natural is what we can touch and see—
The supernatural, life glad and free
In and *over* all, life's " open sesame."

KNOWLEDGE.

PLANTED in midst of Eden grew the tree
    Of knowledge of evil and of good.
  What wonder if the reasoning spirit should
Ask why knowledge should forbidden be
When lower wants had satisfaction free ?
  'Tis pleasant to the eye and good for food,
  And nature's secrets may be understood
By knowledge.   Were our eyes open we could see ;
'Tis good to see, and knowledge gives us light ;
  Then should we be as gods, and it were well
To be as gods in wisdom and in might.
  By knowledge we all lower life excel.
If then on knowledge good and evil grows,
We will endure the thorns to have the rose.

Knowledge of good is always good, but why
    Knowledge of evil ?   Knowing one implies
    Knowledge of the other ; the shadow lies
Among the sunshine, and against a lie
The truth—to see the one we must descry
    The other ; death is but a shadow thrown
    Across our view by life that God shines on.
Good we must know to do ; evil to fly.
Had we no power to choose 'tween good and ill,
    We were, indeed, but worthless clods of clay ;
But having power to choose with a free will,
    We prove our kinship to the Lord of day.
If we would be leal sons of God we must
With all our heart prove faithful to our trust.

STRENGTH.

TRUE manhood centres in free will,
    And muscles gather strength by use ;
  For strength we court the perilous,
Nor count that toil which proves our skill.
'Tis moral gain to vanquish ill.
    We know that victory shall transfuse
    Abiding strength in our soul thews—
Give wings to mount the steepest hill.
To feel our strength is keen delight.
    Swine wallow in a wealth of food,

But man must scale the Pisgah height
　And grandly see that God is good.
To reach the heights we must aspire
By bowing to a life that's higher.

KINGSHIP.

THE strong wise man is kingly, and can make
　All his environments to hew his wood
And draw his water, and freely take
His yoke, and serve him as his subjects should.
But he who is not strong nor wise can only yield,
　And from his feeble grasp let fall the tool
He is too weak and indolent to wield.
　Environments rule him ; he cannot rule.
And he who will not serve and cannot reign,
　Will kick against the pricks and fume and fret,
With rebel temper spending force for pain,
　To wind about his feet a tangled net.
We reign by right o'er all we can subdue,
But kings for service must give service true.

THE WISEST MAN.

'TIS not the wisest man that soonest gains
　The common ear, the loud applause
　That to himself encomiums draws ;
But 'tis the man with common brains

Who speaks what all men dumbly feel,
Who unto them themselves reveal,
And every nebulous thought explains
In words that make men feel that they
The very things themselves might say
Could they have bound the words in sequent chains.
The noblest man is he whose gifts
The common mind from lowness lifts
To wiser views and higher, nobler planes
Of thought. Though bound in iron chains, he reigns.

SLOW TO BLAME.

WHEN in a brother man we see aught wrong,
There may be meaner wrong in us if we
Smile in repeating what amiss we see.
We may perchance be weak where he is strong,
And if, at wrong in us, he smile elate,
We think the cruelty exceeding great.
'Tis this should teach our hearts how pitiless
It is to gloat o'er weakness, when as weak
We are ourselves.   When we have aught to speak
Let us not with black-hearted eagerness
Delight to blaze abroad a brother's shame,
But meekly, with a lowly self distrust,
Speak only, and with sorrow, what we must,
Respecting as our own our neighbour's name,
While trying all we can with love to win
An erring brother quietly from sin.

WEARINESS.

O, HOW the weary yearn for peace and rest
    When aching limbs are bent beneath a weight
Of toils that ever do accumulate,
When nerve and muscle vainly do protest
    Against the burdens that subordinate
    The higher life that should predominate.
It too is weary, and is dispossessed
By lower wants to lower straits compressed ;
    The heart, too weary to be passionate,
Can only feel that sleep, intense and deep,
    Is the one good alone that's understood—
The only harvest that the soul can reap,
    When bowed to earth beneath life's threefold rood ;
O, weary one, the way is short, if steep.

His yoke is easy, and it makes the load
    That thou must bear gall thy bent shoulders less ;
    Learn thou of Him who felt life's weariness—
His yoke was love, and every step He trod
Bound Him more closely to the strength of God,
    As forward still with gentle lowliness
    He went with holy self-forgetfulness,
While from His life a wealth of healing flowed.
And all who bathe within that healing stream
    Shall feel the balm of rest in every sense
Steal o'er their conscious souls like joy's glad dream ;
    While angels strow Heaven's own munificence
On every limb, on tired heart and brain ;
The toil is blest that Heaven crowns with gain.

STORMS.

EXPECT the storms of life while staying here,
  And when they come ye need feel no surprise ;
'Tis good to see all round with open eyes.
'Twere easy on life's open sea to steer
  Were there no storms, no rocks, no privateer ;
  The sailor knows such things exist, and tries,
  With knowledge of the ship, the seas, the skies,
To keep from every hindrance clear.
Knowledge and loyalty to laws concerned
  Give power to reign as kings o'er all we know,
And when such knowledge we have truly learned
  We do inherit earth and all below.
We set our feet on sublunary things,
To know and to obey has made us kings.

DRAGONS' TEETH.

OUR thoughts are seeds we sow with our compeers,
  And folded in each seed there surely lies,
  Strictly exact, the punishment or prize ;
Forgiveness waits for our repentant tears,
But love cannot blot out the sins of years.
  We only can with firm resolve arise
  And on the home star fix our eager eyes—
With sword in hand return through hostile spears
Of serried ranks of armed foes that grew
  From dragons' teeth, sown by our evil deeds ;

But with the sword of God and purpose true
  We may hew down our enemies like weeds,
And with Heaven's help each hindrance base subdue,
  Until our homeward way no foe impedes.

CHARACTER.

WHATE'ER'S the character, it leaves
    It's impress on the form and face,
  Pure heart and seeing eye can trace
The lines of thought and act it weaves,
In face and form as it receives,
    And harbours what is good or base
    Within a heart of guile or grace,
That good or ill itself conceives.
Then let us watch our wayward leaning,
    And keep our lives unstained and straight,
And in God's field still keep on gleaning
    The strength that makes us consecrate
Our lives to life's true aim and meaning,
    And everything subordinate
To service with a love divine,
That makes both soul and body shine.

PRAYER.

WE to our neighbours pray each day,
    And we each other's prayers hear ;
  If I can answer my compeer,
Much more shall He who taught to pray

Hear me and all my fears allay.
   Yea ! shall not He who made the ear
   Hear when I cry for guidance clear ?
And shall not He who made the way
Lead me, His child, by heart and hand ?
All the way His laws like angels stand—
   Each law from Him a delegate ;
And in His name they answers send
   When we with them co-operate,
And with their power our knowledge blend.

FORCE.

TRUE force, invisible, alone is strong ;
   We do not see the wind that waves the trees
Nor yet the will that gives out its decrees,
Judging, choosing between right and wrong,
Steering its course amid the busy throng,
   That from each moving cause effect forsees,
   And by the forelock Time can seize,
And bind the law to will as with a thong.
Matter is but the garb, the tool of will.
   There's nought so flexible as law,
And he who has the key and needful skill
   Can bend it to his yoke and make it draw
His plough, and sow his seed, and turn his mill.
   For unto him that hath is knowledge given,
   And valour opes the rose-wreathed gates of Heaven.

THE OVERMIND.

A MAN can make a watch,
  The steps of time to match ;
But greater than the watch is He
Who measures time so accurately,
And He who with such power
  Of brain and hand
Did this man freely dower
  Surely must transcend
His work, and do beyond what we
Conceive, until beyond the veil we see.

KINDLINESS.

THERE is more kindliness about us than we know,
  We are too apt misjudging reticence
That shrinks from all parade of excellence,
Though underneath the quiet garb doth glow
A kindliness not meant for idle show,
  That we may lean upon in confidence,
  And feel in every nerve the influence
That life with brotherhood doth overflow.
Better it is to do than merely say
  The kindliness that keeps the world in tune,
And gives all needed help without delay ;
  For promptness magnifies the given boon,
And he who gives and he who gets is blest
With Heaven's bright benison on both impressed.

INDIVIDUALITY.

THE man who daily bread doth eat
    Can seldom know whose toiling hands
Have sowed, or reaped, or ground the wheat ;
    But well his need he understands.
And streams refresh all down their course,
Though beast and flower know not their source,
    But when they merge into the sea
    They lose their own identity.
But man, whose thoughts do fill the flow
    Of life, keeps his distinct existence,
Even as the sun dispenses glow
    And keeps its own consistence.
And thoughts may flow into a sea
Of thought and man a man remain
As true in hand and heart and brain.

REVELATION.

GOD'S revelation on our inner eyes
    May come as sweetly as the gentle dawn
Of a long summer day upon the lawn,
To wake the flowers with kisses from the skies ;
It grows upon the growing soul and lies
    All round the pure in heart, a halo bright
    That, imperturbed, reposes in the light,
And with a child-like trust grows strong and wise.
O, blessed light, I hail thee in God's name !
    A father's love to me thy radiance sent ;

By it my heart is kindled to a flame,
    As my work here nears its accomplishment.
The stars flash out their splendour all the way,
To guide my homeward steps with steady ray.

ANXIETY.

DO not be over anxious for the morrow,
    Nor ills imagine that may never be,
  Nor yet imagine that ye shall be free
In days to come of every pain and sorrow,
But take the evil as it comes, nor borrow
    Burdens long miles before they're laid on thee.
  Still be prepared for each contingency,
And put thy fruit seeds in the ground to spring
To sheltering trees, where glad birds build and sing
    'Mid blossoms that delight the glad young year,
And store the summer's opulence to fling
  In autumn's lap the mellow fruits that cheer
Our souls at eventide, as round the glowing hearth
We sit, while outside snow wraps up the frozen earth.

A RACE.

A BAND of men to run a race
    Have stripped off all impediment,
  With soul and body all attent,
And every nerve in utmost brace ;
Turned to the winning post each face
    With hope and courage opulent—

All circumstances pertinent,
And no discounting of disgrace.
Though only one can win the prize
    They start, each one with thought to win—
No thought have they of sacrifice,
    That would seem worse to them than sin,
And for a transient renown
They risk their all to win the crown.

But all who run the heavenward race
    Unfailingly shall win a prize ;
    Though falling oft, they fall to rise
If falling with a heavenward face ;
They help each other in their place,
    For helpfulness is to their feet
    As wings to make them strong and fleet ;
It bears them on with speed and grace,
    And as they help each weaker brother,
The angels bending down from heaven
    To help are vieing with each other,
With help to helpers freely given,
Until they reach the winning post
With welcomes from the heavenly host.

STRICT.

THE Lord, to mark iniquity,
        Is strict, His laws like angels stand,
    Recording with unerring hand
Each thought and deed, to certify ·

That wrong has no immunity
  From justice ; each sin must stamp its brand
  On every thought that's contraband,
And tends the soul to stupify.
But when our pilgrim feet do turn aside
  From the straight road, then angels come
With love our waywardness to chide,
And helpfulness to guard and guide
  Us in the way that leads us home.

THE KEY.

ONLY the fool within his foolish heart,
    (The wish was father to the thought) has said
" There is no God."   The wise man feels and knows
There is a power from whom we come, to whom
We kneel, whose breath we feel in every nerve ;
Who made the soul of man to understand
His kingliness by spelling out the laws
That are, like helpful angels, ever at
The master call of him who knows their secret.
They crush the ignorant, but serve the wise ;
Their secrets they unfold to him who holds
The key—the " open sesame "—of knowledge.
A thousand genii run to do his will ;
He bids them bear him over land and sea ;
They make him tools and turn his factory wheels ;
They bear his words with lightning speed around
The globe, as quickly bear his voice and tone

For many miles, or for an hundred years
Conserve them ; they build a bridge across the sea ;
They weigh the sun and track the distant stars—
All this for him who can command them.
There seems no limit to the power of man
In time or space.   Not only is the earth
Subdued, but heaven above and seas beneath
Must own his sway, and give him service true.
And the mysterious power that bids them serve
Is all unseen as winds that sweep the heavens ;
And may not souls akin to us, though hid
From view, move round us night and day, and be
Protecting monitors ?   For we ourselves
Are known but by the clothes we wear, and by
The deeds that do obey our veiled will.
And even so is He from whom we come
Known by His royal robe, flower spangled and star-
    gemmed,
And woven with the rythmic law that makes
The grand sphere songs that thrill the viewless soul
With visible and audible adoration.

LIFE.

O N this island of the sea
    Of the great eternity
We camp for one brief day,
At even we sail away.

In Memoriam.

A. G.

FROM careless eyes of common men, and all
    The withering glare of all the years to come,
We have thee in our hearts portrayed and hid,
For ever young and lithe and full of life ;
The bright smile in thine eyes shall never fade,
But evermore a sweeter grace, like golden mist,
Shall halo every thought of thee, our friend
Unseen, who walks with God beyond the veil.
    We speak of thee in accents soft and low
Lest we profane, by noise or jar, what God
Has raised to Heaven and rendered holy.
    The books we read together fill our eyes
With tears, but only tears of loyalty ;
For thou, where'er thou art, art still our own.
Brave deeds were loved by thee, for thou wert brave ;
And all brave deeds remind us of thee,
And everything well done recalls thy deftness.
    The register of heights beside the door
Brings back sweet memories of the bypast years
Where grew thy soul up to its present stature,
While step by step knowledge and grace kept pace,

Supplanting ignorance and bringing thee
Nearer to God and nobleness.   And when each test
Of progress was passed " Well," the pride and joy
Were ours as much—and more—than yours.
And as the last dread cloud drew near to take
Thee from our sight, your heart and ours were folded
In the Father's love ; and chastened spirits heard
The Master's words promoting thee—" Well done."
When the veil fell, and we were left alone,
But all the heavens were filled with glory.

*   *   *   *

When the cloud came that took thee from our sight,
We thought the cross laid on our writhing hearts
Was iron, cold and hard and crushing ;
But when the angels came with shining wings
They flashed a glory round thy soul that showed
'Twas gold, and wreathed with flowers, and death was
  but
A rising from the dead to high promotion.

*   *   *   *

Dear friend, our souls look back with weary eyes
 To thy life's dawn that rose so bright and clear,
 When earth seemed fairer for thy presence here ;
We dreamt of flowers, and fruits, and summer skies,
Nor thought the spring-time flower in spring-time
  dies ;
 But soon, alas ; our dreams were blanched with fear
 When death, with sombre wing, to thee drew near,

And smote our trembling hearts with sore surprise ;
The rosy dawn was overwhelmed in night.
  Our souls cried out, as souls cry out in pain ;
But, from the clouds, while passing from our sight,
  We heard thy voice, with high exultant strain,
Praise God ; we looked to earth, 'twas black with
      scars :
We looked to heaven, and heaven was bright with
      stars.

*   *   *   *

Dear friend, thou who didst vanish from our sight
A year ago, a year ago ! how swift
The year has sped from that dark night of pain
When heavy laden moments crept slow on
Like years, canst thou not rend the veil and come
For one short hour to tell us how it fares with thee ?
Whenever, in the past, thy face was homeward turned
Thine eager feet were winged with swiftness—
Thy home is in the hearts that love thee,
And hearts there are in that fair land of light
That ope for thee and draw thee into rest.
  Our weakness claims the succour of the strong,
And thou, ofttimes, perchance, mayst linger near
Though unperceived by horny eyes of sense,
And o'er our wilfulness with Christlike sorrow grieve.
When our weak hearts would stray from God and
      right
Thy pleading love may energise our wills
With healthful rectitude ; and in the heat

Of inward strife, help us to victory.
Ah ! who can tell ? We plod on in the dark,
And trust the stars of God till the day dawn,
When we shall meet thee in thine own bright sphere.

*   *   *   *

O friend, unseen by mortal eyes,
  Though we, mayhap, by thee are seen,
We know not where's thy sphere on high
  Where thou dost work strong and serene.

But faith and reason bids us know
  That whether thou art far or near
Advancement has not quenched the glow
  That warmed thy heart for loved ones here.

And as our thoughts go forth to thee
  Beyond the stars encircling earth,
So thou mayst come to us as free
  When gathered round the friendly hearth.

May thy pure presence drive away
  All thoughts that stain the heart, and might
Unbend the will and lead astray
  Us who on that leave-taking night,
  Promised to meet thee in the light.

*   *   *   *

We pass through days and years as travellers pass
Through lands unknown.   As magnets draw we draw,
And strive to draw only the beautiful and good
That they grow part of us, like nerve and muscle,
To make us worthy of the friend who used
To sit with open face and ready smile
Beside our hearth mingling his thought with ours.
His place is vacant now ; three times we've circled
Round the sun since we went with him to
The mountain top from which he rose and left
Us gazing into heaven.   He circles round
The Sun of Righteousness, and rests upon
The healthful light that nurture's life
Sublime and strong.   We still keep plodding on
Our weary way o'er steep and thorny paths
That end on far-off hills that greet the rising sun,
While he, his prison doors unbarred by pain,
Sped over all impediments to God.
We keep him in our hearts to keep our hearts
Most pure and true, lest we, by harbouring
Thoughts of ill, should grieve the blest in heaven,
And falling from our upward way, be lost
In night, and never see his face again.

*   *   *   *

O friend, within Heaven's affluent light
    With angels for thy peers,
Dost thou remember our dark night—
    Our many hopes and fears ?

The onward flow of fleeting years
　Leave on us their impress ;
Now bright with joy ; now writ in tears ;
　Now sunk in weariness.

All here is change ; we cannot stay
　On time's rough troubled stream ;
Our barque sails on as on the day
　Grief smote our hopeful dream.

But in our heart thou art enshrined
　Unchangéd ; still the same,
And holy thoughts our love hath twined
　Like garlands round thy name.

We, blindly, neither saw nor knew
　Thy wings were plumed for flight,
And that for thee, so leal and true,
　The heavens were opening bright.

We fain would know what thou dost know,
　And see thee in thy place,
And looking up we onward go
Till death shall draw the veil and show
　Our welcome in thy face.

*　*　*　*

The moments calmly glide
　From hour to hour ;
The seasons come and go—
　The summer flower,

The winter snow—
  All, all is change
On earth below.

Time leaves its trace
  Upon the hair,
Upon the face,
  The limbs less lithe,
The eye- less bright,
  All show the day
Wears to the night.

We all do fade
  As fade the leaves,
And in the harvest field
  Death reaps the harvest sheaves ;
But thou, dear friend,
  Whose early loss
Laid on our hearts
  A heavy cross,
Art folded in a love
  That changes not.
Thy face and form
  We treasure to the last,
And dream of thee
  As thou wert in the past.

Death came before
  The harvest field
  Was ripe to yield

Its harvest store.
And in the opening year,
  When the young leaves were green,
  And trouble unforeseen,
He cut the green corn in the ear,
And raised thee to a higher sphere.

And when at night our Father calls
  His children home,
  We'll haste to come
And meet upon life's sunny shore
The friend that Death shall then restore.
  And love's keen eye shall trace
    Through grand development
    Of soul life opulent
  In thy form, in thy face,
  In thy strength, in thy grace,
The friend that vanished on that night
When Heaven received thee from our sight.
And thou wilt reach a helping hand
And bid us welcome to our Fatherland.

* * * *

Flowers cluster round the feet of spring,
Birds on the trees for gladness sing,
  All nature wakes with hymns of praise.

Life, joy, and song are everywhere ;
The voice of spring is in the air
Whispering to sunbeams dancing there.

Seven times round the central sun
The earth its steady course has run,
    And here, again, blithe May comes round,
But he whose step was lithe and free,
Whose laughing eye was full of glee,
We do not hear ; we do not see.

While here our eyes are holden so,
We faintly see and dimly know
    How souls unseen the seen transcend.
At death we do not cease to grow ;
We only leave the husk below ;
    We merge in light and understand.

The concrete soul rays thoughts like light
That round it make a halo bright.
    The soul akin to God is strong ;
And passing swift from star to star
May bring us blessings from afar,
    And make us set our feet on wrong.

We dream of what his life may be,
We do but dream, but we shall see
    When death falls off us as falls from
The chrysalis its cerements rent,

When new life, large and opulent,
　　Shall see our friend with eager feet
　　Rushing through angel crowds to greet
Us first, and bid us welcome home.

REV. ROBERT MUIR.

DIED 21ST DECEMBER, 1882, IN HIS 50TH YEAR.

A CHRIST-LIKE man has laid aside his cross,
　　And weary with the way, has fallen asleep
Among his loved ones here, to wake among
His loved in Heaven, where all the best
Shall hail him brother.

　　　　　　　　　　　For want of him
Earth seems the bleaker ; but Heaven is richer.
　With manly gentleness he bore his cross
Through all the weary years till came this year
Of jubilee, when the ripe soul, ready
To fall into the Master's outstretched hand,
Claimed liberty, and could no longer be
Holden from his beloved Fatherland.
　His life was beautiful ; and all the way
His upward path was strewn with flowers of truth
And kindliness—the sweet forget-me-nots
That grow within the heart and will not die.

M. A.

SO young, so fair, so full of gentle grace,
    And life all opening up with dreamy light—
  Alas, so soon quenched in untimely night—
For memory now, with love, can only trace
On empty air his fragile form and face.

No spectre grim repellent to the sight
    Walked with him till that sacred Sabbath morn
    When he from weariness to rest was borne ;
One sent from God preened his white wings for flight
And bore him far away from scathe and blight.

Promotion comes when evening shadows fall,
    But he was crowned long ere the noon of day,
    As if the angels could not brook delay,
And he, responding to their heavenly call,
Was thrilled with far-off music mystical.

Now dear as are dream songs by angels sung,
    Or flowers that sweetness breathe through morning
        dew,
    Are thoughts of him whom loving hearts best knew.
A halo round his life have such hearts flung
To keep him ever fair and ever young,

REV. ROBERT BLACKSTOCK.

I HEAR the kirk bell toll, but he
　　Who used to answer to its call
　And break the bread of life to all
Hears it no more ; no more we see
His manly form ; his voice no more
　　We hear ; and standing in his place,
　　His flock look on a stranger's face
Through tears, while they their loss deplore.
More sad than all, the heavy loss
　　To dear ones that he loved so,
　　Whose hearts now feel life's winter snow
While writhing underneath the cross.

He is not dead ; he lives above
　　The pain, the wail, the jar, the strife ;
　　And He who oped the door of life
For him, could not be death but love.

JOHN WOODGER,

COACHMAN TO MARK SPROT, ESQ. OF RIDDELL,

FOR FIFTY-EIGHT YEARS.

HIS long day's work is done ; the night has come
　　And his day's wage.　For fifty years and more
He served his master well—no mere eye service his—
No need for that, for he was guileless and upright ;

And there was in his soul the faithful love
That never felt itself.   In all he did
The honest heart made service free and fine.
And serving thus his master here, he served
His Master in the unseen kingdom of the just;
To Whom, from all his many active years
He now returns to make his full report
With manly frankness, and trust the love that never
        fails
To clothe the honest man with grace and happiness.
   His cheerful greeting and his ready joke
Will be remembered long by all who felt
The influence of his individuality,
Genial and robust.   His kindliness
Will always be recalled with kindliness ;
And smiles will kindle round the words he spake,
But now, on earth, speaks never more.

CHRYSOSTOM.

CHRYSOSTOM—mouth of gold—from which
        there fell
Life giving words of God more precious far
Than purest gold ; his heart a temple was,
Where, in sweet truth and purity enshrined,
The holy spirit of the Lord abode
Making his life a consecration and
A beacon light amid surrounding night.

But men on life's high hills must bear the storms
Of life, the burning heat, the searching light;
And he alone the ordeal can stand
Who stands allied to God and girt about
With strength from Heaven, and wisdom which is
        strength.
And Chrysostom was strong ; and loyal as strong
With all the loyalty of love ; brave too he was
And would not flinch an inch though all the powers
Of earth and hell combined against him.
" The floods," he said, " assail, the tempest roars
And breaks above us, but we do not fear,
Because we hold by Him Who is our rock.
The sea may rave and dash its waves against
Our Rock in vain—they only break themselves.
Shall I fear death ?   My life is hid with Christ
In God—to die is gain.   Or shall I fear
Exile ?   The earth belongs to God, and all
That it contains is His.   Nor do I fear
The loss of earthly good ; nothing into the world
I brought, and out of it can nothing take.
I fear not poverty ; I laugh at wealth.
Death appals me not, unless 'tis needful
I should live to work the work of God.
With faith unshaken let us meet whate'er
The time to come will bring of good 'or ill,
When Peter walked upon the sea, it was
Not till the failure of his faith that he
Began to sink.   Let us be strong in trust.
Satan has failed to overthrow our town,

And now he hopes to shake the Church ;
Pillars of faith support its walls of living souls.
Though all the world should rise against my life
My heart is steadfast and I shall not fear.
If 'tis God's will that I should go, I'll go.
Or if He wills that I shall stay, I'll stay.
Where'er He wills that I shall be, I'll be.
I'll give the Church my life if 'tis required ;
Death is the gate of life, and after death
I still shall love the Church of God."
So spake the man of God.   Exile was his,
The last days of his pilgrimage were full
Of cruel pain, dragged on from place to place
Through burning heat, and drenching rain,
Till suffering called on death to bring him rest.
" For all things praise the Lord," he said,
Then fell asleep on earth to wake in Heaven.

JOHN WYCLIF.

WHEN men grow blind by living in the dark,
    God sends a son to give them light, and touch
Their horny eyes with salve of love to quicken vision.
But for a time they neither apprehend
Nor comprehend nor love the light that is
Too holy for their easy lives; they crave
No kinship unto God, but rather say—
" Here is the son ; come, let us kill this troubler

Of our peace, and so the vineyard shall be ours."
But he is sent of God, and must fulfil
His embassage, heedless of consequences.
He does not love the cross, yet does he choose it ;
It bars his path until he takes it up,
When in his hands it grows a Jacob's ladder
With which he scales the heavens, while helpfully
The angels come and go on it for him,
Girding his growing soul with growing strength.
He cannot holden be of any base environment—
" The gates of brass before him burst,
The iron fetters yield."   Zealots may bind
And burn his body, but his soul is free,
And no decree of fate can bind it more than
Could burnt flax bind Samson when the men
Of Judah and the Philistines were on him.
Such an one was Wyclif, the creed that bound
Less loyal souls, to him was as burnt flax ;
Its priests were sons of Belial ; and what
Men called the Church was but a heartless system
Of extortion to glut the sinful priests
With hydra-headed vice and shame.
Wyclif's creed was love to God ; a holy life
Its outcome.   He might misapprehend
The Father's plan ; but love is wise to hear
The Father's voice, and quick to feel His hand
Even in the dark, and so is confident
And fearless.   His heart had caught and loved
The light that holy men of God had stored
For every age, and what his soul had found

So precious, he desired all men to share.
Henceforth his life was consecrated to the needs
Of men whose shepherds fed them not,
But rather preyed on them with greedy jaws.
He, as ambassador from God, must stay
Until his work was done.　Death threw his shaft
In vain, until the hour of his recall.
And once when stricken down even to
The very gates of death before his time,
The monkish rookeries were stirred with joy ;
And, like four hooded crows, four regents
Of the four religious orders came and told him
To recant, for " death was on his lip."
Their creeds sat easy on their lives, and so
Would his, they thought, but their poor souls were no
Meet gauge for his.　With livid lips he made
His servant raise him up upon his bed,
Then fixing his keen eyes upon the priests, said—
" I shall not die, but live and testify
Against your evil deeds."　And testify he did.
Astonished and confused, they fled and left
Him victor.　He rose and gave an English
Bible to the English people.　He sent poor preachers
Over all the land to teach men love of light,
And fill their hearts with peace, although
The monks declared it heresy to speak
Of Holy Scripture in the English tongue.
But their so tender souls could see no heresy
In bartering Heaven and earth for worldly gain.
Blind leaders of the blind ! in vain they strove

Against the light John Wyclif drew from Heaven
And flashed across the land—light welcomed
Into faithful hearts that scorned the burning pile,
Brave martyr souls that now shine bright
As morning stars of England's Reformation.
   Worn and weary through all his latter years
He stood alone steadfast and true,
Maligned by monks, reproved by friends,
In constant expectation of the dungeon
Or the stake.   " Let the blow fall," he said ;
" I wait its coming."   But, like the father
Of the faithful, when his will was tried
The sacrifice was not required, and when
The Master called, He called him as he stood
And ministered before the altar.
   His quest had been the holy grail
Of truth, that precious chalice which contained
The healing love of God for man, and gave
To him who sought strength to triumph
Over all impediments.   The quest
Attained, his soul grown strong rent from itself
The worn-out flesh, and rose to Heaven,
Clothed in the white robes of a holy life,
To mingle with the sons of God, and see,
Abide, and grow in grand perpetuation
The healthful influence of a brave, true man.
Five hundred years ago he entered into rest,
And still we love his memory,
For such as he belongs to every age
As guiding stars in the waste ways of life.

WILLIAM TYNDALE.

FOUR hundred years ago the Church had grown
    A sort of Archimedes' screw to fill
The greedy coffers of the priests, who feared
The Bible lest its light should show
What thing the people's trust was wound about,
When Tyndale came and flashed its light across
The land.   Gentle, brave, invincible,
Loyal and true to his convictions was he.
The kindly Lady Walsh, with perfect trust
In her preposterous judgment, and an air
Of wisdom incontrovertible, lectured
The large-minded, far-seeing, pure-hearted,
Humble man of God.   "What! there are doctors
Worth one hundred pounds—ay, even some worth
Two hundred pounds a year; and think you,
Master William, is it reason we should believe
You rather than such?"   "No, it is not me
You should believe; but then Saint Paul, Saint Peter,
And the Lord Himself confutes them," said Master
    William.
He stood his own successfully against
All cloven-footed falseness.   He loved the light,
And could not hide his all-absorbing love.
A learned priest was sent to win him back
To the dark tortuous ways of Popery,
But soon he shut the mouth that came
To silence him; his baffled foe in rage
Cried out—"Better it were to do without

The laws of God than of the Pope."   Tyndale,
The gentle, roused to indignation, said—
" I do defy the Pope and all his laws ;
If God but spare my life, I shall take care
That e'en the boy that holds the plough shall know
More of the Holy Scriptures than yourself."
    His talents and his learning might have raised
Him up to any earthly dignity,
But his ambition was not earthly.
He only wished for some ten pounds a year,
And some lone Patmos where he might translate
The word of God in peace, and give his life
And work to those who did not know the worth
Of such a gift—a gift like altar fire
To kindle Heaven in every open heart.
But "aye the kingliest kings are crowned with
        thorns,"
And he who gave his life for men, by men
Was hunted like a beast of prey from place
To place until his work was done.
When from Cologne he fled in haste with his
Half-printed Bibles, Cochleus wrote
To Henry and to Wolsey, to hinder
"The most baleful merchandise from entering
Any English port."   Vain thought !   What arm
Of man can keep the sun from shining ?
The Bible entered into English ports—
Ay, and into English hearts as well ;
Its leaves were for the nation's healing—

In spite of king and priest, of earth and hell.
They could but chase the conqueror through
The gates of Heaven, where there was joy to greet
The mighty man who unto God returned
With water drawn from Bethlehem's well,
In spite of all the hostile hordes of Philistines;
And as the centuries roll on, his name
Shall sanctify the lips that speak it reverently.

LUTHER.

IRON lies hid in the dark earth till man
    With kingly 'hest calls it into the light,
And, by fierce heat and heavy blows, forges
The shapeless mass into a thousand forms
Of beauty and utility, to serve
His multiform needs; and so the noblest lives
Are softened by fierce heat of strife, and beat upon
And buffeted by all the storms of life—
Toil, poverty, and all the hydra-headed hindrances
Beset their every upward, onward step,
Till thus tried, tempered, and attuned they take
Command, and act like kings within their spheres.
And kings they are! Strong men that mow obstruc-
        tion down,
Making it food for serving circumstance.

Hindrance wipes out the feeble soul ; but such
As overcome are crowned.
> Luther was strong !
His brave, true soul allied itself to God ;
And from the lowly cot he rose and shook
Kingdoms and thrones. He beat a hole
In every hollow drum*; nor man nor devil he
> feared.
He cared not though it rained Duke Georges†
Nine days running, he would through such a rain
Ride into Leipsic. And he would go to Worms‡
Though devils were as plentiful as tiles
Upon the houses ; he knew whose sword he bore.
All the fierce dragon powers of earth and hell
He scorned and flouted, and yet his heart
Was full of humble gentleness and love ;
He yearned for peace, but never shrank from war.
He fought as one who fights for peace ; and when

---

* Luther, indignant at Tetzel's noisy and shameless traffic in indulgencies, said " God willing, I will beat a hole in his drum."

† Duke George was a great enemy of his, he wrote, " I have defied innumerable devils ; Duke George is not equal to one devil. If I had business in Leipsic I would ride into Leipsic though it rained Duke George's nine days running."

‡ When his friends tried to dissuade him from going to the Diet of Worms he said, " Were there as many devils in Worms as there are tiles on the roofs of the houses, I would go." Devils were very real personalities to Luther.

Death brought the laurel wreath, he gave the king
    his sword
And fell asleep in peace, beloved by Heaven.
And we, who heir the good he won for us,
Do now with grateful hearts remember him,
And thank the king for his brave life and true.

WILLIAM EWART GLADSTONE.

TOLL the bell, and hush the nation's voice,
    The grand old man, full of years and ripe
For Heaven, is raised into a higher sphere
To reap the harvest of his sowing here,
And only dust is left in Death's cold hand.
He was a many-sided man, with firm beliefs,
And courage to speak them fearlessly.
From what he deemed the right he never flinched—
Right was the pole-star of his life.
He fought to raise the trodden down and give
The victims of false laws the freedom of true men.
Spell-bound men listened to his silvery eloquence
And forceful grasp of thought. He never struck
Below the belt. He scorned all mean expediency,
And never yet his bitterest foe could truly note
A single stain upon his moral character ;
And when his sword was sheathed in shadows

All who felt its edge or parried its fell thrusts
Forgotten were as foes, and only loved as men.
While the brave warrior, resting on his shield,
Lay listening for the Master's call
To "come up higher," the Master's will was his.
He praised the Holiest in the heights,
And in the depths he trusted him.
The wide world's sympathy was round
This man of God with wistful eyes, loving
To do honour to the passing of a king,
Whose reign henceforth shall be o'er all
His stainless life has won for Heaven.
And now the loyal soul from the worn body
Is raised from death, and clothed upon
With all the good he did while fighting here
Under God's banner. Peace, perfect peace,
Was his at eventide when the call came
To hear his Master's meed and share His joy.

HENRY FAWCETT.

THE nation mourns a patriot, wise and good,
    Snatched from us in the crisis of our fate ;
A brave, strong man who did not turn aside,
But marched straight on when darkness fell on him
In the full flush of hope in early life.

A meaner man by such a fate had been
Subdued, but he strode over loss to victory.
The sun rose in the east and strewed his way
With good until he reached the west at eventide.
The glad light fell on man and bird and beast
And lovely flower, but his dark eyes were closed
Against it.   The calm clear stars looked down
On him, but met no answering brightness
In his benighted orbs.   The hills and vales,
The rills that ran in music to the broad'ning rivers;
The restless sea ; the rippling lakes that bathed
The mountain's feet, to other eyes were grand
And beautiful, but not, alas, to his.
And when his eager steps were homeward turned
His sunless eyes were never wrought to smiles
At sight of all the dear familiar scenes;
And sweet home faces all aglow with love,
More deeply tender for his sad privation.
Hid from him, too, the changeful light of mind
Upon the kindling face of statesman
And philosopher.

             But though his blindness
With its double lock shut out the light of day,
A grander light responded gladly to
His hungry inner eyes and filled his soul
With power to serve his country well.   And now
We thank him for his legacy of good,
While mourning still a strong man taken from us
In his fruitful prime, when most we needed strength

And skill, that stronger strength to move us forward
In the press of progress. But what he did
Remains with us, his best memorial.

GENERAL GORDON.

WE always need such men as Gordon was,
    To shew what heights humanity can reach,
And by pure force of character to draw us up
To larger freedom with the perfect law.
Brave, strong, and true, with purpose pure he lived
For God and man, scorning all vain
Conventionality of word and deed.
He went straight on where duty led, and never flinched
Or turned aside for any obstacle.
Environments that hindered other men
Bent down to serve him, and ways that seemed
Impassable, straightened and smoothed themselves
Before his wise o'ermastering will; his fearlessness
Was God's best covering for his head when death
Was rained around him. The distant past
Sends glamour to the heroes that we love, but he
Lived in our day, before our eyes, and words
Are poor to praise his many-sided nobleness.
His life was saintly, knightly, kingly,

Cosmopolitan, his soul was never lured
From duty's steep and stormy path by gold
Or honour. Nay! gold or honour never
Lured his straight soul *into* duty He would not
Sell himself; Christ-like he *gave* himself
To all the poor and needy, to king and slave
Alike, and thought not of reward : the work
He set himself to do, when done, was all
He wished or cared for. He was content to toil
In sorrow, could he but smooth the way
For other feet, and guide them Heavenward to
The only peace. A soldier he, who, in
The blessed name of peace, took up the sword
To strike for peace. His single greatness ruled
The fickle, faithless hordes ofttimes surprising foes
Into innocuousness. What he *was*
Lent force to what he *did.* He gave himself
For all, in utter self-forgetfulness,
To further Heaven on earth. The hearts of men
Of every clime and rank were drawn to him
By force of sympathy—a sympathy
That tortured his own kindly heart with sight
Of human suffering. They loved and trusted him,
And were the richer having such a soul
To love, and better they for having loved him.
He set his foot upon the serpent's head ;
It stung his heel, but could not sting his soul
At one with God. Treachery oped for him
The gates of high advancement; and now, at last,
His weary soul finds rest, and all his noble deeds

Like precious gifts flung from a kingly hand,
Do clothe and crown his noble soul with love
While all the angels nearest God rise up
　　To call him blessed.

DR JOHN KER.

AROUND the will of God the circling year
　　Revolves with many a smile and tear—
The spring and summer, times of gladness;
　The autumn, with its golden sheaves,
　Its mellow tints and falling leaves,
And winter with its tears of sadness.
'Twas autumn when earth's fruits were stored;
And through the harvest field the Lord
Of harvest walked, and, well pleased saw
　Among the sons of men, a son whose life
Was woven with the perfect law—
　A man with large, well formed soul;
Rich, mellow, pure, and ripe and leal,
Whose gentle words for human weal
　On human hearts fell soft like rain
From heaven, with easy grace
　And fine simplicity of strength;
While love shone in his face—
　A love that well might win

The souls of wayward men
    From slimy sloughs of sin
To pearly gates of Heaven,
    Where love alone can enter in.

He walked with God while leaves were falling;
He heard the Heavenly voices calling ;
    Death burst asunder earthly ties,
And suddenly he rose to Heaven
    While friends looked up in sad surprise
And saw the streak of shining light
    His life had left below the cloud
That hid him from their strainèd sight.

His soul was weary;
    We may not grudge the rest that's given
To him—another John—
    Beloved of earth and Heaven.

PROFESSOR LAWSON.

HE was a teacher sent from Heaven to show
    How much of Heavenly worth could dwell
In human form.   He was a king and reigned
By right of love divine in every heart
That came within the circle of his calm
Harmonious life.   His heart was large and pure ;

His lips were true, and from them flowed
The mellow wisdom of the pure in heart.
And young aspirants for the staff and crook
Knew that he walked with God and deeply felt
The reverence of deep love.   His spirit was
Reflected in their lives, as he himself
Reflected the pure rays that shone on him
From Heaven, while all through life their souls
Were fed by memories of this gentle
Man of God, in whom there was no guile ;
And through them, ever circling wide and wider,
All the land was blessed by him who so
Did please the Lord with a most holy life.

REV. JOHN LAWSON.

WHERE Ettrick with the Yarrow blends,
        Singing the song they sang in olden times
When Leslie fought against the foes of truth,
LAWSON has been a name revered and loved
For ages.   And now the last of that long line
Of saintly servants of the Lord has passed
Through death's dark portal into light.
He is not dead, but stript of death, and clothed
With the white robe of a consecrated life.
    By forest, hill and hope, and stream,
He tended, with leal heart, his Master's flock.

If any strayed into the wilderness,
With gentle words he brought them back
And laid their tears of penitence upon
The altar stair, and when God looked on them
They shone as shines the drops of dew
When morning sunbeams span the Yarrow hills
With rainbows.
                          With Christ-like touch,
The stricken heart he soothed, wreathing the cross
With flowers that grew where tears had watered them.
And now, at eventide he calmly rests,
While memories of his kindly deeds are poured,
Like precious ointment, round the feet of God.
And love is gazing up to heaven through clouds
That, like the Red Sea waves, parted to let
The King's ambassador pass through
Into his Master's presence, where every
Faithful son receives the meed—" WELL DONE."

DARKLY WE SEE.

SENSE bounds our sight, we cannot see beyond
      The present time except but darkly through
The occult mists that thicken round our view.
Nor can we see how laws to laws respond
Except through mists to where love sits enthroned.
      But what we know grows out of what we knew,

As truth most surely grows from what is true—
  As flowers reveal the seeds from which they grew.
And hearts that loved us here have left a bond
That they, more helpful grown beyond the veil,
  Shall hover round us with an influence sweet,
And guard us well when foes unseen assail,
  And guide from hidden dangers wayward feet.
O friend beloved, unseen, I yearn to know
If this be so, if this be *really* so.

JOHN HENRY NEWMAN.

A LIFE so calm, so strong, so pure,
  Gives out a light that is retained
When Heaven another soul has gained.
The light remains, and shall endure
In many a heart with lodgement sure
  Absorbed as flowers absorb the day,
  Transmuting every kindly ray
To their own bright investiture.
And he who prayed "Lead, kindly Light,"
  Had light enough to walk with God
And trust him in the darkest night
  With willing feet o'er roughest road.
We thank him for the halo round
A holy life, at rest and crowned.

JOHN BRIGHT.

WE mourn the man of peace who fought for peace
          With healthy vehemence and fearlessness
That would not be subdued ; heedless of clamour
He did what seemed the best, and never yet
Did dirty weapon soil his spotless hands.
No meanness stains his memory ; " No speck
Is on his shield."   His was no crooked course ;
Straightforward with a loyal heart he went,
With purpose high, and soul ablaze for right
Against all wrong.   He never grasped at place
Or power, to serve himself, but gave his life
Ungrudgingly to further right.   His heart
Was pure, his vision clear, religion was
For him no Sunday garb for outward show ;
It was absorbed into his soul as bread
Of life to nourish all his noble aims.
And when his heart was sore for loss of one
Whose love lit up his home, he thought of all
The sordid darkness of the hungry poor,
And overgrew his grief in efforts for
Their good ; their griefs he made his own, he was
" The people's Tribune."   Now resting on his shield,
His retrospect is good, and He who gives
To His beloved rest, gives eulogy, " Well done "—
Thou good and faithful one, " WELL DONE."

W. M. D.

THE flush of summer's prime,
   The glow of harvest time
Were past when death drew near,
   Unseen, with muffled feet,
     And touched the weary brain
With rest, when all the leaves were sear.
     And now, though wind and rain,
     Upon the window pane,
Remind us of the heart's November,
Yet gladly can the heart remember
The opening of the fruitful year
   When forth a sower went to sow,
And sowed until the leaves were sear ;
   When, beckoning him to go,
Death raised him to a higher sphere
To reap the harvest of his seedtime here.

His seed fell everywhere,
   And where it fell it grew ;
How large his harvest field
   Mayhap he never knew.
How limitlessly, how endlessly
   Its reproductions grow
   He now may see and know.

The more a sower has to sow
   The more he has to reap ;
The more he fills his neighbours' barns,

The more he has to keep ;
And he who takes most wealth away
    Aye leaves most wealth behind,
For what we get makes rich the giver,
As rain from Heaven fills up the flowing river.
The river flows into the sea,
    The sea is drawn to heaven,
    And to the giver is regiven
In rains that fall upon the lea,
    And on the seed
    Of word and deed
That from the sower's hand
Is scattered o'er the land ;
And on a thousand tiny rills,
Whose crystal streams the river fills—
    The river that grinds the grain
In a thousand mills
That man may eat and live,
And work, and get, and give.

O, happy he who so calmly went
After his task's accomplishment
    To restful heights,
Where, looking on his life's work done,
    He sees how God requites—
How crowns are won.

JAMES MARTINEAU.

JAMES MARTINEAU, thy name is like a star,
    And eyes that love the light look up to thee ;
The great presiding Love has filled thee with
A spirit, large and leal, and pure and good,
And strong to draw clear fire from Heaven into
Thy soul, whose light shines for the human race.
Healing goes forth from such an one as light
That shames the darkness, unasked, unhindered.
The spirit flies where words do lamely creep,
But thou hast winged *thy* words with healing verve,
That permeates the atmosphere we breathe
As light doth search the earth for flowers.
Thy spirit, drawn from God and ripened
Into mellowness, draws what is good in man
Into the fructifying light of Heaven
To bloom and seed, and spread and grow again
In endless harvest fields of loyalty.
The see-er said, in words as true as beautiful,
" They that be wise shall shine as shines on high
The firmament, and they that teach men to be
Wise shall be as stars in Heaven for ever."
Those calm, clear lights that shine upon the dark
And stormy sea of low and fretful life,
Light, wisdom, love, are one—life's trinal star,
That guides the weary traveller home at night.
A higher blessedness we do not know
Than shining 'mid the sons of God upon
The sons of men that fester in low slums,

Toil with hard hands, or strain to meet the light
With eager eyes that widen with the dawn :
This blessedness is thine, James Martineau.
Thy fourscore years and three are beautiful ;
Thou art not old—the growing soul is young
Forever ; years as they come and go but add
A grander grace unto thy soul at one with God ;
And " the declining path of life " is strewn
With palms of victory, and leads through leafy lanes
Of love to opening gates of high advancement,
Where every noble soul with outstretched hands
Shall welcome home their noble brother.

BURNS.

RESTLESS feelings dumbly burned
    In human hearts alive inurned
   Till this man came,
   With heart aflame,
And gave the voiceless yearning name.

The loves of every heart he flung,
   Like birds uncaged,
From his melodious tongue ;
   What man had dumbly felt before
   He coined in words from his heart's core.
So much of love was in the strain,
   It took away the curse of Cain ;

His songs all hearts can understand :
No need to climb the slippery steeps,
Where neither soul nor body sleeps,
  Ere we can clasp a brother's hand.

O, leader of a mighty choir !
  Thy songs from countless hearts are gushing
  Like all the streams of Scotland rushing
From Scotland's hills o'er Scotland's plains,
While other hills sound the refrains ;
  Thy words so fitly speak for all,
  All deem themselves poetical.

Impulsive heart of guilt and grace,
  The weakness and the strength in thee
Make thee exponent of the race ;
  While He who trod the shores of Galilee
Shews to what heights the race may rise
When love its service sanctifies.
  Thus, what man *is* in Burns we see ;
  In Jesus what he *ought to be.*

TENNYSON.—6TH AUGUST, 1889.

LORD TENNYSON has won his lordship o'er
  Our minds and hearts by force of mind and
    heart ;

The seasons rolling round his fruitful life
For eighty years, have caught and stored the tones
Mellifluous that with a halo frames
His wise and precious Kohinoors of thought
That flash on man a rich inheritance.
The thoughts he clearly sees he firmly holds
In reason's honest grasp ; his thoughts hang on
The hearts of men as clear as drops of dew,
And as refreshing ; he winds them not
Through lists of dots and dashes, affecting depth,
With intricacies unthreadable.
No need to hide his thought in language vague,
Making it dearly bought by mental strain,
For it is pure and true and good.　 It glows
With kindly light on open eyes and hearts.
'Tis musical as are the winds of heaven
That blow through leafy trees 'mong singing birds.
No need of laurel crowns for Tennyson ;
His works do crown him with such kingliness
That we do bend the knee before the man
Honoured by God with such vicegerency.

6TH OCTOBER, 1892.

Life fleeing from Death, Death
　　Clutched at the robe he wore.
Life left it in his hand,
　　Only that and nothing more.

"Lord Tennyson is dead," you say ; not so.
He could not die.　 Folded in love, he lives

Within our hearts.   His words so pure and wise
Ray from him as rays the blessed light
From day's great luminary.   He gives,
Nor lesser grows by giving—he larger grows
By largely giving.   He makes men pure
By shining purely on them.   He gathers wealth
By strawing wealth.   Strength nerves his arm
By helping on the weak.   He cannot die,
He has so much of life—his tendrils take
Such hold on human lives Death hath no power
To root him out!   'Tis life that rends the veil
And spreads his wings to soar above the clouds,
And meet the friend who made Death's darkness
          beautiful—
To live with Heaven's plutocracy, and reign
Within the hearts and lives of men below.

When sailing o'er life's sea he strawed
His songs among the ships, and winds and waves
Retain the melody ; and souls that sail
From port to port absorb their beauty,
And grow more good and true and beautiful.
And now, leaving his gifts with us, he sails
Calmly, from friends still on the restless sea
Across the harbour bar, to friends who draw
Him home by love to fellowship with all
The kingly souls of every age and clime.

J. G.

WHEN driving clouds began to lower,
  Oor hearts grew faint wi' mony fears ;
  Love melted into wailing tears
To see the storm burst o'er oor flower—
    Oor ain wee man.

Love lent him for a little while
  To brighten life, wi' prattle cheery ;
  But when his little feet grew weary,
Love took him up at life's third mile
    To rest—oor ain wee man.

But oh! oor breaking hearts were sair—
  We scarce could thole oor heavy loss ;
  We bent beneath the crushing cross :
It seemed abune oor strength to bear
    The loss o' oor wee man.

Now glintin' through the gates ajar
  His memory sends a holy licht,
  That speaks to us o' Heaven a' nicht ;
'Twill guide us ower the harbour bar
    To oor wee man.

Frae winter's cauld and simmer's heat,
  Wrapt in sweet love for ever more,
  He lives, and in life's inmost core
He works to make oor lives mair meet
    For Heaven an' oor wee man.

THE SHADOW OF DEATH.

INTO the shadow of death
  We follow the one we love,
And give her there to the angels
  Waiting to bear her above.

Still while we say "Thy will be done,"
  Our tears are falling like rain ;
But He who knows best, and loves us,
  Makes good have its root in pain.

This day we remember the sorrow
  That wrung hot tears from our eyes,
As we yielded our dear one to God,
  When He called for a sacrifice.

Maybe that glorified one
  May come with the angels of light,
To guard, through the darkness, the soul
  That is passing this night from our sight.

The gates of the new Jerusalem
  Shall open for us ere long;
If now we are parting with tears,
  We shall meet up there with song.

O, why should we look on death
  As aught but the vestibule
Where the children leave their wraps,
  When coming home from the school ?

J. H.

HOR pilgrims at the close of the day,
  Weary and worn and footsore,
When the calm sweet light of eventide
  Shows, at last, the Father's door,
Is it the truest love to wish
  For them even one mile more ?

Where the heart is, there is the home
  That our friend has reached at last,
And we may not grudge the gladness
  That crowns a beautiful past;
She rests in peace where the clear light is
  That no cloud can overcast.

Hers was the heart so leal and kind,
  To the kingdom of Heaven the key;
And hers were the bonds of love
  That make the leal-hearted free ;
And hers the sweetness and grace
  Through which the kingdom we see.

Through all the shadows of life
  Her face was aye homeward bound ;
The shadows are still with us,
  While she is with brightness crowned,
And raised from death to a purer life
  Than ever on earth is found.

And he, the mate of her youth,
  That her heart has missed so long,
Was waiting to meet her there
  With a love 'more deep and strong
Than ever folded her soul in peace
  With a quiet evensong.

W. T. P. Y.

OUR home seems empty since he went who bore
  About with him an atmosphere of love ;
So young, so fair, so full of life's sweet grace,
And, oh ! so dear, we could not let him go.
When first the cloud appeared, no bigger than
A hand it was—a small speck in the heavens,
It larger, darker grew, and all our fears
Grew with it, until our trembling hearts
Scarce dared to look ; but he was calm :
He saw the bow that bound the earth to heaven—
A glory made with darkness, tears and light—
The sweet home light of Fatherland.
The white-winged angels, full of tender ruth,
Came, whispering words that fell on our poor hearts
Like snow on summer flowers. Angels of God
They were, and yet we could not welcome them ;
We sorely grudged to give to Heaven's safe keeping
What Heaven had kindly lent. He was so dear,
His soul so beautiful, no wonder that
The angels loved him, and wiled him from his home

Below to dwell with all the sons of God
In heaven where, sweeter than in mother's love,
His weary soul might rest in perfect peace.
Softly, in dreams, they said—" Come higher up,"
His ready heart made quick response—
" I will arise and go to my Father ; "
And, when his feet grew weary with the road,
Love bore him on up to the pearly gate,
Where ripened for the higher life, like fruit that
        mellows
Long ere the autumn comes to crown the year,
He laid aside his pilgrim staff and scallop shell,
And round him grew the white robe of "a blameless
        life ;"
While, full of faith, love yielded up her treasure,
Thanking the Love Supreme that her dear boy
Had reached his Father's home at last.
We laid him as a flower on God's own altar—
A flower that could not die, and, framed in love,
His image lives, treasured within our hearts
Forever young, and blythe, and beautiful ;
And round his feet are sweet forget-me-nots
Of gentle words and kindly deeds, that death
Is powerless to destroy. These are the charms we bear
About our souls to guard our lives from ill.
He shall be like a star that leads us on
O'er hill, and vale, and thorny brake,
Until the night is gone ; and if men ask
" Why gaze ye up to heaven ? " we shall reply—
        " Willie is there."

THOMAS CARLYLE.

A HUNDRED years ago a child was born,
   Unnoted more than was the birth of such
As lived, and died, and were forgotten ;
Men saw no signs in heaven to prove
The advent of a king of men ; they heard
No angel's song hailing the birth of him
Whom God hath sent to preach the truth ;
No bonfires blazed to show a nation's gladness :
Only a father's care, a mother's love,
Were folded round this " man they'd gotten
From the Lord "—a holy trust most precious—
More precious than they knew.   He grew as grows
The fruitful tree beside the flowing stream
Of life, and his leaves too were for
The nation's healing.   But ere his life
Could write his embassage in altar fire
He had himself to pass through fires that burnt
The dross of life ; angels, with flaming swords,
Led him past doors that ope'd to meaner men,
But shut to him, until he felt like him
Who said—" All these things are against me ; "
While all the time, blindfolded, he was led,
Groping through rough and thorny ways,
By love unseen, into the inner court, to get
Writ on his soul the King's commission
As standard-bearer in the world's broad
Battle-field, where rebels fought against the truth.
Though fools rose up to flout him, unwaveringly

He bore aloft the ensign of the war
He waged with sham ; howe'er hard pressed and
        weary
He never trailed his colours in the dust ;
His master thought was to be loyal
To the trust reposed in him until
Recalled to hear the King's " Well done."   And now
When his true thoughts take root in hearts akin,
We rise to honour him who strove to make
Us honourable by love of truth, and we
Who love him most honour him best
By living true, leal lives, yielding heart service
To the King who gave him his commission.

B. C.

SPRING walks the earth with flowery feet,
    The daisies their white fringe unfold
  To catch the sun in hearts of gold,
Earth waves to heaven her incense sweet.

The trees spread out their tender leaves,
    The streams in many a crystal vein
    Steal through the grassy hawthorn lane,
The swallows build below the eaves.

Full-throated birds their matins sing
    In the grey dawn of dewy morn,
    Above its nest among the corn
The lark exults on quivering wing ;

Its rapt song of ecstatic joy
  With such abandon of delight
  Comes down from heaven beyond our sight
Without a note of base alloy.

The glad spring wreathes with song and spray
The lovely form of laughing May ;
  But through the pleasant leafy glade
  Our hearts perceived a dreaded shade
That wiled our sweetest flower away
And filled our hearts with sore dismay.

Yet nature never ceased her song.
  Why should she? Death but opes the portal
  Of life for souls that are immortal;
To keep them here might do them wrong.

If angels lift them by the way
  Ere they are weary with the road,
  To lay them in the love of God,
'Twere doubtful love to bid them stay.

'Tis want of faith obscures our sight,
  And makes our timid hearts rebel;
  Could we but see that all is well,
Our hearts would make our faces bright.

Through the rent veil could we but see
  The gladness on each angel face
  While clasping in a fond embrace
The soul we love, by death set free,

Our straining eyes might weep glad tears
　　Of only love to see our own
　　Sweet flower, so pure and lovely grown,
Live in the hearts of all her peers.

AT EVENTIDE IT SHALL BE LIGHT.

THE toilsome day is past, and now
　　　In twilight calm
I greet the evening star
Above the harbour bar
　　With a glad psalm.
Supernal love has been my stay
　　And trusty guide,
Through all the weary toilsome day
　　Till eventide.
The watchful love that brought me here
　　Will never leave me now,
But safe into the haven steer
　　My barque, where sweet home light
　　On sweet home faces shining bright
With love's glad welcome waits for me
Beyond life's dark and troubled sea.

Printed by James Edgar, 5 High Street, Hawick.